ANATOLY **KUCHERENA**

TIME OF THE OCTOPUS

BASED ON THE TRUE STORY OF

WHISTLEBLOWER

EDWARD SNOWDEN

A NOVEL

Translated by John Farndon
with Akbota Sultanbekova and Olga Nakston

AD VERBUM

Published with the support of the Institute
for Literary Translation, Russia

GLAGOSLAV PUBLICATIONS

THE TIME OF THE OCTOPUS

by Anatoly Kucherena

Translated by John Farndon
with Akbota Sultanbekova and Olga Nakston

Published with the support of the Institute
for Literary Translation, Russia

Publishers Maxim Hodak & Max Mendor

Glagoslav Publications Ltd
88-90 Hatton Garden
EC1N 8PN London
United Kingdom

www.glagoslav.com

ISBN: 978-1-91141-409-4

ANATOLY **KUCHERENA**

TIME OF THE OCTOPUS

BASED ON THE TRUE STORY OF

WHISTLEBLOWER

EDWARD SNOWDEN

A NOVEL

The plot and main characters of this story are a figment of the imagination of the author and any correspondence with real people and events is purely coincidental.

...May they be damned, these interests of civilization; and may civilization itself be damned if its preservation demands the stripping of skin from living people.

Fyodor Dostoevsky

Those who would give up essential Liberty to purchase a little temporary Safety, deserve neither Liberty nor Safety.

Benjamin Franklin

Water is fluid, soft, and yielding. But water will wear away rock, which is rigid and cannot yield. As a rule, whatever is fluid, soft and yielding will overcome whatever is rigid and hard. This is another paradox: what is soft is strong.

Lao Tzu

The heresy of heresies was common sense. And what was terrifying was not that they would kill you for thinking otherwise, but that they might be right.
For, after all, how do we know that two and two make four? Or that the force of gravity works? Or that the past is unchangeable? If both the past and the external world exist only in the mind, and if the mind itself is controllable – what then?

George Orwell

IN PLACE OF A PROLOGUE

The transit area of any international airport is in some ways a kind of beached Noah's Ark. It is not floating off anywhere. It is not threatened by the rising tide of the next flood. Yet it provides a lifeboat for those who have something to be afraid of in this life of misery and hardship.

Ordinary passengers burdened merely by daily cares, baggage, children, domestic problems and lack of time shoot through transit areas like shoals migrating from one shore of the boundless ocean of air to another. They barely notice those who linger longer here.

The more persistent inhabitants of the transit area – often conforming to the biblical 'two of every living creature under the sun' – try to stay unnoticed, keeping away from the well-trod passenger tracks, slipping away unobtrusively into the back alleys and hidden habitable cul-de-sacs of the airport terminal. For those with means, there are, of course, mini-hotels in transit areas, but the cost is way above the ordinary lingerer's budget.

Yes, they are a varied and numerous community, this tribe of transit area dwellers! There are migrants who, by hook or by crook, made it aboard a plane to escape from poor countries that are not even Third World, but fourth or fifth, in the hope of reaching somewhere they might be accepted as refugees. There are young travellers, who move almost like hitchhikers, without visas and permits. There are old hippies, the last outgrowth of the flower children, on the way to eternal Katmandu. There are shady characters, too – characters on the prohibited lists of different states, defaulters on credits, protestors, false witnesses, deserters, heroes of criminal and political cases; ideological fighters against borders, anarchists, extremists and radicals of all stripes, prophets and false prophets, and also the clinically insane, which may not be so different. And then there are the unfortunates who have simply lost tickets and documents.

All these people are waiting for something. Some are waiting for a decision from the authorities, some for money to be transferred from relatives or acquaintances, and others just for documents, objects, or traveling companions … But there are also those for whom a transit area is the only place on planet Earth where they can feel free.

SHEREMETYEVO
INTERNATIONAL AIRPORT, 07:10 P.M.

Among the transit tribe at Moscow's Sheremetyevo was the young American Joshua Kold – international celebrity, headline newsmaker and also, according to Washington officials, wanted criminal. In the more benevolent English-language media he was referred to as a 'whistleblower'. This means literally 'one who blows a whistle,' of course, but in the USA and other countries the term applies to people who make confidential information public to reveal what they see as violations of laws and ethical standards in their place of work.

To cut a long story short, the concatenation of circumstances conspired in such a way that the transit area of Sheremetyevo Airport became the only place where Joshua Kold could feel relatively safe.

Just what Kold had done to bring him here was little understood by many – even the President of Russia publicly called him 'a strange guy.' But there was no doubt that his revelations had caused a sensation and, in some media outlets, the Kold affair was already described as 'the juiciest spy scandal of all time.'

There is one obvious problem with this nonsense – Joshua Kold's offence was not actually spying...

A spy is someone who works to obtain secrets on behalf of a political system, a state, a group of citizens, or even a religious sect. There are deadly risks of being found out, of course, but this fascinating activity always brings a reward – a remuneration in some form from those the spy serves.

The infamous Aldrich Ames[1], for instance, was said to have sold the identity of his colleagues and numerous CIA agents to the Soviet

---

1   Aldrich Ames was the CIA analyst turned KGB mole who compromised more American agents than almost any other CIA mole. He was convicted in 1994 and is now serving a life sentence.

intelligence services in exchange for a new house and fancy Jaguar. But there are exceptions.

Dmitry Polyakov, a general in GRU (Main Intelligence Directorate), was slipping confidential information to the American side for 'ideological reasons' for 25 years – or at least that's what he said during interrogations in 'the cellars of Lubyanka'. Whatever the truth, there was a hostile Soviet system against him, and it was no accident that the brilliant winner in the Cold War Ronald Reagan asked Soviet leader Mikhail Gorbachev to pardon him – but the request came a little late.[2]

What Kold did, in his own way, was to show the world a unique example of the loner hero.

At least, that's how it looked on the surface. The young man with densely compressed lips and a steely gaze had thrown out a challenge to the mightiest power in the world. A plot like this would be a complete no-no in Hollywood, where the screwed up loner would always be defeated by the anti-hero. In American blockbusters, there is almost never a speech about a fight against the system. Kold threatened the system – and so became a target.

Somehow, he had managed to slip away right under the nose of the countersurveillance department of the National Security Agency and get out of the USA. Beyond that, everything was obscured by a fog of uncertainty. All the same, enough information had filtered through the haze to propel hundreds of journalists to the transit area of Sheremetyevo International Airport in hope of finding the star fugitive.

The fact that Kold had become a star didn't seem to raise doubts for anyone. It was a simple narrative. He had not just tapped on the beak of the American eagle; he had given it thorough, and very humiliating, kick – as if it was not an awesome feathered predator but a feeble country chicken chaotically trying to evade a bike rider.

Feathers flew, and the eagle, making a long chicken neck, shamefully crowed for the whole world. He threatened, he pecked with his beak, he

---

2   General Dmitry Polyakov passed on Soviet secrets for 25 years to the USA where he was known as 'Top Hat' by the FBI and 'Bourbon' by the CIA. His cover was blown in 1987 by Aldrich Ames and others, and he was executed in 1988. CIA officer Jeanne Vertefeuille said of him, "He didn't do this for money. He insisted on staying in place to help us. It was a bad day for us when we lost him."

scratched the ground with his claws, but the reputation of the predator had been dented. Why, even the president of a tiny Latin American country was not afraid to declare that he was ready to provide to 'the brave guy Joshua Kold' with political asylum.

So journalists of all colours, after settling in the transit area of Sheremetyevo Airport, first of all started looking for Kold as for a lost puppy, or maybe even a truffle in the autumn Provencal wood.

The younger ones ransacked every corner and peered at every passenger's face – what if the guy was wearing heavy make-up and/or a false beard? They checked utility rooms, too, because, apparently, several incidents involving employees and airport security service had already occurred.

Their senior colleagues bided their time to give Kold a chance to find them, and spent the hours in what is said to be called, in the vernacular of the second most ancient profession, 'collecting the invoice'. These writing journalists talked to passengers, composed descriptions of airport interiors, surfed the internet, collected information on the notorious capsule hotel where, according to hearsay, Kold had been hidden away together with an assistant sent to him by the professional unmaskers 'Mikiliks'. That assistant was of course a very cute and brisk young maiden, and gave the story an additional frisson.

Meanwhile, the cameramen were shooting general views of the transit area to use in cutaways, and also of the crowds of journalists near the smoking room – to dramatize the importance of the moment.

This crowd generally consisted of the 'golden plumes', the VIP cabinet of the journalistic tribe, the people deemed acceptable to the noblest offices, and entrants to most forbidden doors. Accustomed to gaining information in comfort, they had decided long ago that the saying 'going the distance feeds the wolf' is not about them. Indeed, these golden plumes could not understand why nobody had yet delivered Kold to them on a silver platter.

Time was passing. Tension was increasing. Nothing was happening.

07:16 P.M.

A grey-haired press photographer in a jacket with a Reuters logo joined the group of journalists watching the take-offs and landings. The photographer's eyes were as red as an April rabbit's. He carefully rearranged the wardrobe-like case containing his very expensive Canon, took a sip of dreadful coffee dispensed by the machine in an all-too-thin plastic cup and without addressing anyone in particular said:

"Modern airplanes are literally time machines, especially if flying from East to West."

"Do you think so?" asked the rather middle-aged female journalist nearby, without turning her head, lolling aloof and lanky like a tired hunting dog. It was clear to the photographer, that she, like all the rest of the writing and shooting fraternity now passing their time in transit, was rather lonely, condemned to hours watching the toings and froings of those airborne fish through dusty glass.

The well-heeled photographer smiled, combed his hair and began to chatter with the speed of a boxer:

"Oh, progress has given us what only science fiction writers and poets dreamed of before – to outwit artful and ruthless time. Yes, yes, just so!"

"Scam," a girl with bleached hair butted in lazily. She had just come from the smoking room, and reeked of tobacco. "So what's the secret?"

The photographer laughed.

"To be blunt, *ma chérie*, there is no secret; it is all about the laws of physics and observation …"

"As I said – scam!" the girl snapped back. But she was shushed – and those listening clearly understood that the grey-haired gentleman might lighten the tedium as well as – or rather no worse than – a professional compère or a radio host. And he, being given carte blanche, settled down comfortably on the broad window sill and continued:

"Let's imagine that between eleven and midday you are in the company of the same idle travellers aboard a comfortable airliner – say an Airbus-A330, since frankly speaking, I don't rate Boeings – at the airport of … let's say Bangkok. Yet at five in the afternoon you reappear on the earth at Moscow and inhale its native smoke – which, as we know, is both sweet and pleasant."

Some listeners hemmed, skeptical about the sweetness and pleasantness of Moscow smoke. The others kept silent and so the grey-haired gentleman continued.

"And yet, my friends that flight takes about ten hours! What is going on? Of course, it's the difference in time zones, but, you see, such an explanation is too boring and banal. It is much more interesting to think that, thanks to turbojets and the remarkable mechanics of a wing multiplied by the laws of aerodynamics, you have deceived omnipotent time and ripped several hours of life away from its tenacious claws."

"Yes, but when you fly in the opposite direction, it gets those hours back with percent," the hunting dog interrupted him, yawning and covering her mouth with a narrow yellow palm decorated with a silver Indian bracelet. "Comme il faut."

"But the surprising thing is," the photographer continued undeterred, "That time on the moving plane, as the ingenious physicist Albert Einstein established, is really slowed down. And the quicker the plane flies, the slower time in it passes. Of course, in our case this is virtually imperceptible – some thousand fractions of a second. But if we managed to accelerate a plane near to the speed of light, a person, after staying on board just a few hours according to a place's time, could return to earth at a time when tens or even hundreds of years would have passed. That is, you could make a trip to the future."

"Really?!" the bleached blonde girl was surprisingly excited. "That's amazing!"

It seemed, for a second, that she forgot about the forthcoming hours of fruitless waiting, and found her head filled with the boundless prospects of travel to the future. But the feeble fire in her eyes died away almost as quickly as it ignited.

"But what would I actually do in the future?" she continued despondently. "There'll probably be the same old press tribe working with some totally fancy computers. And I can't even cope with the ancient ones in our editorial office. Maybe it'd be possible to go back into the past? Where there are brave men and beautiful women, and wars, and duels, and hunting – just like in 'The Countess Of Monsoro' series – you can get a box set now."

"Someday science will make it possible," the grey-haired photographer said significantly. "Scientists have already established that in one aspect the great Einstein was mistaken to claim that the velocity of light can't be exceeded. As it happens, it can be. And if we accelerate our plane or, more precisely, our spaceship, to superlight speed, we could reach a remote planet 450 light years from Earth in a few days. Then, if we directed our high-powered telescope back towards the Earth, we would see the slaughter of the St Bartholomew's Day Massacre, or Admiral Kolinyi swearing that he didn't kill his father the Duke de Guiz, or Charles IX firing an arquebus at the running Huguenots, or Catherine de Medici with her poisons. And, of course, maybe all those amazing scenes Dumas père's novel. Though, probably, a lot of those scenes were not absolutely so, or even absolutely not so."

The girl was stunned by the prospect, and made feverish efforts to remember where exactly in her favourite series these names and events occurred.

"You should anchor 'Obvious-improbable'," the Hunting dog observed drily.

"Glad to serve," the old man bowed graciously though it was obvious he was disappointed.

Meanwhile, at the far end of the transit area, near the entrances to the utility and staff rooms, a well-built man of middle age in a bland grey jacket and blue jeans was striding out clutching a black leather briefcase.

If any of the journalists had paid attention to this person, the real Babel in the transit area would have begun. The fact is that the owner of the leather briefcase was none other than the Lawyer, who fortune had made the intermediary between the Russian authorities and Joshua Kold, and who would thus gain international fame through no efforts of his own, a fame very rare for representatives of the Russian legal profession.

As it happens, the Lawyer was rather blessed by luck. From the very beginning of his law career, his mandators – for some reason this is what he called his clients – had been celebrities engaged in improbable adventures. There was the successful media magnate caught trying to walk out of a government residence with a box containing one million dollars taken from under the copying machine. There was the former Minister of Justice whose photos in a sauna in the company of naked girls once filled the Russian tabloids. There was the wife of the opposition leader – a deputy of the Russian parliament – who accidentally, according to investigators, shot her husband on the eve of his carefully planned military coup. There were enough plots in his mandators' list for ten thrillers. And though the possibility of writing them up had sometimes crossed the Lawyer's mind, he'd never had the time to get round to it.

The Lawyer had already met Kold – and nearly all the world media had reported it. Just exactly what these two very different people talked about remained secret, of course, but the international public learned that the Lawyer had given Kold as a gift a Russian abc-book, Fyodor Dostoyevsky's *'Crime and Punishment'*, a small volume of stories by Anton Chekhov, the *'History of the Russian State'* by court historian Karamzin, and, in a makeweight, several words of encouragement transmitted by the Lawyer from the highest Kremlin offices.

Meanwhile, the nervous tension among the representatives of the second most ancient profession reached its apogee. The correspondent of one of the alternative internet portals, a gloomy young man with a bony face – there is a saying about such people: 'not strong, but nervous' – bleated provocatively:

"He's probably under the wing of intelligence agencies in Lubyanka. There 'gutting' gets extreme."

"Well, maybe not 'gutting'," the robust guy from Gazety.ru pompously responded, "It's not '37 now. Now it's called 'debriefing'. But on the intelligence agencies you are bang on, colleague."

The Lawyer grinned to himself because he, unlike these knights of quill and keypad, knew that the one they were waiting for in hope of snapping in a photo, getting a quick quote from, or even a sensational interview, wasn't in Lubyanka. And there was certainly no notorious 'gutting' – the stakes were too high.

"And in the USA, there are no transit areas at all," the grey-haired gentleman from Reuters declared.

"Yes, that's so right!" the gloomy young man added. "There they have such a highly developed transportation system that all eventualities are considered in advance!

"Well – it's the most free country in the world," the blonde girl said, tapping her shoulder.

The photographer smiled sadly, but decided not risk pursuing this unpromising discussion.

07:33 P.M.

The journalists didn't notice the Lawyer. He was nimble and skilled enough to avoid drawing attention to himself. Opening a non-descript grey door, the Lawyer stepped quickly through it and appeared in a small room with a big table in the middle place in such a way that you could only get to other door on the opposite side of the room sideways, squeezing along the wall.

A poker-faced person in the uniform of the airport security police was sitting at the table. The Lawyer showed his ID card and the policeman nodded and pressed the button. The door behind him opened with a quiet buzz.

The Lawyer squeezed past the table, walked through the door and found himself in a space strikingly different from the hi-tech style of one of the world's most modern airports.

Instead of plastic, polished stone, glass and metal, here the tree was king. Heavy oak panels covered the walls and ceiling. The parquet, velvet drapery, leather sofas and floor lamps bearing the coat of arms of the vanished empire helped transport this small hall back into the time when the foundation stone for the Aswan dam was laid upon the Nile, when Soviet rockets in Cuba were put on standby, and Khruschev banged his shoe on his desk at the UN General Assembly in a protest against the Philippines delegate.

The person on duty here had the uniform of an officer of the Federal Guard Service. He double-checked the Lawyer's documents and opened an elevator door in front of him. Here too everything was from the Soviet period with brass buttons with digits for the floors, an ebonite phone and an ashtray wired into the elevator wall. The Lawyer pressed the button with the digit '7' and the elevator plummeted as if into an underworld.

Of course, Joshua Kold was a key player in the global geopolitical game conducted from time immemorial between the largest states of the world. So it would be absurd to assume he'd be simply left to the mercy of fate in the transit area of Sheremetyevo airport. He could not be left as prey to journalists, and, above all to the agents of interested intelligence agencies who might try anything from banal elimination – after all, nobody hurried to hand over umbrellas with poisoned needles to the museums – to no less banal kidnapping (Mossad had great experience in this kind of thing).

So, as soon as Kold got off the plane from Hong Kong he was taken at once if not under protection then at least under intense guardianship, and smoothly but persistently forwarded to that oak hall with floor lamps from where the elevator carried him away into the top secret destination of Bunker A.

The history of this shelter thirty metres down is fascinating and deserves a separate novel. It is closely connected with the history of the creation of Sheremetyevo airport and the destiny of the Soviet leader of that time, Nikita Khrushchev, who intended to catch up and overtake America and complete the triumph of communism no later than 1980.

Awed by the scale of London's Heathrow airport, Khrushchev gazed at the surrounding coppices and woods as he paused on the ladder of the Tu-104 after landing at the drab airfield of the Air Force of the USSR not far from Sheremetyevo village, and muttered: "It will be necessary for us to build something like in London."

Those who needed to heard the phrase, remembered it and took it as a guide to action. The first Soviet international airport quickly accepted Boeings and Caravels, but for the convenience of official government delegations one extra but rather essential trifle was needed – ensuring the safety of the top officials of the state.

Maybe their enemies would rattle the saber, the USSR wouldn't yield, and nuclear warfare could find the country leaders anywhere. Fuel was added to the fire by messages from the USA provided by 'moles' working for the Soviets who had dug into the earthy depths of the Yankee state apparatus. It became clear that under Denver International Airport – the biggest in the world, by the way – the Americans had constructed a huge bunker capable of housing all the heads of the country and members of their families in case of a nuclear attack.

Thus, the need to construct Bunker A under Sheremetyevo airport was determined, and the goal achieved, as well as possible in the country of developed socialism, 'in a short time, ahead of schedule'.

For decades, the bunker stood on 'alert' with all its rooms ready to receive high-ranking guests at any second, with all life support systems checked and ready and every safety system in perfect order.

Of course, one might assume that *perestroika*, and especially that post-*perestroika* time in which hundreds of similar useless objects were destroyed, would not have spared Bunker A. But the democratic leaders of Russia cared as much for their safety as their totalitarian predecessors, and so the bunker continued to serve, hidden under the new terminals of Sheremetyevo as a relic being, a theromorph of another ancient reptile that conjured horror by the mere fact of its existence.

For all these years, none of the highest dignitaries of the Soviet empire ever visited Bunker A – fortunately, there was no need. The same was true of the leaders of new Russia. And so Joshua Kold became the first – and the only – inhabitant of the bunker.

The Lawyer sometimes wondered: how does he sleep thirty metres down? Don't ghosts of the past eras disturb him in this place where six workers died, according to hearsay, in the lift mine of the bunker during a construction glitch?

It is much better to ask such questions over a glass of fine cognac or vintage wine, in a nice, friendly chat. But Kold, it seemed, wasn't willing to be on friendly terms with anybody, and kept himself closed and detached, justifying his surname. Perhaps some positive news might perk him up, or bring him out of his stupor, but the message the Lawyer was carrying to the inhabitant of Bunker A hardly promoted a positive spirit.

The elevator stopped, the next officer on duty opened a door and stood aside to let the Lawyer pass.

In front of him there was a corridor with all the same oak panels, and a thick carpet pathway to muffle the sound of footsteps. The doors were marked only by stark alphanumeric codes, and the dim light glowed from opaque plafonds in the ceiling.

There was one more guard post to negotiate, at which the Lawyer had to open the contents of his briefcase to a Federal Protective Service officer. Then at last, turning round a corner in the corridor, after passing through highly secure isolation compartments designed to protect against the penetration of toxic agents, the Lawyer stopped at a door marked very simply 'Lounge.'

For reasons only they knew, the journalists above, with the special powers of concentration and highly developed cynicism of the all-understanding and all-knowing professional, were sure that the whole world danced to their tune.

But from down here, at a depth of thirty metres, they seemed like the bunch of kids the cunning and artful piper from Hamelin led astray. The piper, as is well-known from the story, very dexterously coped with rats, but also drew children away with no less success.

Then chasing unnecessary thoughts and allusions away, the Lawyer knocked on the door and pushed.

The Lounge was a large room with a sofa, several chairs, a small billiard table up against a wall and an oval table of walnut under a massive triple-armed chandelier with opaque plafonds. A wall clock in a wooden case ticked, emphasizing the silence in the bunker.

Joshua Kold was sitting at the table looking like a diligent pupil with straight back, and hands on the table. He was clean-shaven, except for a small hipster beard, and he was dressed in a grey shirt, jumper, and jeans – all reminiscent of a student concentrating before an important exam. The illusion was supported by the pile of books to the right of Kold. The Lawyer skimmed their spines – reference books on law in English, the Bible, George Orwell's '1984', and also Dostoyevsky's 'Crime and Punishment' and other books gifted by Lawyer on his previous visit.

On the table, there was a metal tray with couple of glasses and several small bottles of water. There was a flat screen TV on the wall behind Kold. In the corner, there was the already familiar floor lamp with the hammer and sickle hidden, and nearby there was a door connecting to another room, most likely, a bedroom.

The lounge didn't smell at all like the rest of the bunker with its thin, almost imperceptible odour of Cold War – a smell of dampness, rusty metal and burnt electrical wiring. Here it smelt quite civilized – coffee, good perfume and fried bread.

"Good afternoon!" the Lawyer said softly.

Kold raised his shining black eyes towards him. Seen through the glasses, they reminded him of olives.

"Good afternoon, hello," the young man got up and shook hands with Lawyer. He had a palm as dry and firm as if turned from a tree. "Sit down, please."

"Thank you." The Lawyer put his briefcase on a floor, pulled up a chair and sat down opposite Kold. "How are you? How do you feel? Where there any requests, wishes?

There was a pause. Kold opened the folder and pulled out a sheet of paper on which there was some writing.

"I'm fine," he said calmly, scanning the writing. "Only one request. Let Ms. Morisson meet me no more than once a day, and only in the briefing room, not here."

Rebecca Morisson was the plenipotentiary representative of Mikiliks, the scandalous international revealers of secrets, and maybe the girlfriend of its founder Augusto Cassandzhi. Cassandzhi had already been hiding for a long time in the Ecuadorian Embassy in London. In Kold, Cassandzhi at once saw a kindred spirit and disciple. How Kold saw 'the great unmasker', as Cassandzhi was called, is unknown, but he obviously didn't favour Ms. Morisson.

The Lawyer remembered that in a lobby of the Presidential Administration there was talk that all the story of Mikiliks and the attempts to catch Cassandzhi were well and skilfully thought-through provocation.

"But there remains the question of what Kold's business actually is," he thought, examining his subject. "In our information century any release of compromising data is a Pandora's box and who gets what out of it nobody knows."

"I'll let them know your request," the Lawyer nodded. "Anything else? How are you fed?"

"Thanks, the food is ok."

"How are the conditions?"

"Perhaps, it might be more comfortable up above." Kold said raising his eyes to the ceiling. "But hardly safer."

"Aren't you afraid to become the new Nasseri?" the Lawyer asked.

"Who is that?" Kold inquired disinterestedly.

"Well, it's a well-known story. Mekhran Karimi Nasseri, Iranian political refugee. In 1970 he was exiled from the country for his participation in antigovernment activities and protests. He wandered for several years between different countries, and finally obtained citizenship of Belgium and, respectively, a passport. In 86, Mekhran travelled from Belgium to London where his relatives lived, but at Heathrow airport it transpired he had no documents – either he lost the passport or it was stolen. The British returned Mekhran to the airport of departure, the Charles de Gaulle in France. There it became clear that he couldn't return to Belgium for the same reason – there were no documents. But then there were also no legal reasons to deport him from France. It was noted that he had entered the country absolutely legally because at that time Mekhran had documents. So he got stuck in the transit area of Charles de Gaulle. Do you know for how long?

"No, I don't know."

"For eighteen years!"

"Why couldn't the Belgians just give him a duplicate passport?" Kold made a gesture of bewilderment.

The Lawyer shook his head.

"No, to put it simply. Under Belgian law, the paperwork requires the presence of the person the passport is issued to, but then it is impossible to enter Belgium without documents."

"Catch 22?"

"Exactly. Though after nine years of life at the airport, having already become not just a local celebrity, but a fixture of the transit area of Charles de Gaulle, Mekhran suddenly received from the Belgian Foreign Ministry an offer by which the country was ready to accept him without any documents. And you know, he…"

"Refused!" Kold smiled with his short, fleeting smile. "I studied psychology. It's so simple: popularity and public attention are like a drug. Once tasted, ninety percent of people can't refuse and try to recapture it again and again."

"True, true," the Lawyer nodded again. "So Mekhran left the transit area and went over to the airport hotel only after he fell seriously ill. The most ridiculous thing is that he moved neither to Belgium, nor Great Britain, but lives in Paris now and feels good.

"Emigrants are always like that: where it is good, there is home," Kold murmured.

"By the way, Steven Spielberg did a quite famous movie based on Mekhran's story "'The Terminal' starring Tom Hanks and Catherine Zeta-Jones. Didn't you see it?"

Kold tugged his shoulder, then nodded.

"Now I remember. Yes, I saw it."

The Lawyer was irritated. He'd just spent several minutes telling this man something he already knew. But, maybe Kold is just too affected and couldn't concentrate?

Mekhran Nasseri was neither the first, nor the only prisoner of transit areas in airports. In this same Sheremetyevo transit area, Zara Kamalfar also spent ten months – after fleeing Iran too, by strange coincidence,.

The husband of this unfortunate woman who belonged to a Muslim sect of dervishes was executed in 2006, and she fled with her two children through Moscow to Germany, hoping to receive shelter there and get political asylum in Canada.

The German officials, however, remained deaf to the tragedy of this family and sent Zara Kamalfar and her children back to Russia. After being forced to stay in the transit area, the refugees had almost no means of support. In a video appeal to the world, Zara said: "Life here is hard, very hard... We fill a bucket of water in the toilet in the middle of the night away from the eyes of the authority to take a bath. I have no place to wash my clothes, all doors are closed to us... A policewoman pushed me, I hit the wall and blood began to flow from my mouth. I don't cry because I have to be strong. Children shouldn't see my tears. I laugh to give them hope, so they can fight, so they withstand."

After a while the children began fall ill from lack of sunlight, scant nutrition and a shortage of vitamins. The daughter developed a skin disease and the son had scurvy. All the same this story ended well since after ten months the Canadian authorities allowed the Kamalfar family to fly to Vancouver and gave Zara and her family residence permits.

But if Iranians were political refugees, then Englishman Gary Peter Austin simply missed his flight at a Philippines airport since his e-ticket had been inexplicably cancelled. The situation was complicated by the fact that he had run out of money and so was stuck ten thousand kilometers from Foggy Albion.

He spent New Year in the airport of Manila, and altogether spent twenty three days there, after turning into a local tourist attraction. In the end the unfortunate Austin's ordeal ended when either a passenger flying to the Netherlands took pity on him and brought him a ticket – or he was helped by the British Embassy.

And the story of German Heinz Müller seems almost a good joke. Müller arrived in Rio de Janeiro to meet the woman of his dreams. They had become acquainted on the internet and agreed to meet, but to the great disappointment of this German Romeo, his Brazilian Juliet didn't want him.

As a result, Heinz ended up in the middle of a foreign country without any money for his return ticket. He lived at Virakopus-Campinas airport near Sao Paulo for several days until he was taken to a local clinic for psychiatric assessment.

There are also some volunteers among the captives of transit areas. Japanese man Hiroshi Nohara stayed for 117 days at Mexico City airport without any apparent reason. His tickets and documents were in good order, and Japanese diplomats were constantly keeping an eye on him, ready to provide him with a new passport at once if necessary.

The story among journalists was that this little Japanese man was simply craving celebrity. And there was no doubt Nohara was happy to be interviewed, pose for tourists, crying out: 'Terminal-2!', with clear allusions to the Spielberg movie. And yet he always refused to explain what he was doing in the transit area.

The final twist in this stationary Odyssey was even more mysterious. One fine day in December 2008 a young Japanese woman called Oyuki literally took Nohara by the hand, forced him to buy a ticket and they departed together for Japan. And nobody heard any more about them.

And if for some transit areas were a shelter, then the famous Chinese dissident Fan Chzhen Hu used them for political struggle. For 92 days, Fan Chzhen Hu lived at Tokyo's Narita airport in protest against the Chinese authorities' refusal to let him come home after treatment in a Japanese clinic.

In the USSR, the People's Republic of China, and other countries with oppressive regimes, dispatching undesirable elements abroad and depriving them of their nationality was by no means rare, but only Fan Chzhen Hu ventured to fight for the right to return. Most surprisingly, he managed to draw international attention to the issue and China relented, their prodigal son back. The dissident was put under house arrest immediately in Shanghai, but this hardly frightened Fan Chzhen Hu who had already spent three years in Chinese prisons for illegal entrepreneurship.

All these various facts flashed through the Lawyer's mind as he collected his thoughts. A tough conversation, with a lot of things depending on it, was ahead of him.

"Mr. Kold, this time I come to you without any gifts, but with news." The Lawyer undid his brief case and took a transparent file out. "There is good news, and not so good news. Which should I begin with?"

Not a single muscle on Kold's face moved. He simply nodded. For some reason, the Lawyer focused on his big ears. From the depths of his memory of a physiognomics course, he dragged up this theory: "Big ears are a sign of independent judgment and determination. They are also a sign of developed intelligence linked to extraordinary acts."

"Let's start with the good news," Kold said at last.

"This is a letter from your mother," the Lawyer said, taking an envelope from the brief case. "It was sent through authorized representatives. Here."

Kold quickly skimmed the letter, then, apparently, started to read it from the beginning, much more attentively. At last, he put the letter aside.

"The Russian side," Lawyer continued, "That is, the Minister of Justice of the Russian Federation received an official letter from the Attorney-General of the USA Mr. Eric Older. This document can be considered as the reaction of the American side to your petition for provisional asylum. Mister Older writes that," the Lawyer glanced at the text of the letter, "You are accused of stealing state-owned property according to section 641 of Article 18 of the Code of the USA; the unauthorized information transfer of national defense interests according to section 793 sub-clause 'd' of the same article of the Code; and also of the voluntary search and transfer of classified information to a person who doesn't have the corresponding permission, as in section 798, point 'a'.

Further, Mr. Attorney-General is convinced, by the way, that your lack of opportunity to leave Russia is reasonably proven by the fact that you, Mr. Kold, cannot leave the territory of Sheremetyevo airport. But at any time the American side is ready to issue to you with a passport with valid for a limited period on condition that you come back to the USA – by a direct non-transit route, it says in the letter."

Kold laughed, practically without unclenching his lips, a laugh resembling that of someone paralyzed, with several short ha-has.

"I share your pleasure in Mr. Older's sense of humour," the Lawyer nodded, "I continue: in addition, he is authorized to report that the U.S. authorities are ready to provide the Russian authorities guarantees concerning the treatment which Mr. Kold, that means you, can expect when you return to the United States.

"And what is that?"

Lawyer noticed that Kold's eyes, usually passionless, glowed strangely, as if he'd been told about the possibility of a big prize on horserace.

"Mr. Older writes that, and I quote: 'Firstly, the U.S. authorities don't intend to invoke capital punishment for Mr. Kold in case of his return to the United States. The nature of the charges brought against him doesn't lead to invocation of such a measure. The U.S. authorities also don't intend to invoke capital punishment for Mr. Kold for other crimes for which capital punishment is supposed.'"

"Funny," Kold unexpectedly interrupted Lawyer. "Are they bargaining?"

"Listen to the end," the Lawyer said softly. "There is still the 'secondly.'"

"Sorry."

"So, 'Secondly, Mr. Kold will not be subjected to torture. Invocation of torture is forbidden by the legislation of the USA.'"

"Swines!" Kold's voice trembled. He turned extremely pale, fists clenched. "Hypocritical swines!"

The Lawyer became silent, waiting until his interviewee pulled himself together. Kold's reaction surprised him – perhaps, for the first time he had dared to give vent to feelings.

"May I continue?" Lawyer asked, at last.

"It isn't necessary," Kold shook his head and looked aside. "I know what is coming – that my case will not be considered by a military court, that I will be able to hire any lawyers and all interrogations will be carried out in their presence, that a trial jury will judge me in open court, that I will be able to appeal a judgement in the appellate court of the USA and so on, blah blah blah. Isn't that true?"

"True," the Lawyer nodded. "I will add only that in completing the message Mr. Older believes that the guarantees given by him are sufficient to completely deprive you of any basis for you to consider yourself a refugee and be provided with temporary or any other shelter."

"They want to catch me at any cost," Kold pulled a mouth corner. It was probably meant to be a smile, reminded the Lawyer more of a grimace of pain. "'He won't be subjected to torture', 'it is necessary…'"

"Mr. Kold, there is more to come," the Lawyer put the papers and file away in the brief case. "As you understand, after this letter the Russian side is obliged to react and make a decision on your application for provisional asylum based on the guarantees provided by the Attorney-General."

"I … I understand," Kold took off his glasses, and swept his hand across his face. It was clear he was hanging on by the skin of his teeth. "When will the decision be made?"

"I can't tell you definitely, but I think in the nearest future. It is now 20:24 by Moscow time. By the morning everything will be clear."

"The last night…" Kold whispered and tugged hard on his elbows. He stared at the table. "The last …"

"I understand that in this situation words of consolation look a little fake, but nevertheless – don't worry," the Lawyer stood up, patting Kold's shoulder. "Don't imagine the worst. Anyway, if you don't mind, of course, I will be with you to the end to protect your interests."

"Until the morning?" Kold raised his head. "Will you stay here with me until the morning?"

"If you need me."

"Please, don't leave me! I am lonely … And still this girlfriend of Cassandzhi tries to learn what information I have. She gives me hints, do you understand? And I am tired."

"Perhaps, you should have a drink?" the Lawyer asked.

"No, I rarely drink and even if I did, now is definitely not the time to deceive myself with alcohol," Kold looked out of the corners of his eyes at the Lawyer. "And anticipating your next question: medical means of calming nerves don't interest me either."

"What do you want?"

"To talk. Just to talk. However, if it isn't interesting to you, of course, I don't insist..."

The Lawyer slightly loosened his tie and leaned back on his chair.

"Mr. Kold, I have told you, I will be with you to the end in any turn of events; it is my professional duty. And believe me, I am speaking absolutely sincerely: you are one of the most interesting interlocutors I have ever met."

Kold nodded, took a small bottle of water from a tray, unscrewed the cap, poured out a glass and took a sip.

"Interesting," the Lawyer thought, "What if he now suddenly declares that he actually doesn't want shelter in Russia, and wants to take off for Venezuela or Uruguay? Or wants to meet the wordsmiths upstairs and put all the information he has out there in real-time? Or just says: 'I have realized the wrong I have done and the depth of my treachery. I now want to return home and be punished according to the guarantees of the Attorney-General of the USA Eric Older.' What will this mean for those who make decisions at our end?"

The Lawyer knew who made the decision, and didn't doubt for a moment that the decision would be made, and that from the point of view of safety of the country and its geopolitical interests the decision would be correct. But the destiny of the guy sitting in front of him was not enviable. How did the alternative journo describe it – 'disemboweling'? God forbid he hear about the particulars of this especially as Kold didn't react entirely comfortably to the words in the letter on torture to which 'disemboweling' must only partly compare…

The clock jingled out half past nine in the evening. Kold frowned.

"You don't like loud sounds?" the Lawyer asked.

"Not when they are imposed on me."

The Lawyer stood up, opened the clock and stopped the ticker.

"So what would you like to talk about, Mr. Kold?"

"What? I don't know … Everything. Or more precisely, about lots of things. I am at a crossroads, a bifurcation point, and to me it is important … important to understand what is happening. Both to me and to the world, as melodramatic as that sounds."

"You need to get it off your chest," the Lawyer nodded. "Well, it is good. For us lawyers, the principal who makes contact is always better than those who stay tight-lipped. You know, I don't like the word 'client', so popular with American lawyers – it always reminds me of a phrase from an old Soviet comedy movie: 'The client has ripened'. What does that mean? Well, it's a long story, and has no relation to our business. Would you mind if I turn on a voice recorder? Recordings can be useful in this work."

Kold grinned, genuinely this time, and waved a hand around the room as if specifying some objects invisible to Lawyer.

"Of course, turn it on. At least, you do it openly."

He waited until the Lawyer had set his smartphone up then started talking:

"You asked what I would like to begin with? Probably, with rats."

"With what?" said the Lawyer, surprised.

"With rats. Rats, small animals, rodents. Grey backs, beady eyes, naked tails, you know? The omnivorous creatures that can get anywhere and everywhere. Those scurrying beasts that since time immemorial have lived near human dwellings, where life is quieter, more reliable and more nourishing. By nature, a rat is an egoist thinking only of its own benefit and pleasures. In a dense forest, in a dried-up steppe or in some tundra it doesn't get to live, but merely survive, and the rat doesn't like it. Are you already recording?"

"No," The lawyer shook his head. "I will turn it on now."

"It isn't necessary. This is just a preamble, a prologue. When I give you a signal, then you can start to record, but now it isn't necessary. So, about rats. The Ancient Romans, who were big experts in the destruction of civilizations, called rats by the short word 'rattus'. By the way, contrary to popular belief, this has no relation to the Latin word 'pirata', though it seems conformable and, above all, similar in meaning. But I'm wandering off topic...

So...warm cellars, tasty garbage, darkness, silence – human cities became rat paradise. Especially tolerant people call it symbiosis, normal ones parasitizing, but, in fact, neither care much about nudicaudate rodents. They exist, and as long as they don't transmit plague as in old times, that's fine.

But everything changes when He appears. The Ratcatcher. Nobody knows who he is nor where he is. Nobody has seen him. Well, almost nobody. Nevertheless, the Ratcatcher is material, perceivable and corporeal. On the one hand, he is like time, existing regardless of our knowledge of him, and on the other hand, we, the people, we can observe the results of his actions, and empirically we watch the Ratcatcher carefully, framing conspiracy theories about him.

But while we are framing them, the Ratcatcher takes his pipe and he begins to play ...

The sound of his music is at first heard only by rats. You can call it magic, neurolinguistic programming or exact calculation, but once they've heard the pipe of the Ratcatcher, rats begin to change. They leave their daily affairs, cares, entertainments and begin to gnaw ...

'Grrrum, grrrum, grrrum!' This is not the shod boots of red-faced fellows in grey shirts clip-clopping on a cobblestone road. This is tens, sometimes hundreds, of thousands of yellow gnashers piercing basements and foundations. Of history and culture, of family and practice, of belief and traditions, of literature and music, of architecture and painting. Of language. Of education. Of the memory of a nation. All of it turns to dust, to garbage, to slime, to mud and ashes.

Rats gnaw! Precepts and principles are subverted, heroes and feats are discredited.

Rats gnaw!! White becomes black, and black white. Everything is turned inside out, remade, upside down, back to front, simple becomes difficult, and difficult is simply destroyed. The truth is replaced by a lie. The truth is drowning … no, not in wine – but in the streams of this lie.

Rats gnaw!!! Sharpen, crumble, and grind to powder. On radio stations and TV channels. On pages of paper and virtual media. In blogs and social media postings. Every day, each hour.

'Grrrum, grrrum, grrrum! Grrrum, grrrum, grrrum!', in tune with the melody of the magic pipe. 'The worse "the better!', is the slogan of the rats. Or the Ratcatcher's?

Ultimately it isn't important. On a lovely day, the castle of civilization once so firm and unapproachable, long undercut by rats, suddenly begins to be unsteady, then cracks, founders and stops being a stronghold and a citadel. Walls and towers fall, buttresses turn into taluses of crushed stone, and gates turn into dust. And then no more rats climb into the breaches and holes, but in their place, the real predators, greedy and hungry, and after them come the night deathbirds, numerous and dangerous.

The rats become the first, easiest prey of the newcomers. Weakened, exhausted by gnawing, but still captivated by the song of the Ratcatcher, the rats can't perceive reality adequately. They are devoured alive, even while they are gnawing to the last gnaw the already decayed and useless walls.

But the acts of the Ratcatcher aren't at an end because after the rats, the turn of the children always comes.

On the ashes, on waste grounds and heathlands, among crumbling gravestones and fallen statues, children dance wild dances to the music of the Ratcatcher, and around, in the darkness, predators and deathbirds whirl. From time to time, they rush in on the dancing children and drag away a prize which cries out in horror through the darkness, but the cries cannot be heard by the rest since their ears are ringing with the sound of the Ratcatcher's pipe.

The finale of the Ratcatcher's symphony, the end of his time, comes when nobody is left on the ruins, either children or rats. Fields grow with tall weeds, sand skims marble steps. Where life once thrived, wires buzzed, and the pulse of steel hammers roared, now wind whistles through bare branches and wild dogs prowl. This is what I wanted to tell you before you turn the gadget on to record!"

Kold was walking up and down the room for a long time, and as he finished his speech, his hands were shaking. The Lawyer looked at Kold if not with amazement then with considerable surprise.

The usually pale face of Kold turned red, and his nose fluttered a little. But noticing the Lawyer's surprised look, he smiled simply, with a guileless smile, took a seat on the chair and almost cheerfully waved a hand.

"Turn it on, come on!"

Lawyer turned the smartphone over in his hands thoughtfully and found himself recalling Brodsky, from 'Letters to a Roman Friend':

> *Yes indeed, Posthumus, a chicken's no bird*
> *But a chicken brain suffers its own misery.*
> *If you're born in an empire, you mark my word,*
> *It is better to live far away, by the sea.*
>
> *Far off from Caesar, far away from the blaze*
> *Where there's no need to scurry and cringe all your days.*
> *You say that all governors are thieves in the night*
> *But I'd rather a thief than a vampire that bites.*

Kold was confused, but in his eyes something doglike flickered, sad and fateful. But there was no turning back now; recording had begun.

FILE 001.WAV

"My childhood was spent in the State of North Carolina. I was born in Elizabeth City, but we moved to Wilmington, where the Cape Fear River drains into the Atlantic Ocean. Yes, there still is a cape, and it is indeed called Cape Fear and somewhere in these regions in old times pirates earned their living, with Edward Teach the Blackbeard at the top.

The coast here is extraordinary, with vast sandy beaches, dunes and old boarding houses and tourist hotels. If you've seen Scorsese's movie 'Cape Fear', you can imagine what I'm talking about. But the cape doesn't get its name from the movie, of course. In the 16th century the English seafarer Richard Grenville – he was a corsair, I think, and a friend and accomplice of Francis Drake – well, he nearly went down with his ship here. Then, my father said, such places were called the graveyard of the Atlantic. It's easy as pie to run aground even now, and in those days when seamen were guided only by compass, sun and stars, they were wrecked in great numbers here, so you really should call our beaches 'The Skeleton Coast'.

North Carolina is quite a remarkable state, if you don't know. Many key historical events happened here. For example, there was nearly a thermonuclear Armageddon. I learned about it when I worked in the Agency when the information was strictly secret, though now it is available to all.[3]

I know it's kind of strange to be proud of their homeland for such a reason, but you need to understand that American patriotism has a rather different flavor from, say, European, French or English.

It's like with Italians when they are proud of something – maybe some quaint local pub called 'The Cheerful Guinea' where a moustachioed Giovanni makes delightful pizzas with no less delightful mozzarella.

Why? Because the entire ground in the neighborhood of 'The Cheerful Guinea' is larded with historical relics – because in the house opposite Pope Saint Leo I stayed and in the belltower next door Leonardo da Vinci made sketches, and down the same road Hannibal's elephants walked.

For locals, all this is not just a reason for pride; it attracts tourists, too, like honey attracts bees. But of course nectar is also needed for honey, and that's where moustachioed Giovanni with his pizza comes in.

But in America – not only in North Carolina but all states – there are occupation layers where you find charcoal from a fire the Apaches

---

3   This is the crash of a B-52 carrying two 3-4 megaton nuclear bombs at Goldsboro, North Carolina in 1961. Documents released in 2013 revealed that with one of the bombs just one of the four arming switches prevented it detonating. If that last switch had gone the result would have been catastrophic. The bomb disposal expert there, Lt. Jack Revelle, said "As far as I'm concerned we came damn close to having a Bay of North Carolina. The nuclear explosion would have completely changed the Eastern seaboard if it had gone off." Each bomb had more than 250 times the destructive power of the Hiroshima bomb, with a 100% kill zone of 23 km.

started no longer ago than the 18th century. So in effect, we are like immigrants to another planet where there was no human history before, only Martian, vague and little understood.

Probably, if the Lord had done things differently – if the Mayan pyramids stood in the State of Washington, and Machu Picchu was in Boston – then we too might be a little different. But our ancestors had only the 'five civilized tribes', and all the rest were 'savages'. Yes probably not such blood-thirsty devils as they've sometimes been painted, but still savages.

However, even this Indian component was enough for us to make a cult of it. White boys and girls ran with plastic tomahawks, wearing carnival costumes of Indian chiefs, and on Independence Day they shoot bows in the park at targets stylized as pumas and bisons.

It is natural that in this earth, poor in historicity, then in each state, in each county and each district there are constant searches for something that can be lifted on to the board of the imagination and proudly proclaimed: 'Here, look, we are also a part of world historical process!'

And so the 'Mayflower', 'the pilgrim fathers', 'the Salem witches', 'the Thirteen Colonies', 'the Boston Tea Party' and others have become symbols of real resonance, and Trenton, Princeton, Yorktown and Saratoga are revered no less than Waterloo or Austerlitz in Europe.

Of course, sometimes these desperate searches for reasons for pride get rather comical, and you'll find a set of attractions like 'The biggest cord hank in the world' in remote places in America, monuments to 'The most gigantic teflon frying pan' or 'the house museum of local hunter John Smith who killed the largest beaver on the planet.'

However, the story of the North Caroline Armageddon has no relation to this provincial exotic. It is real and awful because of its reality.

What I'm talking about is the so-called 'Goldsboro accident' or 'the crash over Goldsboro'. It occurred in 1961, on 23rd January. I remembered this date for life thanks to Pa, who once said:

'Josh, all residents of our state have to consider this day our second or maybe our main birthday.'

My Pa would never speak frivolously, he wasn't that kind of a person, and for this reason 23rd January was etched in my memory forever.

1961: it was a hard and heavy time. The CIA had tried an invasion of Fidel Castro's Cuba which ended in humiliating failure. A year later there was the Cuban Missile Crisis, in which both the USA and the Soviets, as the journalists say, 'developed muscles' as they limbered up for World War 3.

B-52 bombers with nuclear weapons on board were constantly plying the East coast at that time. In the event of armed conflict and attacks by Soviet ships, they had to destroy them in the ocean away from the United States.

I read the secret report prepared by Parker Jones, an employee of the Sandia national nuclear laboratory who headed the department to ensure operational safety of nuclear weapons. The report was written on the basis of a thorough investigation of the incident. It said that all of us, I mean the United States, miraculously managed to avoid a 'catastrophe of monstrous scale.'

At first, there were no signs of trouble – the B-52 rising from the Seymour Johnson base near Goldsboro, made a planned flight along the coast and circled back to its turn point, ready for mid-air refueling. On board at the time were two Mark 39 hydrogen bombs with a capacity of four megatons each.

During refuelling the patrol-tired crew lost control of the huge plane, and as a result the B-52's wing came off. Still flying at high speed, the bomber began to fall apart. Three of the eight crew members were killed instantly, and five escaped by parachute.

Both hydrogen bombs dropped right out of the bomb bays and plummeted to earth. One fell on heathland near the settlement of Faro without any harm; but in the second one detonation mechanisms activated.

A special landing parachute had deployed over the bomb. The surviving pilots, seeing it, begun to pray – they were sure that in several moments there would be a vast explosion.

In Parker Jones's report, it is stated that three out of the bomb's four safety mechanisms failed, apparently because of the concussion of the crash. So when the bomb hit the ground near one of the neighboring farms, a detonator activated and the process to detonate the bomb's core was almost launched. Millions of lives were saved only by the last, fourth, fuse, the so-called low-voltage switch.

One can imagine what the locals thought when they saw the crash of the B-52, and then the descent of the bomb on a parachute. At that time in our country there was real hysteria – they were all afraid of Soviet attacks and nuclear war. People dug shelters, stored weapons, daily necessities, and other things. But they just didn't know enough about the consequences of a nuclear explosion– many hoped to go into the forest, into remote areas and thus survive.

Perhaps farmers, seeing the bomb on the parachute, took it to be the first signs of a Russian invasion. Maybe they thought of gathering their relatives, maybe, even their cattle, and heading for the trees, without even suspecting that if a nuclear device activated, they wouldn't outrun the blast wave even in racing cars.

The Mark-39 hydrogen bomb was, of course, not as powerful as the Soviet AH602 'Tsar bomb' with which Khrushchev threatened the whole world. The power of 'Tsar bomb' was fifty eight megatons, and the Mark-39's only four – but even this four was two hundred times more than the power of the atomic bomb which destroyed Hiroshima in 1945.

And if the Mark-39 which fell near a North Carolina farm had blown up, not only would numerous villages and towns nearby have been destroyed, but also Washington, Baltimore, Philadelphia, and even New York. The report's author estimates that the number of dead would rise beyond one million and if you add the wounded and the victims of radiation, then there would have been tens of millions of casualties.

Naturally, all information on the incident was at once coded. The Mark-39 was deployed five more years, despite its unreliable system of protection against accidental triggering of the detonators. This, I found out, was down to the fact that at that time we just had no other powerful nuclear bombs.

However, all this was long before I was born and is now ancient history.

Because Wilmington stands between two rivers flowing into the ocean bay, there are many channels , islands and moorings. From the windows of our house, especially from the second floor, you could always see ships sailing past Cape Fear and they constantly reminded me that everything in this world is changing, moving – that nothing is permanent, except time, which, as I said, exists regardless of our knowledge of it.

I was very fond of this house and everything around, and I want you to know – America is a great country, and I never betrayed it. On the contrary, it betrayed others, those who fed the octopus with human flesh. I'm probably speaking a little chaotically, but you will understand later. Now I come back to my childhood.

I remember one time when I was about eight or nine. It snowed – and snow is not the most frequent winter guest in North Carolina. The snow fell hard, forming real snow drifts, like in Canada. And, of course, everyone was delighted, children and adults, and for all the town it was like another Christmas, especially since it was Sunday.

That day Pa had a day off, and we all ran out into the yard and began to play snowballs. We didn't just throw snowballs at each other, though; we imitated the assault of Umurbrogal mountain on Peleliu Island during the fight for the Palau archipelago[4]!

Pa had often told us about this operation in World War II in which his father's elder brother took part – and always quoted vice admiral Sherman (not the one who used to beat confederates, another one). He learned Sherman's words from school: 'The steep slopes of this hill were broken up by strange edges and spokes, and marked, like a grid, by a system of caves. Our foe had used the area with devilish ingenuity and created such a strong position that the American marines still hadn't managed to take it. Among the maze of rocks the distance moved by the army in an entire week was measured in yards and feet.

On these islands, thousands of Americans died because the Japanese had created such tough fortifications here. They'd dug through the earth and rocks, made caves into bunkers, set guns and machine guns everywhere, and were so prepared it was as if they wanted to beat off the army of the Apocalypse. All the same our marines managed in the end to pick the Samurais out from their holes and dens and set up the American flag on Umurbrogal's top.

---

4   The Battle of Peleliu is the World War 2 battle of late 1944 that is featured in the video game *Call of Duty*. It was a controversial engagement because of the high loss of American lives for no huge strategic advance. Moreover, Major General William Rupertus, (USMC commander of 1st Marine Division) promised it would be over in four days – it lasted over two months.

The role of Umurbrogal was played for us by an old pickup truck filled up with snow. Pa got inside and became all the Japanese at once, and the rest of us – Mom, Judith and me – were our marines, attacking in three parties. It was terrific. I even had a flag to raise! A real American flag, though not very big.

Gee, it was so tough breaking through to that pickup truck! Snowballs flew. Everybody was covered in snow. There wasn't a dry place left on me, nor the others. Pa was standing in the truck driving us off like a multi-armed Shiva god, laughing at the top of his voice with horrible samurai laughter!

But then finally he gave us a chance to get closer. And as we moved in we managed to plaster him in snow and tumble him in a snowdrift. Then I solemnly set the American flag on the pickup roof. We started singing the anthem, and Pa climbed out of the snowdrift and joined in.

But right then I burst into sobs. Real hysterics. I cried in great spasms. Mom stroked me in the face, and Judith wet my head.

Everyone thought that it was because in the middle of the fight Pa had caught me on the nose so hard with a snowball that my nose started to bleed. But no, I endured that bravely and Pa even said I was a real soldier, that I was no worse than the heroes of the fight for Palau and that he was proud he had such a son.

But actually I was crying for another reason. If Pa hadn't given in, we would never have captured the pickup and set the flag on the roof. So it turned out that our fight for Palau was won not by America, but Japan. At that time, this idea was for me simply impossible and even intolerable.

I can't even imagine what it feels like for people of countries which have lost a war, been occupied or lost independence. To be a citizen of this unlucky country dooms you to a sad existence, to become an outsider, and with no way to improve the situation quickly.

In sport, even if you or your team lose, there is always a chance to strain muscles, to gather your will in your hands and to achieve a new result, to achieve a victory. We are taught this at school from the earliest age. To be successful, to be a winner, is the ultimate goal in life – only this way can you become the master of your own fate.

For this reason, I am grateful to God that I was born in the United States – in the richest, happiest and safest country of the world. Naturally,

I love my country. That's not sentimental at all. I don't understand how it could be any different and I was actually surprised to learn that in other countries there are people that despise their Homeland.

It wasn't for nothing that the Lord granted human beings freedom of choice in everything in life – everything except for the three things given us from above: country, family and race. They can't be chosen. These are the choice of God and people have to be proud of His choice whichever it is. Only like this can you live constructively and work.

Work – in particular, hard work – built a small group of settlements into the strongest and most powerful state on the planet in two hundred years.

Work, money and capital are the basis of freedom. Only a wealthy man is really free. The pitiful runaway and the poor derelict without a cent to his name will be slaves forever. The beliefs of the pilgrim father's told them: 'Work, create, fight to find your house and to become the owner of it!' They trusted, they worked, they fought …

But I got it. Americans are essentially immigrants – and they include many who came to the States to work for a better life. And these Americans have become the ones who worked, who believed in freedom and were ready to make any sacrifice for the sake of it.

Of course, if you think about it, it's all completely logical and corresponds to a success algorithm – people with initiative aim for a beacon of success and prosperity just like moths are lured to a light.

Anyway, the USA is a unique or rare phenomenon on our planet. Once again: I want everyone to know, I am proud of the fact that I am an American and that I am honoured to fight to make my Homeland an even more free and happy country.

When I was a child, we often played Elvis Presley's recording of 'America the Beautiful'. I remember the lyrics so well:

O beautiful for spacious skies
For amber waves of grain
For purple mountain majesties
Above thy fruited plain

America, America!
God shed his grace on thee
And crowned thy good with brotherhood
From sea to shining sea.

America, America!
God shed his grace on thee
And crown thy good with brotherhood
From sea to shining sea!

For amber waves of grain
For purple mountain majesties
Above thy fruited plain

America, America!
God shed His grace on thee
And crown thy good with brotherhood
From sea to shining sea.

I am ready to stand by every word in there. That's all. Enough of that.

My first and probably only early childhood friend was Ron Stout, though nobody called him that. To residents of Elizabeth City where we lived then, he was known as 'The Iron Hand'. No that's not an Indian name at all, though there were enough of them in North Carolina in earlier times.

The truth is Ron's father was a mechanic, or more precisely, the owner of an auto repair shop attached to the gas station, you know, just an ordinary gas station with a big Shell banner over the entrance. So he had a big tin shed, with lots of machines, devices and tools. And, well, Ron had spent all his time there since childhood, tinkering with all these pieces of iron, always twisting something, soldering, drilling and welding. And once he made an iron hand for himself as the Terminator in the old movie, and even went to church with it – where he ripped the deputy mayor's new suit when it got hooked. That's why ever after Ron was nicknamed The Iron Hand.

We were pals even before school. Well, companions… We sat together in preschool in the sandbox under the supervision of Mrs. Boyd and we wouldn't give this 'Galactic Star' cargo spaceship to fat McFlynn. Then the other McFlynns always came – three brothers – and took over the box and chucked sand in our faces.

Later, in grade school, we were joined like salt and pepper – always going everywhere and sharing breakfasts. We did just about everything together, and even fell together into an old maintenance shaft – that's the kind of friendship we had.

When the war against Iraq started, the first, Operation Desert Storm, Ron's father hung out a poster saying 'I Do Not Serve Militarists' over the entrance to the auto repair shop.

Pa, I remember, got really angry, and his friends too. They considered that 'Old man George'– that's how they called President Bush Sr. – is doing everything right, and Saddam needs to be punished for his friendship with the 'reds' and his aggression against tiny Kuwait. Generally, they thought: 'Go ahead, sons of America!'

Once my old man and Ron's began to argue about it ferociously in the street. My Pa shouted that an American can't go against the president, because then he is not an American any more but a pathetic turncoat and a sluff. Ron's Pa shouted that it is all about oil and those babblers on television had just filled the heads of people like my old man with guff.

Well, and then the auto repair shop suddenly burned down, with Ron in it. Police officers said he was making something in there, maybe a new iron hand and couldn't get out – he'd inhaled smoke and poisonous fumes and then the roof had collapsed. Only bones were found.

After that Ron's family left the city, and we left not long after too because Pa's reassignment took us to Wilmington. But in Wilmington, I had no real friends, only occasional playmates.

Maybe of all the people I met in childhood besides my parents, Mr. Stanford, the history teacher at our school, was the most interesting. He was tall and grey-haired, with the ruddy face of a Santa Claus and a wrinkled neck. He invariably wore an American flag on the lapel of his no less invariable striped jacket. He constantly joked around with us, set up voluntary groups, took us on excursions, told us about things.

Once he took thirty or so of us little ones to the *USS North Carolina*. That was the name of a huge battleship that had been laid up at a pier in Wilmington in 1961. We just called it 'Ship', with a capital letter. 'Let's meet opposite Ship', we'd say, and everything would be clear at once.

The *USS North Carolina* was an impressive construction. As a child, it seemed to me that it was no less than a mile long, and its steel masts looked taller than the skyscrapers of New York. Then I looked up the true dimensions of this battleship, and its length was actually 728 feet – which is still, you must admit, considerable. And I still remember the massive, just incredibly massive, guns with barrels so big an adult could climb inside.

There was a museum on the battleship, and Mr. Stanford led us there to tell us about the fighting history of the *USS North Carolina*. This steel monster was constructed in 1942, and more than a thousand people served on it. In the war, he told us, Japan attacked us and their planes bombed our ports and cities all the time, and their troops occupied all the islands in the Pacific Ocean and were coming for California and Portland. Then all the American people followed president Roosevelt's lead, and said in unison: 'We can!', and we began to build new ships and planes.

The *USS North Carolina* and other cruisers, battleships and aircraft carriers sailed out into the ocean and began to attack Japanese military bases and ships, and assist landings to free the cities and islands.

I am telling this now as I remembered Mr. Stanford telling it – vividly, his arms swinging, acting out all the parts – wise president Roosevelt, the blood-thirsty Japanese, our courageous seamen, and even the storm and fog that lead the ships towards the enemy.

The *USS North Carolina* did a lot of fighting, together with the aircraft carriers *Enterprise* and *Saratoga* – and then received a torpedo hit from a Japanese I-15 submarine.

Only two seamen died but the forward part of the battle ship together with a main gun turret were damaged, so it was withdrawn from military operations and was sent to Pearl Harbor for repairs. Once repaired, the *USS North Carolina* was in the war for a long time, reached Japan and Okinawa, but this isn't interesting.

What's interesting was that those dead seamen became ghosts!

Mr. Stanford always told us about this down below, in the dark cramped space beneath the front gun turret, and in such a sinister voice that some of the little girls began to squeal in fear.

The first time ghosts were noticed on the battle ship was in 1961 when the money was raised locally to redeem the battle ship from the Navy and it was towed to Wilmington to make a museum from it.

That's when everything began! Every year, it seemed, somebody managed to imprint on a photograph a blurred silhouette in some corridor or doorway, while awful groans and a lingering howl were repeatedly registered on tape recorders – and everyone could listen to the recording for twenty five cents at the cash desk of the museum.

I remember all this distinctly because I have always had a very good memory for information. In Elizabeth City, I was even called a marvel.

Once, I memorized twelve pages of the Gospel of Luke for a bet and didn't make a single mistake when I repeated the text aloud. I can say it all even now.

But back to the museum. When he spoke about the ghosts, Mr. Stanford transformed himself, turning into an infernal creature. He lowered his voice to an ominous whisper, cried out as if he was attacked, distorted his face into horrible shapes and grinned like B.B. King.

The unfortunate sailors from the *USS North Carolina* were soon joined in his string of narratives by European ghosts such as the Canterville Ghost and the White Lady, and by the Salem witches and spirits of Indian leaders and shamans.

If Mr. Stanford hadn't been a teacher, he would have been a preacher or a salesman. He was the kind of guy who could persuade any American to believe in anyone or buy anything.

By the way, Mr. Stanford's second favourite topic after ghosts was Indians. He knew everything about the history of development of our state and the Indian wars which Cherokee, Croatoan (those said to have slaughtered the 'Lost Colony' on Roanoke Island), Maskoki, Chickasaw and others, those 'red-skinned devils' who were moved on from the Indian territory to beyond the Mississippi letting us, in a sense, more civilized people, live settled lives.

Mr. Stanford never stinted on color, painting vivid pictures for us school students of the awful atrocities done by Indians on our unfortunate ancestors who brought the light of civilization to these savages. Once the pilgrim fathers landed on the East coast, Mr. Stanford said, there was nothing else to do but exterminate them entirely.

The sad story of the colony on Roanoke Island, he told us, is one of the best confirmations. The slaughtered colonists carved the letters 'Cro' on a column to identify their ruthless murderers, the Croatoana, who painted themselves with black and white paints. But other tribes were no better, killing colonists in ambushes, attacks on farms, burning houses, and cutting, forcing and tearing off scalps.

And to the glory of our great, courageous and generous ancestors, Mr. Stanford said, they managed to curb the damned devils, beat the tomahawks from their hands, and then humanely move them to a place where they threatened nobody. To Oklahoma, for example.

Then, much later, I read the documentary book by Dorris 'Dee' Brown, *Bury My Heart at Wounded Knee: An Indian History of the American West,* in which I found out the real history of the Indian people and understood that Mr. Stanford had lied. Lied – deliberately and insistently – because it is simply impossible to be so mistaken. Of course, it was 'the children's lie' because we simply wouldn't understand the truth.

Maybe I'll come back to the Indian topic later and for another reason. But here I'd like to tell you about the Cherokee because this tribe, one of the five so-called 'civilized tribes', always seemed to me that part of 'the real America' which had to be in the present United States.

And so the Cherokee somehow managed to create a small, but quite real state, the Cherokee Nation, with its own parliament or tribal council, a constitution, written laws and a nationally elected president referred to as the 'Great Leader'.

By this time, the end of the 18th century, they had already become Christians, led a settled life, lived in houses, cultivated plantations, raised cattle, and even had black slaves – in a word, they were no different from their white neighbors.

And from bad to worse: it was the Cherokees who, for the first time on the continent, created a free school system, with more than thirty schools, and their president Sequoya, named in English George

Guess, created the special Cherokee alphabet in which even a Cherokee newspaper *The Cherokee Phoenix* was issued in 1828.

The Indians had a newspaper, do you realize? If Mr. Stanford was to mention it, he'd probably say it was a forum for discussing scalping techniques and how to cut the hearts out of white men.

Our ancestors didn't like the competition with the Cherokee. Civilized Indians threatened the existence of the young country which not so long before had achieved independence.

And everything ended in 1838 when, under The Law on the Removal of Indians, the Cherokee were sent on a 'Trail of Tears' to a new homeland in the desert valleys of Oklahoma.

On the road more than half of the tribe died of cold, hunger and disease.

Interestingly, their black slaves, and even some whites living in the Cherokee Nation, moved with the Cherokee. And so our ancestors breathed a sigh of relief, having finally got the lands belonging to the tribe.

Just to say a few words about scalping, since this is considered a purely Indian atrocity – ripping skin with the hair off the head of an enemy. I deliberately checked on it, and it seems to be nothing of the kind.

Scalps were remove by ancient Scythians, who hung up triangular pieces from the heads of killed enemies on the reins of their horses. The more of these leather fringes there were on their reins, the more their owner was respected.

In the Dark Ages, according to various chronicles such as that of the 9th century abbot Emmanuel Dominic, Anglo-Saxons, and Goths and Francs, all tore off scalps.

Then when the war of independence broke out on the territory of the future USA, the English Vice Governor Henry Hamilton declared that he would pay any person for a killed American immigrant. And how would you prove the murder has happened and the white person was killed? Ingeniously simple but nasty: with a piece of skin and the lock of hair cut from the head!

Soon Hamilton received the nickname of The Famous Hair Buyer among trappers and Indians. Scalping became a very convenient way of reporting on killed enemies and during the Frontier wars with the Indians and, during the Clearing of the Great Plains, our civilized pilgrim fathers counted killed red-skins by scalps. Thousands, tens of thousands of scalps, men's, women's, children's…

But I learned all this much later, after college, and for me as a child, Mr. Stanford was a real idol. Lao Tzu was right when he said that an eloquent person is often false whereas a moral person is usually not eloquent. But Mr. Stanford then could compete in my eyes for authority with Pa or Aunt Prist.

Damn, I had totally forgotten about her! When we still lived in Elizabeth City, I liked to visit Aunt Prist.

She was not really my aunt. She wasn't a relative at all. It's just that when grandpa, my pa's father, employed her as a servant, it turned out that she saved his and all the family's lives.

She noticed two robbers climbing into the house at night and called the police. The robbers were caught, and it turned out that they were in fact 'the Black Devils', a couple of cold-blooded murderers who sent to glory nearly thirty people in four states down the East coast.

They got into houses at night, killed everyone in the house with a gun with a silencer, then quietly took away all the valuables and slipped away before dawn. Needless to say these devils were called 'black' because both were Afro-Americans.

So, Aunt Prist received an official message of thanks from the police department, an award from the state governor and a tidy sum of money from our old man.

After that she worked for us a long time and when she became old and our own family affairs went downhill, she lodged in the neighborhood. My sister Judith and I often dropped in on the old woman, and she always treated us with gingersnaps and tea like in England.

Aunt Prist loved everything English, except their movies. She watched American films, but old movies, not color. She had a big player for videotapes, apparently, in a format called VHS, and her TV was old too, with a picture tube, with polished wooden sides and a convex screen.

She often showed us her movies while we had tea and dangled our legs under the table. They were mostly comedies about a little man with a short moustache and a ridiculous gait. He was called the Tramp, and he constantly got into some silly situations. Ju and I laughed loudly as crumbs of gingersnap fell from our mouths.

Then for some reason Judith stopped going to Aunt Prist, so I watched the movies about the Tramp alone, while Auntie knitted in the corner – she knitted all the time with a smile in the corners of her wrinkled mouth – and glanced at me over her glasses.

Of all the movies I saw at Aunt Prist, the two I most remembered were *Modern Times* and *The Great Dictator*. Well, the dictator was Hitler, that was clear there, and in *Modern Times* the Tramp kept going to prison because he couldn't fit into the conveyor of life, though once he even was drawn into a huge car factory.

Then he fell in love with a poor orphan girl and tried to arrange her life for the better, the girl got arrested but he saved her. There was a lot about the Great Depression, about strikes and the people's fight for their rights. Anyway, the Tramp and the girl were forced to leave the city to look for happiness in another place.

Of course, I didn't understand at once what this movie was about. I watched it absolutely as a child, but once, when I was six or seven, I suddenly realized that in order for people to be happy, you need to break all these cars and factories, and then everything will be good.

I went and told that to Father. Pa… he, well, let's say didn't approve of my idea and… And he called Aunt Prist the old hen. My Pa is in general a severe person – I'll return to this later.

So I didn't tell Pa about *The Great Dictator*. And I started going less often to Aunt Prist so that Pa didn't see me going, because if something or someone isn't pleasant to him, and I am on friendly terms with them, then that could only bring further trouble.

Then Aunt Prist died. She had no children and no relatives, and was buried at the city's expense – so we, in a sense, our family, allocated something.

She bequeathed all her property to our family, but Pa gave the order 'chuck this stuff out.' So workers in blue coveralls came, took out all her furniture, threw many things in sacks and took it all away on a big truck. All that was left was on a windowsill – some flowers in pots and three rows of those big videotapes. I grabbed my two favourites, *The Great*

Dictator and *Modern Times* and took them away home. We had nothing to watch them on – we already had a DVD player – but I kept those tapes until Pa noticed them by chance.

'What shit is that?' he asked, shaking *The Great Dictator.* "What's it for?"

'For memory...' I mumbled.

'Memories are here!' Pa tapped himself on the forehead with his finger. 'And this is rubbish and shit the red madman made for fools and idlers. Throw it out at once!'

I threw out both tapes. Because if Pa called someone 'red' things looked bad.

Charles Chaplin was indeed red, or more precisely, or most likely, a socialist in beliefs, but my Pa used the word 'red' not only in the ideological sense.

'Red' for him was first of all the enemy of all that he loved, appreciated and protected. Of all things American, correct and true. 'Reds' wanted to destroy them all, to delete, wipe out and if possible erase them altogether.

There was a time Pa was in the CG – that's the Coast Guard – and on Fridays over beer they'd all discuss 'reds', and it was better not to get involved. Everyone was subjected to severe punishment – both 'stupid Chinese', and 'narrow-eyed Viet Congs', and 'hairy Russians', and 'whacked out Latinos', and even 'the mumpish Brits' which welcome 'dirty Muslims' and had 'strongly reddened' in recent years – just like 'those French frog-eaters'.

I should tell you about my father. His name is George. George Alan Kold, his full name. He is a real American – strong, energetic, self-assured in his person and what he does. Always so sure. I remember, since I was an infant, he would say:

'Josh, if you want to achieve something in life, never doubt yourself. Doubts are like fear, and for a man there is no worse accusation than cowardice.'

Once I asked him:

'And what do you do if you aren't right, Pa?'

'Stand your ground!' he answered firmly and thrust his chin out. It was his habit at every trifle to thrust his chin out and to look with a squint as though he wants to hit you.

'Even if you're not right at all?'

'Precisely, Josh, quite so. Even if you did something wrong, you behave as if you won the biggest discount at a sale. People love confidence and can't stand doubting whiners. And remember, little Josh: if you do something, never be afraid of a result, do not be afraid to finish your deed, you understand? Like President Truman with the Japanese. The weed must be weeded out with its root! If Kennedy hadn't tucked his tail between his legs in '62 and had instead given the reds in Cuba a big thump on the head, he'd be alive, and the world would be absolutely different.'

'How?'

'Entirely American!' Pa's chin thrust even higher. 'Nowhere would have stayed red and the whole world would live like us. That means right and happy.'

Pa's friends were like him. They called themselves 'the real guys'. Not all of them were from the Coast Guard. Big Bruce, for example, headed the fire team, and bald Walter served in the police.

On Fridays, as I said, they gathered either in a bar on the embankment, or at our place, drank beer and discussed any news and problems, and the next day, on Saturday, they went to a shooting range because all were members of the National Rifle Association.

Of course, all these 'real guys' voted for elephants, that is the Grand Old Party, and hated donkeys, that is the democrats, for their liberalism, cleverness and love for any strange minorities.

Perhaps from my story you might get the idea that my Pa and his friends were gallant soldiers who enjoyed singing the national anthem and marching on Independence Day, and spent the rest of their time in a bar or in front of the TV or shouting at the wife?

Well, no, my old man was not that way at all. He read much, especially magazines on the military and history and he regularly executed tough work. The Coast Guard in Wilmington doesn't catch Mexican smugglers like in California or on the beaches of Texas, but there are plenty of real problems on the Eastern coast, especially during the storm season, and Pa had several commendations for excellent service.

I was always proud of my old man and I am still. He is a very good person. Yes, his character is no bowl of cherries, but it depends how you carry it, doesn't it? At least, a lot of what is in me is down to Pa's strengths. He taught me to be a real American, and I always remember him when things are hard or I need to make an important decision.

Maybe you're surprised that I still haven't mentioned my mother? Well, of course, Judith and I have a mother; we aren't orphans! And Mom is a remarkable woman – kind, lovely, and we love her…

But somehow when I was a child she spent all her days at work without a break. She's a lawyer, and I can't remember ever seeing her on weekdays – during the week Pa often stayed at home because he was on day duties, and two days he had a rest. So I remember Pa, but Mom – no.

During week-ends, of course, like any real American family, we gathered round the dining table, prayed, ate, discussed things, but I remember that during these family lunches it was Pa who always led everything, and Mom only smiled.

I can't tell even now whether she had the quality of brevity, rare in women, or just didn't want to talk to us – or rather, didn't see the point or wasn't interested. Anyway it's hard for me to understand what united her with Pa – they weren't just different, but like entirely separate physical particles.

They divorced soon after I left school. Judith was already in college by that time and, remarkably, studying to be a lawyer. Mothers and daughters seem to know better how to pull together. Psychologists may say it happens the other way – that fathers gravitate toward communication and affection for daughters, and mothers towards sons, but in our family Pa was lukewarm with Judith. Frankly, she didn't like his morals and his categorical way of making decisions, and he… well it seems to me that he doesn't really believe in natural equality, but that's only a politically incorrect guess.

Mom works in the Federal Court of Pittsburgh now… Or Baltimore? We sometimes correspond by e-mail or exchange calls on Skype, and she always sends a big paper card with spangles on holidays.

Well, that's all I can tell you about my family and childhood. Well no, of course, there were many different situations, both ridiculous and sad. Once, for example, there was a fire at our house and Pa and I and the neighbors had already put it out by the time Big Bruce's firemen arrived.

Or there was the seasonal sale in Nordstroms – when we arrived during the night to grab first place in the queue. Pa always loved to be first in everything – but it turned out that nearly half the city were already there!

And one day on TV it was declared that the wreck of the ship of the notorious pirate Edward Teach the Blackbeard, full of treasures, had been found on the North Carolina coast, near our city[5]. So Pa and I and one of his friends, red-nosed Rick, went out there on a boat to have a look at what was what, and, maybe, try our luck. But of course we were intercepted by the Coast Guard from the next base who mistook us for marauders. Who knows what would have happened if uncle Ric hadn't had acquaintances among this Coast Guard.

I never loved school, mainly because of the teachers. Not all of them were as eloquent as Mr. Stanford. Some couldn't even connect two words, and there were those who didn't teach us anything, but derived pleasure from their power.

We had Mr. Ivan Isenberg, the owner of a very extensive bald head and the academic degree of the doctor of philosophy in the field of applied informatics. Now I think that if someone with a PhD is working as a schoolteacher, there's something is wrong with him, and it seemed to us that Mr. Isenberg was a red terrorist fascist who just hadn't been finished off by our heroic soldiers in Vietnam or in Iraq, or The Maniac and Dr. Evil in one package.

He was average height, always dressed in a faultless suit, always shaved – and always scented with sweet cologne, so sweet it seemed like a perfume for women. Like all the other teachers, he liked us all to do everything similarly – similar dress, similar studies, similar behaviour. 'Similar', in a word, so nobody needed to be individually catered for – so convenient!

But, unlike other teachers, Mr. Isenberg called this similarity 'standardization', which he thought was necessary for children. He was like some ancient paladin, a gallant knight whose sole purpose was to eradicate the sedition of originality and dissimilarity in erring, innocent youth.

---

5   The wreck of the Blackbeard's ship *The Queen Anne's Revenge* was first discovered in 1995 off Beaufort in North Carolina, where it went down in 1718. But it wasn't until 2011 that it was finally confirmed to be the real thing.

He had many methods of eradication, some trickier than others. 'Collective education', for example, was when all the class suffered because of one pupil. If someone was five minutes late for a lesson, say, then all of us would have to stand up and stand till the bell rang. And so, during the break, the exhausted classmates would become brutes and give the late student a 'friendly chat' to make he was never late again. During this chat, they usually beat his legs and stomach so there was no visible bruise. And Mr. Isenberg spurred them on.

He also had a method, called 'personal participation', in which the guilty pupil stayed after lessons and Mr. Isenberg read aloud to him excerpts from the *Tortures and Punishments* encyclopedia by Brian Lane.

From him, I learned about ducking-stools, the rack, the 'Judas Cradle', the 'Spanish boot', 'the heretic's fork', 'the qualified execution', decimation, castration and decapitation. Some of my schoolmates felt dreadful during 'personal participation', but I usually stayed calm, since I am rather phlegmatic by nature and not so imaginative.

All the same, one of Mr. Isenberg's conversations, I remember, did make a strong impression on me. It was about China, and I had always, since early childhood, been interested in China, its culture and history.

It was about Chinese women who, according to medieval standards of beauty surviving into the 20th century, had to have small arc-shaped feet reminiscent of a new moon or a lily petal. Mr. Isenberg pointed out that it was hard for a girl who didn't possess these signs of beauty to marry.

To get that arc-shaped foot, girls from six years-old had all toes, except the big one, turned in and bandaged to the sole. Twice a day, bandage was tightened firmly. This continued until the sole took the arc-shaped form.

This procedure caused extreme pain in girls, their legs often grew numb, and there were problems with blood circulation. The toes pressed into the sole completely lost blood supply. In adult Chinese women, they looked like white rectangles inserted into the skin of the sole.

As a result, adult women had the small foot of a six-year-old child, with only the big toe developed and providing support for walking. Because of this millions of Chinese girls couldn't move easily, fell on ladders, on slopes or in a strong wind, but were considered 'graceful' and 'distinguished'. Mr. Isenberg emphasized that they were 'standardized' and willing to suffer great torment for it. Not without reason did the Chinese people have sayings such as: 'Beauty demands suffering', 'A pair of bandaged feet costs a bathtub of tears'.

I also learned from Mr. Isenberg that the famous Chinese politician Sun Yat-Sen, as a little boy, went through anguish because of the tortures his little sister suffered as her feet were bandaged by their mother.

The poor girl couldn't sleep at night. She groaned and cried and only at daybreak went off into a leaden sleep. But almost at once, mother came and changed the bandage on the girl's feet and the torture continued. Shocked by all this, Sun Yat-Sen addressed his mother one day:

'Mother, it is too painful for her. You shouldn't bandage the legs of my little sister!'

I don't think that the daughter's suffering pleased the mother, but she was forced to answer:

'How can your little sister have lily-feet without pain? If she doesn't have little feet then, when she becomes a young lady, she won't marry and she will condemn us for violating of customs.'

Sun Yat-Sen, the future revolutionary, continued to campaign against bandaging, but only succeeded in getting his mother to invite another woman to bandage his sister's feet, telling him:

'It is the custom. Everyone does it.'

Mr. Isenberg gave this example and always stressed that the destruction of traditions and 'standardization' was the work of mad revolutionaries who as a result destroyed the state as Sun Yat-Sen had destroyed the Great Middle Empire and led millions of Chinese to death.

Sometimes, listening to Mr. Isenberg, I thought that one of us was mad – either he was, because of what was saying or doing, or me, because I was listening to all this.

And I couldn't really understand how and why in the best and most fair country, in the center of the world, in an era when distances between continents were reduced to a several hours flight, and electronic communications have made it possible to contact anyone and anywhere instantly – when the future which science fiction writers dreamed about had arrived – nuts such as Mr. Isenberg lived there.

Some children wanted to send a complaint about him to the State Department of Education and even began to collect signatures, but what is known to two is known to everybody – someone informed and the complainants received additional sessions of 'personal participation'.

To be honest, my dislike of school was cultivated not only by the teachers, but also by my schoolmates. As I said I had no real friends, and plenty of enemies.

I was rather thin, but I wasn't a puny creature at all, and in sport I did everything I should, so it was no standard healthy-fellows-against-the-puny-nerd situation.

It was rather the contrary. The guys that snubbed me weren't on friendly terms with sport. They were big, even fat guys, fans of chips, cola, burgers and movies with Bruce Willis.

They wore rapper trousers with low crotches, black caps with long peaks, undershirts with skulls, and portraits of Jam-Master-Jay and chains as if they were black.

And of course, they listened to rap, rough rap, Onyx, D.I.T.C. and Tupac Amaru. They called themselves 'whiggers' – well, like 'white niggers' though they were typical 'white trash'...

Yes, and they spoke among themselves in rap slang as well they understood it. You know, all those words: 'Hey, dude, high five, brazza, everything is cool, break off to the bro a couple of dollars on heating', and other garbage.

I wore chinos and polo necks and didn't listen to music at all. These 'whiggers' latched on to me, but I usually told them where to get off or simply ignored them. Once they came up to me and began to mutter something in their slang like 'dude, brazza, everything is great' and so on in their 'ebonics'. So I answered them: 'Speak white, guys!' There were four of them, but I could only answer two or three times before I was shoved to the ground. And then it began…

They hated me, and their hatred was shown at every opportunity. Pa guessed that something was wrong for me at school, but all his advice came down to 'if you clench your fist right, a punch won't break your fingers' or 'if your opponent is taller or heavier than you and has big muscles, hit him in the throat and in the balls, where there are no muscles'.

Well, I didn't graduate from school. Are you surprised? Actually, I was surprised too, but on the other hand, I now think that the 'whiggers' were sent to me by God so that I could reasonably and legitimately get rid of Mr. Isenberg with his sweet cologne and infinite stories about disembowelment, dismemberment and 'Saint Augustine's tie'.

Pa, to my surprise, did not really react. I told him that I would finish the last grade externally – that I intended to enroll in a college and that I had a lot more important things to do, much more important, than stay in the company of morons like our 'whiggers'. Actually, the relations between Pa and Mom were by then so thoroughly messed up probably just didn't give a damn about me.

But I wasn't lying about things to do. From an early age I'd been drawn to computers, game consoles, electronic gadgets and other cyber-thingummies. It was my world, a world run according to exact and strict laws without emotions, without excess and unnecessary words.

Bytes, kilobytes and megabytes of information were carried away in a split second over vast distances, converted into text, into pictures, into moving objects. With their help, it was possible to operate all kinds of processes and mechanisms – and even launch ballistic missiles.

It was real magic, scientific magic, and it attracted me much more than riding a bicycle, inhaling dust on a basketball platform or cuddling schoolmates at a dance-party.

I was fond of programming. I played games. I tried to make my own, unpretentious working toys. Computer systems seemed to me a real leap into the future, something like a fairy tale in reality, and their era had come with the advent of the internet. Here everything fell into place: it was mine, it's what I was born for."

09:08 P.M.

Kold became silent. His eyes dimmed. The Lawyer switched off the recording. The silence was thick, deep and impenetrable. It was clear that Kold regretted his frankness or wanted to pretend so to make an impression on his interlocutor. This thought came to the Lawyer's mind and seemed to him not entirely baseless.

"Communicating with people like Kold, you always need to remember that they aren't so simple as they seem at first and even second glance," he thought, then said aloud:

"All this is very interesting, but maybe you wanted to speak about something else?"

"Do you want some coffee?" asked Kold instead of answering. "Two coffees and a couple of hamburgers? Ok?"

"I won't refuse. It's warm here, but kind of…dampish, isn't?"

"I set the climate control thermostat at nineteen degrees. And that isn't just about my surname," Kold smiled. "Just my brain melts if it's too warm. Figuratively, at least."

He got up and vanished behind the door. No more than a couple of minutes passed during which the Lawyer checked that Kold's story was safely recorded and the battery on the smartphone had plenty of life, and then the inhabitant of A Bunker returned with a plastic tray with a glass coffee pot, a carton of milk, two cups and a plate with sandwiches.

"Please!" Kold put the tray on a table, pulled up a seat and started eating.

"And still…" After taking a sip of coffee, the Lawyer looked at Kold closely. "Something oppresses you… besides your own fate. What?"

"'Nature never hurries, but everything is accomplished.'" Kold ate a sandwich, drank his coffee and then put the cup aside.

"Lao Tzu again? Are you fond of the Chinese culture?"

"Yes, but most of all Taoism.

"Then Zhuang Zi also has to be close to you. I always liked his directness. 'Small swindlers in dungeons; large in the throneroom'" the Lawyer smiled.

"It seems that all Russians must like this statement," Kold smiled too.

"Do you consider that human nature is identical only between modern Russians and the Chinese in the fourth century B.C.?" the Lawyer responded ironically.

"No, of course, not." Kold sighed. "But if you remember Lao Tsu, then 'the great person holds on to the essential and lets go of the inessential. He does everything truly, but will never be guided by laws'.

"We have a national expression in which this thought is expressed more simply," Lawyer said: "'The winner isn't judged.'"

"Was it created by the people?" Kold asked. "Then your people learned Tao."

"No, of course. It was said by the empress Ekaterina the Second when with just 800 soldiers commander Alexander Suvorov conquered the Turkish Turtukay fortress garrisoned by 4000 -against the orders of his commander Count Rumyantsev. Suvorov was to be judged by court-martial and sentenced to penal servitude or even to death, but the empress intervened …"

"Was that the great empress?" Kold asked: "I know so little of Russian history."

"Not so little," Lawyer nodded. "She came to the throne by chance and she was German, but … but finally deserved the honourable title of 'Great.'"

"So, she was Taoist precisely!" Kold solemnly raised a forefinger and both of them burst out laughing.

Suddenly, the Lawyer's phone began to vibrate. There was a call from the office. His secretary reminded him that on the *Russia Today* channel a broadcast of a press conference with the former director of the Central Intelligence Agency and National Security Agency Michael Wyden was about to start.

"Mr. Kold, would you mind if I turn on the TV?" the Lawyer asked. "We can watch a program you might find rather interesting."

"Go ahead," nodded Kold.

The press conference had already begun. The smiling face of Wyden appeared on screen. The former director of the most powerful intelligence agency in the world resembled a Baptist preacher or a paediatrician from a prestigious clinic speaking at a charitable meeting.

"… He is definitely not a hero. At the same time, I don't think that he fully fits the definition of 'traitor' as it is formulated in our Constitution. But with his actions he has undoubtedly caused huge harm to our country and he, most likely, has a major problem with his mentality. So the truth, most likely, lies somewhere in the middle," Wyden said. The Lawyer smiled and looked at Kold.

"He thinks you are loony."

Kold squirmed:

"I'm not interested in what this person says."

"Why? He was your immediate superior and is still a very influential figure. I think Washington is speaking through his mouth now."

"That's not so," Kold rubbed his chin doubtfully. "You see … Wyden reminds me… of your leader Gorbi, Mikhail Gorbachev, yes. Look, he even looks like him, only there is not a birthmark. And he is the same… a demagogue. Blah blah blah is his power. You listen!"

Kold took the remote control from the table and put the sound up. Wyden was answering a question about how he would behave as head of the NSA if a young specialist came to him and told him that they had problems with the BRISM program:

"And that is where the shoe pinches! Exactly. This is what most disturbs us – why didn't Kold act this way? If someone wants to be a real whistleblower, then in a similar situation he is obliged to go to the chief, to the chief of the chief or to address a general council of the department or the General Inspector or even a Congressman to state his claims. Our country has a certain hierarchy allowing him to do this."

"As I said: demagogue!" Kold said contemptuously.

Wyden meanwhile continued:

"And now let's have a look. I am ready to be the first to recognize that such an act demands a lot of courage. People can be different, and we can't exclude the idea that among us there are those who would subject such a brave employee to pressure. But this is only correct in such situations. In my opinion, if an employee comes to the chief with similar doubts, you have to take them seriously. If someone comes to you, led by conscience, you have to postpone other matters and talk to such a person very seriously, and you need to understand the details as far as his concerns are proved."

"And was it really acceptable to express doubts about the correctness of conducting intelligence activities to the higher administration?" The Lawyer was deeply interested, but Kold caught the ironical notes in his voice and guessed this was a game:

"Indeed! I suspect Mr. Wyden will tell us about it now."

Meanwhile a new question was heard from the screen. The young newswoman asked:

"I remember that in 2007, when you headed the NSA, there were other whistleblowers, similar to Kold. Did these people address you with the doubts before making them public?"

"It's as if they overheard us!" the Lawyer cheered up.

Wyden leaned into the microphone and without a trace of uncertainty said:

"Actually, I left the NSA in 2005, and those events in 2007-08 happened after my departure. In my time, I didn't face any complaints, except for some connected with the solution of some technological problems in the NSA. So I had no knowledge of any processes that could lead to the appearance of whistleblowers."

"So that just indicates that they work badly," Kold shrugged his shoulders.

Meanwhile on the screen, Wyden was getting excited and began to gesticulate, supporting each statement with a wave of his hand:

"In such cases, you need to understand who exactly bears responsibility for the incident. That does not necessarily mean you find the guilty person. You need to get employees to be frank with you so they tell you in detail how everything occurred. You want to help people to comprehend a situation, to draw lessons for yourself out of it, so you have the chance to prevent a repeat of similar situations in the future or, at least, to considerably reduce their probability. To talk about Kold, then here you need to know the details to reveal the entire scope of his relations, and you need to talk to all people who communicated with this young man. What, in their opinion, pushed him to such actions? You'd need to talk to his chief. Was there something in Kold's behaviour that could lead to some suspicions? Perhaps he did something unexpected? Perhaps there were some signs indicating that something is wrong with him? And after that you need to carry out a comprehensive analysis and assessment of the damage caused."

Kold burst out laughing, this time quite sincerely, without holding back. The Lawyer realized that it must be very amusing for Kold to listen to what a person of such caliber as Wyden broadcasts for the whole world.

And that, meanwhile, continued:

"Let me designate three main areas in which the damage was done. First, Mr. Kold revealed our capabilities to potential opponents. He told them what we can do and what we won't do, and this itself can be very dangerous. Secondly, it will damage American companies which cooperated with the NSA. They will suffer damage though everything that they did, performed by American laws and protected the United States. Thirdly, if in the world there are still governments or individuals or information sources which would like to cooperate with the USA, then on what basis will they believe our assurances that we are able to keep secrets? All this has caused us damage."

"Isn't that too much for a loony loner, Mr. Wyden?" Kold whispered, looking at the TV. His face at the same time acquired quite a spiteful expression.

"Maybe time to switch off?" the Lawyer asked.

"No, it's interesting," Kold said abruptly, without turning his head. It was clear that he had become really engaged in the press conference. A new question was posed:

"What is happening to the programs Kold made public – for example, the BRISM program for data collection? Have they been curtailed, or is the NSA going on with them, do you think?"

Wyden passed his hand over his bald head as if in confusion, but at once he found the right words:

"I see no reason why any of those programs which he revealed – let's say, the BRISM program for collection of metadata – should be stopped. They are legal, they meet a need, and they are effective. But their efficiency is the element that suffered most from his 'revelations'. Besides, now our opponents know what we can do and what we won't do, it's about what restrictions are imposed by our legislation and our policy. Most likely it will allow our opponents to protect their communication systems from the intelligence services of the USA as they attempt to intercept their messages."

Straightaway, the journalist threw a new bit of firewood into the fire on which Wyden was to be roasted:

"In spite of the fact that BRISM has a very broad span and actually turned the USA into one big database with access to Facebook, Google, Yahoo, and Microsoft, it, nevertheless, 'missed the boat' with the online correspondence of the Barayev brothers on the eve of the explosion during the Chicago marathon. Do you, perhaps, scatter networks too widely?"

Wyden for a second seemed to lose control and through the kind paediatrician mask another face appeared – stern, domineering and with the prickly, cold, shrill look, which is necessary for a professional intelligence agent. However, by the time he began to answer, control had already been restored:

"Actually, the Barayevs weren't identified by means of one of these programs because BRISM isn't intended for the detection of the type of communication which the Barayev brothers used on the eve of Chicago marathon explosion. I mean that BRISM is intended for tracking foreigners. Confidence in the NSA is necessary because the people we want to watch are foreigners or have potential value as foreigners. And we must prove it in at least the most general form in the American courts before insisting that one of the internet companies helps us with it.

"It seems that the journalists are well prepared for this briefing," Kold noticed.

The Lawyer grinned.

"Most likely they had the benefit of helpful consultants from certain services. By the way, I've long wanted to ask – how was your communication with the representatives of these departments?"

"Practically non-existent. I am not the carrier of any important information. All the data which I can publish is there, on remote servers, and will become property of the public anyway. Already practically nothing depends on me."

"Nothing at all?"

"I don't want to talk on this topic now," Kold evaded the question and turned to the TV. The next question came out:

"President Obama declared that surveillance programs have allowed us to prevent 50 terrorist attacks. Taking into account that these programs started soon after 9/11, how many terrorist attacks were prevented due to information collected by programs similar to BRISM which couldn't be obtained by other means?"

"He won't answer that," Kold quickly told.

Wyden answered carefully:

"Yes, that is a good question and I don't want to be evasive, but I am forced to be. I don't know how correctly I can answer your question about the number of terrorist attacks prevented only by means of these programs. Usually, when we talk about the success of one or another intelligence operation, we cannot claim that this success was provided by means of only one program. One of the main achievements of U.S. intelligence over the last ten years has been the fact that we could connect various flows of information, each containing separate data. We connect this separate data to give an informative picture. It's as if you have splinters of colored glass – separately none bears any significant information, but connected together they can create a very informative mosaic."

The journalist took out several papers, shuffled them and said:

"I will quote Kold: 'The agreement of citizens with the actions of the authorities can't be considered an agreement if citizens are not informed properly what these actions are.' I think, we must accept that many citizens are appalled by the content of these leaks, since the impression is given that you enter each house by violence, you listen to telephone conversations, you read private e-mails, private SMS, without notifying citizens that you are doing it. And you call all this the 'War on Terror'. I want to ask, can you wage war on terror and at the same time preserve private life, my private life?"

"I think that the President was right when he declared that a responsible government faces a choice," Wyden said gravely. "You can't ensure absolute personal privacy and absolute safety – a balance has to be reached between them. And this balance, frankly speaking, depends on circumstances. What is the nature of the threat? How real is this threat? How effective are the tools available for us for the detection of this threat? I think the President is right. It is necessary to aim to achieve balance. But I would like to emphasize that much of what we, in your opinion, do, and what Americans speak about, is actually 'the fruit of misunderstanding.'

Unfortunately, when stories of this sort go public in the USA, they are at once surrounded with a depressing aura. So it is very important that American citizens understand what we are actually doing. If you go back to the quote from Kold about the agreement of citizens with the actions of the authorities, then remember we're not living in ancient Athens. We don't have direct democracy where all the population collectively makes decisions on all questions. We have a representative democracy. And national representatives knew about these programs, and voted for them. They were approved by two presidents. They were approved by the American judicial system. In the American system, the separation of the authorities into the executive, legislature and judiciary guarantees the legitimate interests of citizens to the maximum degree."

"We have a saying: 'spinning like a grass-snake in a frying pan,'" the Lawyer commented.

"Again the Russians?" Kold was interested. "And do people eat snakes in Russia?"

"In your country people eat the tails of beavers and syrup from a maple tree," the Lawyer shrugged. "And the French eat frogs and snails. National cuisines are a subtle thing. For me, no less subtle than intelligence."

The press conference meanwhile was about to finish. Wyden, vigorous and young-looking at first, now seemed slightly emaciated. Spots had appeared on his face. There were beads of sweat on his brow – and there was nobody to dry it. In the end, age had told. But, despite everything, he was clearly determined to stand up.

The journalist meanwhile vigorously referred to a piece of paper:

"What does the fact that your own citizens notify the world of its danger say about certain malfunctions in your system? This is not the first case."

"No, not the first," Wyden nodded firmly. "But I already said that, in my opinion, Mr. Kold is not a hero; he committed a crime. But he also has problems with his mentality, if you'll allow me to express it delicately. What arrogance must you possess to believe that your own moral estimates outweigh the estimates of two presidents, two chambers of Congress, the American courts and about 30,000 of your colleagues. I am ready to accept that in American society, and in Russian society, there is a new generation of young people whose ideas of transparency go much further than those of my generation and even generations of my children.

Our intelligence agencies, like the Russian intelligence agencies and intelligence agencies worldwide, today employ people whose ideas of privacy and of openness differ a little from ideas of those in intelligence agencies before. And so here we see Mister Kold, and we see Corporal Benning show almost romantic love to a dehiscence of secrets. But in both these cases their commitment to absolute transparency caused significant damage to the safety of people worldwide.

"That's not true!" suddenly Kold cried out, seizing the table edge. "A lie! They were the ones who threatened the safety of people!"

"Calm down," the Lawyer moved a glass to Kold. "Drink some water. He can't hear you."

"Yes, yes, you're right. Sorry…"

Wyden meanwhile answered the last questions:

"I wouldn't like to comment on current operations of the American intelligence services, but I would like to emphasize that all countries of the world have legitimate foreign intelligence interests, in addition to the war on terror. It is not only about the fight against terrorism, but also about foreign intelligence activities. I am repeating: all countries perform foreign intelligence. I can predict that these two programs, taking into account that the program of collection of metadata and the BRISM program only to a minimal degree affect the private life of Americans, will, I think, be continued. They won broad support from both sides. They will be continued. But what we discussed today, what my country and the whole world discussed in the last two weeks – all this, I believe, will generate a global discussion concerning what is meant by private life in the internet era, what reasonable rules are, what legitimate hopes for private life can there be in an extremely interconnected world. I headed the consulting department under the CIA and I set complex problems for them. One of the most difficult problems I set was a search for the balance between safety and transparency. I formulated the question as follows: 'Will the USA be able to perform intelligence activities in the future within the broader political culture which every day requires more transparency and more public reporting in all areas of national life?' They studied this problem, and came back to me with this answer. It was as follows: 'We are not sure.'"

"Not sure..." Kold repeated. "Well, I am sure."

FILE 002.WAV

"I won't tell you any more about my childhood. I've left this time forever, and you know I am glad of that. I didn't like being a child, and not only for the reasons which I have already spoken about. The fact is that ever since I recognized I wanted to be an adult, I have had a desire to grow.

What for? It's quite simple – to have those opportunities and rights which an adult has. No, it's not about sex, alcohol, drugs or gambling institutions (especially since all of us get acquainted with these things at a pretty early age.)

An adult has access to what I call the 'real deal'. You don't understand? Well, it's like in economics, there are parasitic sectors, such as the sphere of entertainment, while there are some things the economy can't exist without: heavy industry, high technologies, the primary sphere, food, army, police, medicine.

Childhood is kind of a parasitic sector, with all its toys, pictures, training sets, puzzles, Batman and Spiderman suits, bicycles and kites. To me, it was always uninteresting, and all around slobbering affection and ah that kid Joshua, ah, he'll start off a new helicopter now!

I read that the fashion for hypertrophied childhood and for subsequent infantility – now twenty-year-old men and women are called teenagers – began rather recently.

Even in the 1930s, there was no mass industry in the service of children. Girls and boys wore adult clothes that were the exact copy of the clothes of their parents, just smaller. And their toys weren't bright and ugly hypertrophied images of the real things; they were copies of transport ware, household items, and weapons too...

I saw on the internet, a photo of the nursery of the children of your last emperor Nikolay, and in the photo you could see their toys. The dolls of the girls reminded you of real people. They were not ugly baby dolls with the exaggerated heads and protruding eyes of gigantocephalics. Their dresses, hats and boots looked like real clothes and footwear, only reduced, too. And the locomotive and cars were exact copies of real locomotives, not bright yellow monsters with a mouth and eyes, or a transparent tender and a big 'Happy Train' written on one side, like mine in childhood.

I know that for Alex the Russian prince, the only son of your emperor, the gun and saber, exact copies of real weapons, were just made small. And he had the same military uniform in this khaki-colored cloth or whatever it was made from at that time.

And now this would all be made from safe, nonflammable, certified by the World Health Organization hypoallergenic material, bright fluorescent orange in color so it's obvious to all that it's for children...

Do you understand what I'm getting at? If you make a child a moron or a clown, he'll grow up that way. If he from birth he lives in a world of unclear, nonfunctional, senseless and incredibly safe things, he won't want to move to the adult world where absolutely other laws and rules work.

And on the other hand, maybe, the adult world will finally turn into a kingdom of idiotic entertainments, foolish design and infantile acts. This process, actually, has already started.

I escaped from childhood when I was thirteen. I had a telescope – a big cylindrical thing on a tripod covered by various finders, counterbalances, eyepieces and other mechanical-optical trash. Pa gave it to me when I was nine, when I joined an astronomical club.

For a whole year, I regularly froze at an open window, examining the Galilean satellites of Jupiter, Archimedes crater on the Moon or some comet of Halley. Then I got bored and the telescope just stood a few years until suddenly it became much in demand.

I won't beat about the bush. You, probably, guessed what happened. Yes, I found out that with this telescope I could to look into the windows of other houses! This discovery beguiled me to stand at the eyepiece for whole nights.

In America, it isn't normal to use heavy blinds or curtains, just net, because neighbors have to know you have nothing to hide from them because you are an honest and respectable person! And if the sun bothers them in the afternoon, there are always rotary blinds. Well, and on the top floors you don't need net at all.

Thus I opened for myself a kingdom of others' passions…

At home, people don't behave like in the street, in shops, at offices, medical institutions or other public places. At home, they become as they were created by God. Well, or Mother Nature. Real.

Behind closed doors, solid, adult businessmen turn into jumpy hysterics beating their children and shouting at aged parents.

Good girls, exemplary schoolgirls, hide (as they think!) on a garret balcony from the whole world, smoking the cigarettes stolen from mothers.

Comely grey-haired gentlemen take cover in the long cooled matrimonial bedrooms and masturbate over old numbers of Penthouse.

And last, the basis and support of American society – the housewives over thirty. In the absence of children and husbands, they do things that I don't have the nerve to tell you. I will only say that I never thought that the ordinary vacuum cleaner, a hair dryer, or a cylinder of hairspray could be used with such sophisticated ingenuity.

During the days and in particular in the evenings I watched without a break the secret lives of my distant and nearer neighbors, gradually turning into a juvenile cynic who was undeceived in life.

The most terrible suspicions, the most awful hints I had read somewhere or heard on TV had suddenly became true and real.

My Pa, despite his rigid male character, was a man with strong principles, one of which said: 'The soldier will not hurt a child'. But witnessing abuse for me became a nearly daily reality.

As soon as I went outside and met a person of any gender or age, my new experience began to cry out in me: 'There goes one more pervert, house tyrant, or a voluptuous freak who is only pretending to be the normal person.'

But I couldn't give up this forbidden, yet oh-so-fascinating occupation. Every evening, after saying I needed to do a school project or prepare for exams, I locked myself in my room and hurried to the cold eyepiece of the telescope.

Now I understand that at this time we in our family were going through a very intense, bad period – my parents were getting divorced, or more precisely, their relationship was going completely wrong, and to everyone, and first of all to them, it became clear that a crack had developed that couldn't be stuck together, patched, covered or eliminated in any other way.

But I didn't notice any of that, entirely absorbed by my secret, shameful, but devilishly fascinating hobby.

In time, simply looking became boring, and once I had the idea of writing down the names and addresses of those people who were performing illegal actions at home then reporting them to the police. I don't remember precisely why I didn't actually do it, but most likely it was the fear that I would be found and revenged.

However, there was nobody special to revenge Mr. Chandler, who beat his daughters at home but in the day was a quiet and modest accountant; and nymphomaniac Ms. Bryant wasn't especially suited for the role of blood-thirsty avenger, and I could have beaten off the pervert Paul Harden even then in spite of the fact that he was about forty years old – because from birth he had suffered from cerebral palsy.

Anyway, the main object of my visual fascination was old man Coburn, or more precisely, his young wife Ellie. Actually her name was Espina, and I don't remember her surname, even though Pa mentioned it several times. The fact is that Ellie-Espina was a Mexican of twenty something years and worked for old man Coburn as a housemaid.

Worked – worked – and married him. Coburn himself, a stately man of 70 with a white beard, was extremely happy about this and terribly proud of 'my Ellie' who 'brightened up the declining years of a patriarch.'

And Espina herself was even more happy with her new status. This large girl with a shock of black hair and size five breasts had now become 'an absolute American'.

But I knew that happiest of all was old man Coburn's grandson Sam, a restless boy of my years working at the post in a suburb of Wilmington.

From time to time he visited his beloved grandfather. They sat in the garden, drank a glass or two, then old Coburn fell asleep, and Sam and

Ellie went upstairs to the second floor guest bedroom, and indulged in what in books is called carnal joys.

The window of the guest bedroom was a quarter of a mile from my window in a line of direct visibility. Naturally, it was completely impossible to discern much from such a distance with the naked eye, and even ordinary tourist binoculars would hardly help, but the telescope is quite another matter!

In my big pipe I could see everything, up to the sugar skull tattooed on Ellie's forearm along with the Spanish words: 'Perpetuo socorro'. Well, and all the rest I saw fairly accurately too.

You must admit it's one thing to hear about what is done by a man with a woman alone from peers or to see it in photos in magazines, but absolutely another to study it with your own eyes!

Now Sam was quite a puny creature, and maybe he blackmailed Ellie with something – otherwise why on earth she would need him? On the other hand, the old man Coburn could hardly be surprised at her – she was in her prime and wasn't remotely like the chaste maiden Conchita in any way.

So, while the old man was dozing, they rough and tumbled on the bed, sometimes using handcuffs, or toys from the adult shop, and even a whip. I don't know why they needed all that stuff, but maybe they couldn't explain it either if anyone ever asked.

The only problem, which was a real pain, was the fact that the telescope showed everything upside down! When you look at stars or at Jupiter, that doesn't matter at all, but when you are watching Sam and Ellie, it can feel distinctly uncomfortable.

For a long time I pondered how to eliminate this annoying defect, and tried to make a system of mirrors, or find lenses with a focus that turned the picture over, but nothing really worked.

Then it suddenly dawned on me – the video camera! Pa had just bought a new Japanese camera few months ago, and we wanted to take it with us on a trip to Illinois Park, but something went wrong and the camera had mostly laid in the storeroom on the shelf. Judith took it out several times to shoot our old cat Clothespin when she came, but beyond that the camera was unused.

After fitting the camera to the telescope eyepiece on radial knife-edges, I waited for the next occasion of Sam and Ellie's meeting and prepared to record. Just in case, I not only locked the door, but also propped a hockey stick against it. Then I rewound the cassette and pressed start.

What I then saw in my usual house porn shocked me. Because now what I had watched upside down in the telescope eyepiece before had become a full record, material evidence of the misbehaviour of the Mexican and Coburn's smart grandson. Anyone could see it now. And with this anyone could blackmail them.

My hands sweated, and the inside of my head began to pound. It was inexpressible with words, this new feeling, not comparable in its excitement with anything in the world. Power, yes, yes, exactly power – this is what I experienced when I looked at the folding screen of the Japanese video camera.

I laughed and jumped about the room like mad, imagining how and what I could make not only with Sam and Ellie, but also with all those freaks.

I was like the gods or demons from ancient myths, able not only to see what nobody saw and nobody knew, but also to transfer those visions to a tape and make them material.

Power! I had in my hands a real power over a load of people now! It was only necessary to make a quantity of records and to think up a plan for inducing the heroes of my documentaries to do what I needed, to guarantee I didn't arrange a meeting with the police for them.

Did I think at that time that blackmail is a serious criminal offense? Frankly, I didn't. The prospects in my inflamed imagination absolutely hammered away all thoughts of ethics – hammered them away with the justification that who, frankly in this age, thinks of ethics, except ten hypocrites?

I don't know how all this story would have ended if the divorce of my parents hadn't burst on me like a bolt from the blue.

It was a beautiful summer day, with the sun striking through the window and through the nets and painting orange rectangles on the floor, like the Windows logo. My parents were sitting on chairs at different ends of the room, and on a table there were several boxes of Chinese food that my Pa had bought to... well, probably, to sweeten the pill. He always wanted it better. And Mom too.

Then they told Judith and me everything – that they couldn't live together any more, that they are strangers now, that Mom would move to another city, and that Pa would stay here with us, well, more precisely, with me, since Judith was already studying at law school in Norfolk. For me, the whole world just collapsed.

That familiar world in which all of us lived. I mean that. It became empty and lonely.

And what's interesting, as I have already said, we weren't especially close with Mom, but when she just disappeared it was like the chromaticity was taken out of a film. Everything became black-and-white, dirty and dim.

And my interest in the telescope, in that forbidden video, in my plan for blackmail, didn't just die away – it also grew dim, covered in dust and shrunk.

For days Pa hung out with his service pals, and Judith went to college. And I stayed at home and played on the computer. I played for days and whole nights, generally strategies, shooters, and RPGs.

At that moment, it seemed to me that in those games was the whole meaning of my life, and yet now I can barely remember the names. Still, I'm grateful to their creators because those games helped distract me and endure a difficult period in my life then – and as it seems to me, still help, by giving the illusion of the infinity of being. That sounds complicated so I'll try to explain a little.

The world of virtual heroes and computer landscapes seems simply illustrative at first sight. But it is not about the quality of plotting or 3D graphics, but about the depth of setting, and the believability of the heroes' characters. Sometimes they are made with such stunning realism and charisma that one is reduced to tears – 'why can't you penetrate behind the screen?'

Of course, computer games are, first of all, an escape from reality, and who would argue with that. When there is sleet outside the window, not a cent in your pocket, you've a bruise under your eye and no prospects ahead... When you are not just a low ranker, but The Most-Low-Ranker of all low-rankers...When even such an 'important' thing as the timing of the walk to the mailbox for a fresh newspaper doesn't depend on you... In fact, when all life is bullshit, there is a huge desire to escape from it.

To run away anywhere – to another city, to another state, into narcotic nonsense, to death, eventually...

And in this scheme, computer games are true salvation, or I would even say, therapy, a special valve, a fuse that stops your mind shattering into millions of pieces of colored glass.

In fact, when you're a teenager of fifteen years, and you have it real bad... How bad, I won't explain in detail, I've just spoken about that. And if you don't stand up and blow your socks off, you just go off aimlessly wandering. And there you go, you spend a day, two or even three. But more than likely you will be found, the police do their work well. After all, you're just a lonely white teenager, not a needle in a haystack.

And you were found, returned and everything began! Juvenile justice, it's like a tick – once it's got its tail into you, you can't tear it off. Psychologists will drive you crazy with their little chats with you. Various inspectors from various organizations which patronize and watch over children at risk will visit your house again and again because since the moment you left your home, you became precisely a child at risk, and also mentally unbalanced. And this is branded on you for a long time, possibly forever, and many roads in life are now blocked for you by the barriers of the state system.

What's more, they can take you away from home and find you new parents. That is, you have to leave the places where you were born, grew up, which are dear to you, and move to some 'promised land' like Mount Clemence in the State of Michigan to start everything from scratch, from a blank sheet. And what does it mean to start from scratch at fifteen years? I can tell you that it is much more difficult than at five or twenty-five because when you're fifteen, you're like a target at which everything flies – views, words, spittle, fists and lumps of crumpled paper.

And computer games were invented, it seems to me, to avoid all these problems. You just sit at a computer, put on your earphones, launch the program and say so-long to reality for a while. The main thing is that it isn't necessary to run anywhere.

And crucially, in a game you can be anybody. That's vital, it's a gift from heaven – to realize your dreams! Yes, in reality you have weak arms and terrible eyesight, and you can barely make it round the track in the school stadium, you shuffle along in a stoop and even the little girls from the junior grades laugh at you.

But in a game you become that nimble hunk with elastic muscles, a square jaw and a heap of skills, from archery and axe-throwing to 'light magic' or 'blood magic'.

And you go on your journey through uncharted lands, you meet friends and foes, you face terrible dangers, join fights, find treasures, save beautiful princesses or great princes – it all depends on your personal choice at the beginning, and no matter how the game ends today, you stay happy because tomorrow your hero will be alive, healthy and full of strength again.

Nothing hurts him, he is always ready for heroic deeds and adventures. He is perfect … the ideal American, to be plain. And here you are – not ideal. And all the adults around you stick your nose in your not ideality. It's clear they mean well, but it turns out just the opposite, and you're angry because of it, and get a heap of complexes. And you already very much want to become what you are wanted to be, at least once, in real life. But offline it is impossible because…

Yes, it is simply…impossible, and all! And in the game, so easy. Of course, it is an escape from reality, pure escapism. But fans of computer games are not innovators at all, they weren't treading any new tracks – all those beatniks, hippies, rockers, bikers and other punks, they ran from reality too, they were escapists too. To live in the real world and not know its problems, this lot came up with their own imaginary world, their 'Strawberry Fields.' Of course, the entrance fee was more expensive than for gamers. For gamers, all it costs is money for the internet and time… well, and may be sometimes conjunctivitis, carpal tunnel syndrome and scoliosis. But for them it was necessary to poison their organism with various forms of chemistry, clouding the brain so that sitting on garbage you could believe you are in paradise.

No, the computer in this respect is more honest. The main thing is that there is electricity, and that is almost everywhere and almost always now. There are, of course, blackouts, but they're about as likely as dying from a meteorite.

A meteorite is a prohibited reality – literally a guest from another world. Here, in Russia recently you had such a gift from the Great Space

Fall. I watched many videos of it because in Russia car owners have this excellent habit, or tradition – I don't even know how to call it – of equipping their cars with dashcams – and I was surprised to see the courage and composure of your people.

Nobody panicked, nobody was running around crying: 'Oh, my God! Save us, save us!' People just looked into the sky, they were filming, discussing it, and then when the explosion blew and the windows in lots of houses, offices and schools were shattered, everybody just made sure everyone was safe. Nobody died! All got help in time. While watching the video, I even had a feeling that they were training videos, and everybody was prepared.

I remember one particularly amazing video. The class teacher, seeing the flash outside the window, orders the children to hide under their desks. The explosion knocked out all the windows, but no child was injured, not one cut! The children leave school in an organized way, and they're even laughing…

I reflected on such a reaction, and realized that for you, Russians, escapism isn't necessary and even harmful, because you already live in another reality…

Your world can't be destroyed because you're always ready for any surprise, because no rules nor regulations for life exist.

Churchill wrote about you: 'Russia is a riddle wrapped in a mystery inside an enigma.' Perhaps it's like that, but it seems to me that you shouldn't look for hair on a tortoise shell and horns on the head of a hare – everything is simpler.

Your reality is similar to computer, a virtual reality. It is the world of inexplicable things and acts, the world of boundless opportunities. I don't know how the philosopher Thomas Carlisle got scent of all this in the middle of the nineteenth century, but he wrote then: 'Russia is indifferent to human life and to a current of time. It is silent. It is eternal. It is indestructible'.

That's an exact description of the virtual world, the world of the computer game where fatalists ready for everything live! Here the Russians, I guess, approach living by the Buddhist principle: 'Do what needs to be done' and 'come what will'. When I understood that, not so long ago, during my life in Hawaii, I became fascinated to look at your country with my own eyes. However, I am getting ahead of myself.

At the beginning Americans were engaged in hewing a civilization on wild land. They had to win a piece of the earth from the wood, the prairie, and heathlands, to fence it off from wild animals, to banish or exterminate Indians and predators, to build a house, to plant European plants. That is the United States – a created world.

It's largely artificial – but not virtual – because everything is firmly regulated here and everybody lives guided by an infinite number of laws including unwritten ones. If you walk down the street in any American town and don't smile at passersby in response to their dutiful 'smiles', you've already broken these laws, and the world around won't be polite to you. So you sometimes get a strong wish to run away from all this – especially at fifteen years!

So that's why I played. For hours, at nights, days around the clock. I didn't go to school. I simply couldn't. The moment I had to leave the house was real torture for me. It seemed to me that everyone I met in the street, from children to police officers and road makers, was aware of our family problem, and felt sorry for me, and I owed something to all of them, and I felt like a target – and here I was, a hair's breadth away.

I didn't want them to feel sorry for me. I wanted to go on living here as if everything was the same, as though nothing had happened. Mom had left, Judith had left – so why were Pa and I left on the ashes, on the ruins of our family? We needed to go somewhere too, and it didn't matter where, just away from here."

09:57 P.M.

The Lawyer stretched to the remote control to switch off the TV. There was some night show. But suddenly, the door leading to the corridor swung open and in the doorway, completely filling it, was a real mountain of a man in a black suit with a tie.

He had huge red hands, so broad-chested and tall he reminded me of a two-door bar refrigerator, yet his shaven head grew directly from his mighty shoulders and seemed disproportionately small. The overall picture was completed by the headset attached to his left ear and the radio set sandwiched in his left hand.

"Gentlemen," the man-mountain said with an unexpectedly high-pitched voice. "I ask you to remain where you are. We have an emergency situation."

Kold jumped up, overturning a chair, and moved back to a corner. The man-mountain stepped into the room and stood beside the door. After him several members of spetsnaz in masks and grey 'city' camouflage slipped in like fleeting shadows, armed with small submachine guns with extra thick barrels. Two raced into the bedroom, while the others – five or six of them – took up positions around the table, directing their weapons at the door.

"Look, what is going on?" the Lawyer asked, trying to speak quietly and calmly.

"Maybe an unauthorized penetration,'" Mountain replied without looking at him, squeaking in ultrasound. "Keep calm, gentlemen, I am asking you. Mr. Kold, sit down; it will be more convenient for you at the table…"

The radio set came to life, made several rustling sounds, croaked a muffled phrase and then went calm again.

"Roger, waiting," Mountain growled quietly.

Grim minutes past. The spetsnaz men stood still and silent. Kold pulled out two jade *baoding* balls from his pocket, each the size of an egg, and began to roll them on his palm, phlegmatically looking at a wall.

"Perhaps, it is better for us to move to another room?" the Lawyer asked.

"This is the most suitable room for ensuring your safety," Mountain answered.

The Lawyer knew he was asking in vain for in the bunker for sure there were countless additional tunnels, technical corridors, ventilation systems and other passages connected with each other, and the security people know best. But to just sit there and be silent when beyond the door, perhaps, there was someone who came here for Kold's life, was very hard, if not intolerable.

It was obvious to the Lawyer that the 'unauthorized penetration' was connected with Kold. If nothing had threatened the life of this man, he wouldn't have been hidden straightaway from journalists, diplomats and others. Of course, he had made things safe, having securely hidden the compromising evidence and making sure of its publication in case something happened to him, but at the same time no one has repealed the old maxim, as old as the world, attributed by the writer Anatoly Rybakov to Stalin in the novel *Children of the Arbat*: 'No person; no problem.'

Kold's death would also instantly lower the amount of scandal hanging over the activity of the U.S. National Security Agency, and significantly reduce the belief of people in the accuracy of exposed materials published in the mass media.

It's one thing when it's done at the instigation and with comments of a real employee of the intelligence agencies, someone who actually worked with the surveillance programs, and absolutely another when behind revelations there are only questionable journalists of dubious reputation, who are also no doubt homosexuals.

No sound reached them from behind the locked door. The spetsnaz men stayed as still Madame Tussauds waxworks. Man-mountain snuffled. And the *baoding* balls tapped in Kold's hand. Minutes passed.

The Lawyer had not touched alcohol several months but suddenly thought that nothing could be better now than a glass of good red wine –

for 'nervous anaesthesia', as one of his high-ranking clients, the famous specialist and expert on body relaxation, used to say.

Red wine was much better for this, than, for example, cognac or whisky, because it kept clarity of thinking and in moderate doses didn't impair coordination. The Lawyer realized that coordination might really be needed at any moment, if there was any chance of getting out of this mess alive.

The most reliable way to destroy an objectionable person is with an explosion, and the more powerful it is, the better. Both the mafia and terrorist organizations around the world have made it their choice in recent years, having graduated from training snipers to training high quality demolition engineers and suicide bombers. The fact that the technologies and techniques for programming a normal person to suicide and transforming him into a walking weapon came to terrorists from their curators in the intelligence agencies of various states was no secret.

"If a drugged fanatic with about ten kilos of explosive on his paunch gets into the bunker, there'll be hell," the Lawyer thought. "But there are different explosives. Some plastic explosive will rip everything to shreds here, though regular TNT can do a lot of damage in a closed room…"

The Lawyer knew firsthand about TNT and closed rooms from the time he had served in the Strategic Missile Troops of the Soviet army, where they'd had classes in case of attempts to capture command bunkers by enemy saboteurs.

The Lawyer cast a sidelong look at Kold. He had closed his eyes and was twirling and twirling the *baoding* balls, representing Buddhist renunciation of the world, but his skin was very pale and his thin nostrils trembled, indicating that he was literally shaking with tension.

A muffled thud several minutes later from the corridor made the Lawyer flinch. One of Kold's jade balls fell on the table, rolled and banged against a glass.

"Easy, everything's under control," Mountain made a soothing gesture with his free hand as if he was parting waves, and then reached into his jacket and pulled out a square black pistol.

Kold gulped noisily. The spetsnaz clanked their safety catches. Along the corridor hurried footsteps pounded, and it seemed to the Lawyer that he heard a stifled cry. At that moment Mountain, who was listening to something on his headset smiled a child's disarming smile and said with obvious relief:

"That's it, all-clear!"

The Lawyer barely noticed as he and the shadow soldiers with their automatic machines left the room – he was suddenly visited by a thought about this pale guy with the jade balls in his hand that now sat opposite him at the table on the minus seventh floor in the secret Cold War bunker: around this one guy, thousands, if not tens of thousands of people, were participating in the most highly complex intelligence, diplomatic, geopolitical games, the results of which no one could undertake to predict.

But the fact that no one will undertake it doesn't mean that in such a game it's all left to chance. No, no there are no accidents, it's all too weighty, and even experienced players are burnt. There's too much effort and money spent on training, and it is even possible that someone gave their lives so that the game took place.

"And I'm not sitting here accidentally. It is very possible that my appearance in this bunker was predetermined long before Kold even boarded the Hong Kong Airlines plane and set foot in Russia," the Lawyer mused.

Kold got up quickly, went to the bedroom and a few seconds later returned with a big-bellied bottle of Irish whiskey. He thumped it on the table with a look as if he was going to drink until he was unconscious.

"But you don't drink?" the Lawyer was surprised.

The surprise was sincere. In the data-file on Kold he had read before the first meeting, it was specifically stated that Joshua practically never drinks alcohol.

"In this case it is medicine," Kold said in low tones and unscrewed the green lid from the bottle.

"Couch syrup?" said the Lawyer, whose conversational English left much to be desired (although he perfectly understood Kold and quite clearly stated his thoughts), deciding to flaunt the slang phrase which had recently got to him in some article. But right there in these circumstances it was hardly relevant and he apologized: "Forgive me if this joke isn't entirely successful."

"I appreciate your diligence in studying English," Kold parried icily. "But it is better to refrain from using doubtful idioms until you master English perfectly. Sometimes they can be taken wrong."

He poured himself and the Lawyer two fingers, lifted a glass and then instead of a toast gave a quote from Lao Tzu:

"'He who overcomes others is strong, he who overcomes himself is mighty.'"

"'Nothing is softer or more flexible than water, yet nothing can resist it,'" the Lawyer responded with a quote from the same source and gulped down his whiskey in one go.

The fiery stream slipped down his gullet and blew up in his stomach like a thermal bomb. The Lawyer looked at Kold. His companion drank standing, in small sips which made his sharp Adam's apple twitch, threatening to tear the skin from his thin neck.

After dealing with the whiskey, he looked at the Lawyer with eyes watering, and noisy breaths and asked:

"What do you think? Will they come back?"

"I think they won't."

"So strange," Kold sat down, rubbing a cheek with his palm. "Why would they want to kill me... It is meaningless!

"I think not all think so."

"Yes, you are, it seems, right. If your government denies me asylum, I will be forced to surrender to the U.S. authorities. I've already guaranteed... No, this is not an option. It seems I am in a desperate situation..."

"Don't rush things," the Lawyer said softly. "Don't back yourself into a corner. A way out will always be found. I am asked sometimes why I undertake fruitless cases. But I always answer that there are no fruitless cases. Anyway, all my experience confirms this truth."

FILE 003.WAV

"So, having passed all school assignments externally, one fine day I went to study at AACC in Maryland. AACC is 'Anne Arundel Community College', in Arnold, near Baltimore. However, in Maryland everything is 'near Baltimore'.

Why there? Firstly, AACC wasn't a pretentious place, secondly, they had a computer science course and… why hide the truth – I just wouldn't have gotten into a more prestigious college, my grades weren't up to it.

The first feeling that visited me in college – loneliness. Maybe, if our school psychologist had learned about it, he would put me down as a deviant teenager, registered, and would prescribe some rehabilitation therapy and antidepressants. But firstly, I wasn't going to tell anybody anything, and secondly, the school remained in the past, and I was inexpressibly glad about that.

Some time, maybe for three months, or perhaps half a year, I lived in an invisible space suit, like some surprising protective overalls that separated me from others.

Life bustled on around me, crowds of guys and girls communicated, kissed, smoked, drank, ate, copulated, quarreled, reconciled, danced at parties, watched movies, played computer games, attended classes, organized draws and played sports – and I observed all this through a hidden, but very strong cover that hid me from their eyes.

Nobody addressed me, or asked me about anything, invited me anywhere or demanded anything. I wasn't…you know?

First it amused me, and then it began to anger me – what, am I worse than others? For me, as for any guy at that age, there was a desire for communication, I wanted credibility and popularity among my peers … I wanted pretty girls to notice me, damn it! But for half a year no girl at college ever stopped near me to have a quick word, let alone to 'chat.'

Gradually, I began to develop a loser complex. I didn't sleep at nights. I stopped eating normally and for days on end without a break, I vanished behind my computer.

At the time, I was fond of cryptoprograms linked to data encryption and breaking passwords. I had a cipher, the animated image of a green rabbit, a series of alternating pictures creating the illusion that the rabbit danced. Access to the 'Dancing Rabbit' program was password-protected.

I wrote a program that created passwords which were updated every ten, five, then three, two and one seconds, using a random number generator, and then another program which, using the same MFG[6],

____

6   Medium frequency generator.

generated passwords to try to crack my first program. I got really carried away. I could watch for hours on the screen the monitor columns of digits changing, changing, changing, with inhuman speed. They say there are people who can enter into a trance with a mirror pendulum and a candle. I entered into a trance with my 'Kraken' programs.

Once I took a disk with a couple of password generators to college and in a class on information security, I secretly logged in and 'screwed' my program into the final table in which the results of the lesson were noted and marks were given. So, if you tried to display the table on the screen, you got my green rabbit dancing and, with the most innocent look, asking you to guess three figures from zero to nine.

If you could only see how diligently they all tried this seemingly trifling task! All those blockheads tapping on the keypads of their personal computers! All those 'Mr. Touchdowns' and 'Mrs. College-2001s', and other lard-asses that didn't even think that the combination from three digits gives one thousand combinations and they would spend several hours guessing it not the few remaining minutes till the end of the lesson.

I chuckled quietly, furtively looking at this until Mr. Thewlis, one of the teachers of information systems, came up to me.

'I have been watching you for a long time, young man,' he said quietly. 'I see you are making progress down your chosen path. We have a small community here…more precisely, a club of fans of programming. Would you like to join?'

'With pleasure, sir,' I answered, 'But my knowledge levels are quite low and I will hardly be able…'

'You'll be able, you will be able,' Mr. Thewlis calmed me. 'And now remove your spell, please, from our system – I need to finish the lesson.'

I already had a program for hacking the password generator on call, so I started it under comments from Mr. Thewlis and an ovation from my classmates who had at last noticed me. The green rabbit danced its final dance, the table opened and against the name Kold a capital letter A appeared.

It was the day of my triumph. Joshua Kold, 'College Superstar!' They shook my hand, patted me on the shoulder, called me by name – it seemed they knew my name!

But the most important thing was ahead. Neolani approached me in the corridor. Usually she was called Abigail, Abigail Svaysgud, but she said her parents gave her a second, Hawaiian name as well, Neolani, which means 'heavenly girl'. She was one of the alternatives who hung out in the 'Garage' and she was cool, very cool.

Even externally Neolani made such an impression that guys on the street twisted their necks to see her – short leather jacket, leggings, a magnificent miniskirt, a brilliant belt with rivets, sneakers with bulbs in the sole... Add a hairstyle like Robert Smith's, make-up like the replicants in *Blade Runner*, a pierced lower lip and a whiplash tongue that could snub anyone – and you get the portrait of this 'heavenly girl'.

And so she approaches me with that special walk that makes you go dry in the mouth. She had rings in ears, bracelets on her hands with baubles, and she says:

'You are cool, you should hang out with us! Savvy in computers?'

'Like a shot,' I say.

'Well, come to the Garage this evening. Our computer's giving out trouble. Will you come?'

I nodded – there was no force left for words.

'Well, then bye!'

And she left. And I stood as a statue, except my ears burned. Neolani had talked to me! I was invited to the Garage! Probably, it was one of the happiest moments in my life. A celebration moment, the moment of fulfilled expectations and the emergence of absolutely new ones. The line of my destiny at this moment made a sharp turn, an abrupt zigzag and I...

Damn, I became another person, get it? The Garage – it was a gate to the new world, the portal to the delirium pastures of Heaven. By hearsay, they not only smoked grass, but also snorted coke, and sniffed the Mexican brands, and beer flowed like a river. And of course, all the best girls in college went to the Garage not only to dance there were many secluded corners with soft sofas.

Of course, it was not a garage, but a former hangar for seaplanes on the bank of the Severn River. It belonged to the father of one of those guys that hung out there, Bach. Bach is not a name, but a nickname, in honour of the old composer who created the 'Pa-ba-ba-ba!' song; all 'garagers' had nicknames, some catchier than others.

To get to the Garage, you could go along a footpath on the coast. When it rained the path became muddy, and wet branches hung low over it, but I liked this way much better. If you go along the road, you inevitably pass houses rolling in thickets where there live some gloomy old women and loud mammies eternally complaining that along their precious lawns and mailboxes 'all kinds gad about'. Well, some garagers once accidentally knocked over a couple of those boxes – so now you need to call the FBI?

Semi-darkness always reigned in the Garage. The door was locked – one of the Three Main Rules. The first: 'The door is always locked!', the second: 'You disturb nobody, nobody disturbs you', and the third: 'The garbage from the Garage can't be taken out'. Certainly, in the third rule it was not talking about empty beer bottles, crumpled cigarette packs, boxes from pizza or packaging from condoms, but information, and in translation into the language of our ancestors it meant: 'What happens in the Garage stays in the Garage'.

There were always five people living there, generally guys. Their dens were in the east part of the Garage separated from the 'Central Station' and the 'Waiting Room' by racks and a black tarpaulin curtain on which it was written in silver paint 'Iron curtain'.

In the Waiting Room there was a bar, a gallery and a dance floor. In the Central Station there were compartments for couples who wanted to smoke grass in private or get on with something else. 'Nirvana' was the iron box with a door where those who got enough marks or 'passed on the three paths' could 'fly'. The 'Senior Flight Control Room' was the personal apartments of the head garager, who, to my astonishment, was not the phlegmatic fat man Bach, but a puny, short, short-haired guy with an unpleasant, even angry, face called Pincher. It as Pincher who owned the computer which was giving out trouble. On it, Pincher had made some music clips of the Cure and mounted porno-videos filmed in Nirvana in his spare time.

The computer, by the way, appeared so-so – weak and carelessly looked after – the case was wet with beer and the screen splashed with goo whose origin I don't even want to think about. But the machine was a working one, so I just rebooted the operating system, much to the rough delight of the garagers.

'Look at you, pro!' Frisbee tapped me on the shoulder, a thin smiling blonde of six foot. 'Perhaps you could also fix the amplifier?'

'Wait a moment, Fris. We didn't even ask the man whether he has time for this,' Pincher interrupted. Unlike the majority of garagers he rarely used slang. 'Josh, what do you say?'

I looked at Neolani, who suddenly smiled at me. I was at a loss and just nodded, agreeing that I have time.

'Does that mean you want to join us?' Pincher asked bringing his face so close to mine I wanted to push away him.

'I wa-want...'"

'Initiation!' the girl with green hair laughed loudly. She was called Pipe. 'There will be an initiation! Bach, bring some cream!'

And everyone around – about ten of them – whooped with delight. Someone turned on Quadrophenia and the entire Garage was flooded with the Who's guitar riffs. Pete Townsend ripped strings, Roger Daltrey wailed over the unfortunate destiny of Jimmy, and the garagers dragged me from the office of the flight controller to Central Station, pulled up a table and set me on it, all the while yelling raucously.

The music ceased. The lights went out completely.

'Joshua Kold, worthless college boy, are you ready to change your life, expand your consciousness and learn the beauty of the inner world of the Great Beaver here, in our monastery of Chaos and Gloom?' Pincher said in a solemn and rather ominous voice.

'Y-yes...' I answered quietly, but in the Garage there was suddenly total silence and I could hear the waves of the Severn River rolling onto the coast behind the iron wall of the hangar.

'Do you agree with the Three Main Rules imprinted on the Big Wall opposite to you?'

'Yes.'

'Are you familiar with the Doctrine of Time?'

I shook my head 'I just heard about it for the first time.'

'Lani,' Pincher turned his head towards my benefactor, 'So you didn't explain anything to him?'

'Slipped,' Neolani shrugged her shoulders. 'Not enough time. You do it.'

'So!' the voice of Pincher filled with epic force. 'World governments by means of science lie to people about everything that surrounds them.

The world is not such as it seems to all of us at all. And first of all this concerns time. They din into our ears that past, present and future exist. They do this so that all of us – all mankind – are slaves to time. We are forced to look back all the time at the past which allegedly contains the experiences endured in ancient times by previous generations. So we work, work hard all the time, and stoop for the sake of the future which will come after who knows how many years and allegedly will be light … It is a lie!'

'A lie?' I said, surprised.

'Everything is a lie!' Pincher confirmed. 'To the last word.'

I looked at Neolani and she smiled with her contemptuous and haughty smile – the smile of the person who knows all.

'Remember,' Pincher summed up solemnly, 'There is no Past. Absolutely. It has already passed, it was carried away back, absolutely back and therefore does not exist. I have said this phrase, and so it has already stopped existing, understand? That's it, there is no past! Every second, each fraction of a second, the past disappears, melts like ice, evaporates into vapour, and is gone. So everything that was in it ceases to exist and has no value. All this experience, all these learned mistakes are nonsense and rubbish! Remember, Joshua, college-boy, others' mistakes never taught anybody to do something. The free person learns from their own mistakes! Learns because there is no past. But there is no future either. It is absent for another reason – it hasn't come yet.

Everybody today says you need to work hard and strive to bring the future we want but this is a double lie. The future can't come, it can't arrive because the moment it arrives, it becomes the unique condition of time which is the present. The present is that instant in which you live, in which you exist at present. Only the present is material and real. So live in the present! That is our motto! And now tell me, computer master with a chilly surname, do you want to spend the fleeting present working, sitting in stupid offices, for shares and transactions, for courts and reports?'

'No,' I said.

'Louder!"

'No!"

'Life is short!' Pincher began to yell. 'Learn yourself, learn the true world! Have fun! Create! Have a good time! Live in the present! Yeeha!!'

'Live in the present! Yeeha!!' the garagers shouted and began to leap in the air. Stroboscope lights flashed and dazzled. The music began again – this time the contemporary band Shadow Gallery, and Pincher ordered sharply:

'Lani, on the table! Bach, cream!'

Neolani, still smiling, threw her jacket onto the floor, revealing a red crop top. She got up on to the table, crawled to the middle, sat down, and, coiling all her body, pulled off her crop top with a quick tug. There was nothing underneath! She lay down on her back.

My heart stopped, then was driven on in a beat, driven by the frantic pounding of the music.

'Hey, hey!' Pipe cried, twisting her shaggy green hair. 'Why her, not me?"

'Because I said so, baby!' Pincher grinned. 'Bach!"

The fat man approached Neolani and began to smother her erect breasts and their ringletted nipples with whipped cream from a barrel. When he had finished, the smiling 'heavenly girl' looked like a cake. Pincher pulled a bag of white powder from a pocket and strewed it over the cream.

'What's that?' I asked.

'Vanilla sugar!' Bach answered and laughed loudly.

'Eat!' Pincher ordered me.

'What?'

'Lick! Eat! Guzzle! Guzzle!

'Guzzle! Guzzle!! Guzzle!!!' the garagers chanted.

I bent down over the table and, avoiding looking at Neolani's smiling face, licked the cream, trying not to touch her skin with my tongue. For some reason it seemed to me that the white powder, surely ground tablets like amphetamine, must taste bitter, but that cream really did taste like vanilla.

'You need to eat with appetite!' Neolani sang, suddenly seizing my hair and pressing my face firmly into herself. I choked, swallowing the sweet mass, and rested my hands against the table, trying to escape, but she held me tight. The rigid nipple of her breast with its corrosion-proof steel ring slipped into my mouth and…

And I calmed down. A strange languor spread through my body, and I wanted to laugh and eat this cream forever. I hugged Neolani, nestled on her and froze, feeling her body shuddering with laughter. It was … good. That good. Maybe for the first time in life it was so good. As if I had found a family. And maybe, I really had found it.

Do I need to say that that evening I became a man? But I don't remember much about it itself, because Pincher had filled the cream with too much 'magic powder.' I was blown away very far and for a long time, and in the morning I felt so bad I swore never to use drugs again.

<h1 style="text-align:center">10:12 P.M.</h1>

"Mr. Kold, I'm sorry, I need to interrupt you," the Lawyer made a helpless gesture of apology. "I've had an urgent message about you…"

"What is it?" Kold said after a small pause, tightening his lips, and turning his eyes to stare at a point in the distance.

The Lawyer paused his phone, took out a tablet from his briefcase and logged into his email.

"The source whose name I can't tell you, writes that forces interested in your extradition to the USA have intervened in the decision on you. The scales are not inclined in our favour…"

"I was ready for this turn of events," Kold said firmly. "But it's all in God's hands."

"Don't you regret you casting your lot with Russia?" the Lawyer switched off the phone. "You had other options…"

Kold rubbed his chin, and unexpectedly smiled.

"Would you like to have supper? I'll order pizza and salad."

"Thanks, I am full, though to keep you company I won't refuse a couple of sandwiches. But you didn't answer my question."

"One minute …

Kold picked up the internal phone and dictated the order, but the Lawyer could see that all this time he was considering his answer, and pushed him:

"By the way, several countries in Latin America wanted to accept you and grant a shelter directly?"

Kold hung up and nodded.

"Yes, actually, the way Cassandzhi was supported by Ecuador gave me the first hope that everything will turn out ok. I was wanting to tell you about it, but those people appeared… Are you ready to listen? "

The Lawyer inclined his head, turned on the phone again and laid it on the table near a bottle.

"Well," Kold took a half-full whiskey glass, shook it in his hand then set it down again. "Then I will continue. Time is moving. It's already nearly eleven, and I would like to get to the end of my story by three o'clock, telling everything in order…"

FILE 004.WAV

"That Pincher, he was abnormal. Now, after some time, I am absolutely convinced of it. He didn't just have pathological interests, but pathological tendencies. He needed to spoil, befoul, vulgarize and pervert everything he touched.

I remember, during one performance called 'Stewart Little has breakfast in heaven' he put thirty live white mice in a big empty aquarium, then climbed inside himself and began to squash them with his legs, at the same time noisily reading aloud the description of the posthumous destiny of some unfortunate princess by the name of de Lamballe who was torn to pieces by a mad crowd at the time of the Great French revolution:

'That hapless body was dragged through all Paris. Her mutilated genitals were sliced off with a sabre like a military trophy and set up on a pike. And the crowd, jubilant and drunk with blood, carried her severed head with its flying hair and her ripped out heart on pikes too, like army standards. The procession made its way to the Temple, the prison where they had imprisoned Queen Marie Antoinette, the dearest girlfriend of the torn-to-pieces princess.'

When almost all the mice had been crushed to death, and Pincher's legs were soaked red with blood, he ordered Frisbee to pour some gasoline from a canister into the aquarium. While all this was happening, Pincher continued to read the description of the appalling punishment of this time:

'The first slash of the sabre sliced the hood from her head, letting the long blond hair scatter on her shoulders. The second slash sliced through her forehead to the eye, and the gushing blood instantly filled her dress and hair. Fainting, she began to settle to the ground. But the crowd wanted the show to go on. She was forced to rise and walk over the corpses. She fell again. Perhaps she was still alive, so a woman called Sharla decided to snuff her out for good, and walloped her with a cudgel. And, as if it had waited for its moment, the crowd now furiously attacked the body, slashing with sabres and piercing with pikes until it turned into a bloody, shapeless stump. The violence and gore made the crowd dizzy, it seemed, for there was no limit. The butcher's helper, a boy known as Donkey, bent down over a corpse and cut the head off with a huge butcher's knife.'

Then at a sign from Pincher, Bach lit the gasoline and the surviving mice began to squeak desperately, burning alive, but their squeaking was drowned out by Pincher's voice:

'The pen cannot describe in detail the execution of Madame de Lamballe. She was tormented in the most terrible way for eight hours. With her breasts torn off and her teeth pulled, she was kept conscious for two hours by all means, so that she could better feel her death.

Waving their terrible trophies, the cortege went on their way. The corpse was dragged along pavements by ropes tied to the legs, first to the Parisian residence of the princess, then to Temple where the royal family was imprisoned. One eyewitnesses describes that cortege as follows:

Some villain bore on the point of a pike the head with blonde hair matted with blood. A second, following him, had in one hand the blood-dripping heart of the victim, and in the other her guts, which he wound around his wrist. The monster boasted that today at supper he would treat himself with the heart of the princess de Lamballe!

Two men dragged the legs of the naked and beheaded corpse of the princess de Lamballe with the stomach ripped to the breast. The procession stopped in front of the Temple. The mutilated body was set upon a shaky scaffold, as if trying to give it a respectable look. All this was done with such composure and efficiency that it begged the question: were these people in their right minds? To the right of me, one of the leaders swung the pike with the head of madam de Lamballe on it from side to side, and on each swing her long hair touched my face. To the left, another, even more awful, with a huge knife in a hand, pressed to his breast the guts of the victim. They were followed by the coal miner of huge height bearing on the point of a pike shreds of a shirt impregnated by blood and dirt.

A barber was quickly found to arrange the princess suitably for an appearance in front of the queen. He had to wash the hair matted with blood, comb it and powder it as demanded by court etiquette. The cheeks were rouged in the fashion of that time: 'At least now Antoinette will be able to recognize her.'

Coming up to the Temple, the crowd demanded that the royal family come to the window. They couldn't wait for Marie Antoinette to look at what remained of her beloved girlfriend. The young officer of the municipal guard sent this request to the King. Hearing it, Marie Antoinette fainted, and the crowd raged, demanding the head of the Queen. Then the cortege went to the Palais Royal to show the corpse of the princess to the Duc d'Orleans, her brother-in-law. Around seven o'clock in the evening the crowd were finally tired and drained of emotion and got rid of the body by throwing it into a ditch close to a building under construction near Châtelet. At sunrise, the body of the princess was buried at last in the Cemetery of Foundlings.'

I don't remember that during this or other performances (and there were some even more disgusting!) anyone in the audience or any of the participants felt bad. No, there were those who crashed out, vomited or went bananas, but that's because of various drugs for 'consciousness expansion.'

Before I became acquainted with the garagers, I knew almost nothing about modern art. Actually, not almost – I didn't know anything at all! Pictures, sculptures, painting, graphics – all these were totally unfamiliar to me..."

10:34 P.M.

Kold's phone rang unexpectedly and the Lawyer was forced to switch off the recording.

"Hallo!" Kold answered laconically. "Yes. Yes, I am busy. Mrs. Morisson, I can't accept you. No, I am not obliged to report to you … Well, I have a meeting with my lawyer. No, everything is all right. Yes, all the best."

He switched off his phone, leaned back the chair and sighed.

"Sometimes it seems to me that Cassandzhi deployed Morisson to spy on me. Who does she transfer information to?"

"These people help you, don't they?" the Lawyer said, surprised. "In my opinion, it was they who managed to contact diplomats from Ecuador…"

"Ok!" Kold moved forward suddenly, interrupting him. "This is exactly why I don't want … I have to be careful, you understand, and there… there everything is too simple and too much like a baited trap. You asked the question: why have I chosen Russia? For the moment, I'll just say this: prospects. Here there are prospects. Room for manoeuvre, do you see? And I have a feeling that I can just get so lost here I won't be found by the CIA, or MI6, or archangels of our Lord. But Latin America is the backyard of the United States! No, after giving it some thought, I realized I wouldn't like to be there. And one more important point – I would maybe consider offers from Ecuador and Venezuela more carefully if I wasn't pushed by Cassandzhi…"

FILE 005.WAV

"Before going on with my story about the Garage and the incidents that came after, I just want to say a few words about 9/11. When it all happened, I was just beginning college. It was an ordinary day, a Tuesday, with nothing untoward going on. Then suddenly all the TVs around the college hall and in the snackbar – even in the security guards' room – began to show the towers of the World Trade Center and these planes crashing into them.

Everyone was crowding around the screens. There were lots of people crying. And some just asking: 'What do we do now, what now?' And when the message came that more planes with alleged terrorists were in the air and one of them was heading directly for the White House, there was almost panic. Two ambulances arrived as one of the schoolgirls and the teacher, Mr. Hopkins, felt ill.

For some reason, this didn't make that strong of an impression on me. No, of course, it was awful that people died – innocent and civil, as my father used to say. Yes, people died, but this death in the air seemed to be designed for salesmen and housewives. In a word, it looked as though it had been written in advance cinematically according to a scenario. Maybe, though, my muted reaction to the terrorist attacks in New York was linked to the divorce of my parents and internal experiences which eclipsed them. I don't know.

Of course, I read lots about it, and watched the films shot by supporters and opponents of various versions. Then at last, when I worked in the National Security Agency, I tried just for the sake of interest to learn the 'truth', but encountered a very powerful system of concealment of information.

It was organized in such a way that anyone who wanted to delve into the facts came up against what seemed to be mere coincidences, pieces of a puzzle scattered on the floor in the dark room on which Confucius's cat seemed to have scampered about. The creators of the TV series *The X-files* were right – the truth is still somewhere nearby.

Anyway, let me go back to the Garage. It regularly arranged exhibitions and open days of contemporary art – well, in the way that garagers understood it! I've already told you some examples and that's enough because it is really not too appetizing! But I will say that the Garage gave me a lot of knowledge about various movements in painting, sculpture and graphic and other arts.

Before knowing Neolani and the others, I had heard only about surrealism, and that thanks to the reproduction of Dali's *'Dream Caused by the Flight of a Bee Around a Pomegranate a Second Before Awakening'* hanging in Judith's room. But to be honest, it was the naked woman that drew my attention to the picture, not surrealism.

In the Garage, I was very simply and intelligibly, with examples, introduced to the way one style of a contemporary art differs from another. Frisbee and Neolani taught me.

'Here look,' said Neo, quickly sketching the contours of a horse on a piece of writing paper. 'I am drawing a stallion the way it is, with dirty hoofs and a throbbing dick – this is realism. Now…' she took some felt-tip pens, 'We will paint our horsey in a blue with scarlet hair. That will be expressionism. And now we will add a shovel to the dick, skates on the hoofs, and on its back we will paint a portrait of the Pope. That is surrealism. Pass me the charcoal, Fris!'

With the charcoal she sharply delineated all the contours of an initial horse, then divided it into geometrical figures, after slightly modifying the positions of the head and tail.

'That's cubism. And if I turn everything into a black square with a white circle and write 'horse' sideways, that's suprematism. Oh, I forgot – if right at the beginning we painted the horse with various pastel tones and blurred contours, that would be impressionism.'

'If there is only a circle tracing out the horse's hoof, that's minimalism,' Frisbee intervened. 'And if all of it is smeared with horse shit. Then it is 'active painting' mixed with Dadaism. Do you get it, Joshy-boy?'

'In general,' I laughed. 'And do you want me to tell you something useful about programming in the statically compiled language 'C-plus-plus' or about html design?'

'Buddha forbid' they yelled in unison and ran off in feigned horror, leaving me alone with the image of a horse.

Besides art, the garagers were involved with various social and political movements. We regularly wrote trials for the renegade websites, picketed the local chemical plant, supported Greenpeace, printed Che Guevara's portrait on red teeshirts for the antiglobalists who were going to go to fight the police somewhere in Europe and illegally replicated disks of musicians like Manu Chao because he was singing songs of protest.

Once I went with Neolani and other garagers to Baltimore on a demo in support of Dmitry Sklyarov, the hacker from Russia. This pretzel wrote the 'Advanced eBook Processor' program, which easily bypassed the protection of PDF files, designed by ADOBE specifically so that nobody could copy anything from them.

Under American law what Dmitry had done was illegal, but it wasn't under Russian law – so his firm quietly traded the program created by him, and everything was good.

Then Dmitry was invited to a computer conference in San Francisco, and even wrote a paper, but he was arrested by FBI agents there and thrown into prison.

Well, of course, normal people all over the country were strongly indignant – because if this Russian was jailed today just for doing his job well, then tomorrow one of us might be jailed just because we've written something on the internet. Something 'not acceptable' from the point of view of the authorities, I mean.

However, I always felt there was some wormhole in this story, something hidden from the spotlight, some nasty twist you couldn't quite express.

In fact, Dmitry's program allowed you to steal information, and theft is always bad wherever it happens – in a shop, at a BP gas station or on the internet.

But on the other hand thousands of people claim that information has to be free. Do people pay for something that they hear on the street, on the train, in a wood or in a field?

I didn't really think that deeply about it, though. For me, it was enough that Neolani and the garagers, my friends, were for Dmitry – so, then, was I.

We went in two cars. The guys went in an old Ford with a big panel saying 'Release Dmitry!' and Neo and I went in a small Toyota. We were picking up some weed from some acquaintances of Neo's so after the demo they could really get their rocks off.

We chatted and made out all the way and a few times we nearly came off the highway. Neo's little beast was as fast as a track car, though she said it was a cheap Japanese model.

After Pasadena, we turned left before Glen Bernie onto the street with the amusing name Avahart Road. But there was nothing else amusing in that street. In fact, nothing in that whole district. It was 'frankly shit' as Pincher would say. But it's in exactly that kind of place that drug dealers live.

Neo stopped the car near a two-storey house covered in plastic plates. This, it seems, is called siding. In Wilmington, only snackbars or municipal buildings are sheathed that way.

'Come on,' Neo said and dragged me along. I smiled – I'd learned a cool smile to say, don't worry about me – and got out of the car to follow her. Of course, there was always the thought that drug dealers aren't too keen on extra eyes and ears in their work.

When Neo pulled out a key to open the door, I was really surprised. Then she took off her shoes, presumably because there were mats everywhere. I took my shoes off too.

We went into the house, passed through a big room with a sofa and fireplace, and slid between a curtain with Chinese bamboo bells and dream-catchers into another room. Here, probably, lived a mad hippie-nymphomaniac artist. All the walls were covered in drawings and pictures in which naked women were depicted in obscene poses. Women were fucking with live snakes, giving birth to toads, vomiting severed dicks and other activities which made me genuinely nauseous.

'Look at the books here. I'm going to the attic for weed,' Neolani said, and I listened to her bare feet pad up the wooden steps of a ladder.

There were certainly books on the shelves, a lot of books. I'd only seen so many in the school library before. Well, except perhaps in Mr. Isenberg's office where he had a huge case.

We didn't have books at home and none of my friends did either. No, the Bible doesn't count. My schoolmate, Mathew Turkle still had some ancient books from Europe, either his great-grandfather brought them, or his great-great-grandfather. Pictures in these were black-and-white, creepy – various demons with a skeletal knight on a horse fighting against them. The book wasn't written in English, and I didn't understand the name, but something was about Don Quixote de la something else.

Neolani's books were very different. I read the names of the authors on their spines: Huxley, Camus, Heinlein, Orwell, Ortega y Gasset, Fukuyama – and realized they meant practically nothing to me. Besides that there were some books that seemed totally nonsense to me: Huang-di, Lao-Tzu, Gian Daolin, Ge Xuan and Five Pecks of Rice.

My attention was drawn by a big, black book with the intricate, clear name of *The Anarchist Cookbook* by a certain William Powell.

I opened it at random and read: 'Cooking with marijuana. Many people throw away the seeds, stalks, and branches after purification of raw materials. I strongly recommend you to keep them since there are many recipes for using this waste'. And there followed simple and detailed instructions for making marijuana tea. I turned the page. Here it gave a recipe for narcotic desserts. 'This Mr. Powell was rather inventive,' I thought, flicking through the book. 'But what have anarchists to do with this? So what next?"

The answer came with LSD, where it explored Artaud's and Huxley's experiments with mescaline and peyote and talked about Artaud's idea of the creation of a great society based on psychotropic drugs. Peyote changed Artaud. He found he could comprehend and understand ideas on another level. He could depart from rationalism, and even the modern truth. Artaud found his own truth and own structures. But they locked him up.

I died at Rodez under an electroshock.
I died. Legally and medically died.
Electroshock coma lasts 15 minutes.
A half an hour more, then the patient breathes.
Now one hour after the shock, I still had not
                    awakened and stopped breathing.
Surprised at my abnormal rigidity, an attendant had gone to get
the physician in charge
Who after examining me found no more signs of life in me.
The coma after the electroshock lasted 15 minutes.

The lines were so-so, of course, but the story is about a person who describes his own apparent death, under the influence of LSD. It interested me, and I began to read further: 'Preparation of LSD in laboratory. To synthesize acid, you need knowledge of fundamentals of chemistry and access to a laboratory'. And Powell went on to give a simple recipe.

But I don't understand chemistry so this was boring. Flicking through further, I came across peyote. It always seemed to me some dull Mexican cactus. But the author of the book revealed that this nondescript plant contains the strong psychedelic mescaline, and described his first powerful encounter with it.

Neolani was taking a long time. I listened to the sounds from above, but I could hear nothing but faint muttering, including a woman's voice. It was baking hot and I was thirsty. We needed to get to the rendezvous point for the demonstration and time already was short.

I was going to call Neo, but decided to wait five more minutes for decency, and I was again engaged in the book. My next finding was a chapter named 'A Treatise About Toads' in which he described the extraction of a hallucinogen called bufotenin from the skin of toads...

'Here,' I showed her. 'Interesting book.'

'Second-hand stuff,' she contemptuously pulled her shoulder. 'Compositions of Uncle Billy and his disciples. Ok, let's go, I have the weed. Real Mexican, from Chihuahua!'

I put the book down, and we went out.

'Whose house is it?' I asked when Neo closed the door.

'Oh, just...' she fell silent then answered abruptly as we got near the car: 'My parents.'

All the rest of the day in Baltimore, we horsed around, drank beer in the lanes and gateways where there were no police officers, then we were dumped on by some local citizen. Or a few locals. Some nose in a window saw that minors were drinking beer behind a store, and called the cops. They arrived, but we ran away. It was a riot!

As we ran, we ran into a procession of evangelists and got lost in the crowd, just as in a film. We slipped away from the cops. So all of us got lost in the melee.

We hung out with some goths and some gays from Washington, and marched through the streets with posters and shouted: 'Freedom for Dmitry, May he screw up together with his shitty Rushka!'

Do you think we had much interest in this hacker? Absolutely none! We were just having fun. Yes, there those principled people at this fucking demonstration who raised fists and were ready to dive under the wheels of police cars. But did we care? We were free artists, we lived in the present.

After the demo, everyone – except me, you remember the oath – smoked weed on the riverbank, hiding under the bridge. Seven or so black guys leaned over the bridge and kept taunting us, sneering: 'Whad-ya-lookin-at, snowballs?' But we were a big group, and there were the goths and gays from Washington, too. So they didn't pursue it – and anyway the guys were stoned, and none of us gave a damn.

At night we ripped flags off buildings. They were hung on every building in Downtown Baltimore in triplets – the US national flag, the flag of the State of Maryland and a flag with a municipal coat of arms. Pincher was the first to jump up, grab all three at once and yank them off with a noisy rending sound.

I remember at some point I flinched from the cognitive dissonance, yet all my life, all my eighteen years, everything around me, at home and at school, in the street and on TV, had drummed into me (and other children) that our star-spangled banner was our key and almost sacred symbol.

From my first days in school, I had learned the rules of what can and must never be done with a flag of the USA by heart! It should never be dipped to any person or thing even if the flags of states, military banners and other flags are dipped in their honour. It should never be raised upside down, except as a distress signal. It should never be raised so low that it touches something beneath it: the earth, a floor, water, other objects. It should never be borne on a flagpole with the pole horizontal (the flag shall always be carried at an angle). It should never be raised so that it could be damaged or soiled. One should never write or draw something on a flag; or wrap something in a flag; or use it as clothes, bed linen or draperies, or in a suit or on sportswear – though at the same time the image of a flag can be sewn for members of the patriotic organizations, military, police and firefighters. One must never use a flag for advertising and promotion of goods or print its image on napkins, boxes and other disposable objects.

Pincher broke several of these rules as he wrapped himself in a flag, blew his nose on its hem, then tore off a strip and put it in his trousers in the manner of a diaper. I wanted to tell him that, probably, he shouldn't do it. But Frisbee shouted that Pincher looked like Casper the Friendly Ghost, and everybody laughed loudly, including me. And as my friends were under the influence of weed, they just couldn't stop.

We hobbled along the street and tore more flags off. Some tied them as scarfs, some as Roman togas or Superman's cape. For some reason, I tied a flag on a belt as a Scottish kilt and danced a wild jig with Neolani, yelling that we were from Clan Macleod and that there can only be one.

Of course, the police were called, as people peeped from their windows to see us up to all kinds of tricks, and breaking the peace and all kinds of state laws. But it was dark. And as the sirens wailed from the next block, we scurried into the slums and away.

Well, not slums really, but warehouses down by the railroad. We spent the night there on boxes and containers covered with tarpaulin, smoking weed before sleeping.

Under the tarpaulin, it was warm and easy to smoke. Some puffed smoke, others just breathed it in and felt high. They also invited me in, but I got out and sat down in the wind. Firstly, because of my oath, and secondly, it had all become rather revolting…

When we got back to college, life swept on indifferently. The ripped flags were nothing to most of us, a prank with no consequences and leaving no memories.

It haunted me, though, and once when Neo and I went to the Garage together, I suddenly told her it is wrong behave like this with a flag. I didn't expect an answer, I just needed to express my feelings. But she did answer, and seriously, without any of her favourite words, like an exam:

'Flags, anthems – these are all external symbols. A transferral of concepts. Do you understand?'

I shook my head.

'Well. Fabric alone. Words alone. They mean nothing. But you can create fetishes out of them. 'Don't create an idol for yourself' remember?'

I shook my head again. It wasn't that her words were unclear; I just didn't want to agree with them.

'Oh, well!' Neolani stamped her foot in indignation. 'I'll get you the book, and you can read everything…'

And she really did bring me the book. I don't remember the name, but it was about Buddhism, about its various trends, about philosophical schools and wise men who lived a thousand years ago. Why was I interested? Probably because Neo liked it.

Not that I got the idea of all these allegories and abstract definitions straight away. How could I, an American teenager, understand what Tao is, especially if you consider that even now, as a thirty-year-old, I don't really get it. I'm absolutely sure that no one in their senses and sober will say to himself: 'I have learned Tao!'.

All the same, there were different scientific definitions, using clever words like immanence, and transcendence and undifferentiated emptiness, but what are they to me?

To me, as an IT specialist, it is clear from Lao Zi's words that Tao generates one, the unit generates a pair – Yin and Yang – which generate three and reveal the entire world.

So Tao is a binary code, a source of all forms. But according to Lao Tzu, Tao is at the same time the energy which forms all processes of creation, and creation itself. It is the creating spirit which creates and destroys – but creation and destruction equally create and maintain this world, ensuring its existence in the form we know. Tao is also the balance of good and evil, again a binary code, and, I think, is also love, because how is anything possible without it?

I enjoyed reading the Taoist sages much more than the Buddha. Neo brought me the book of the writings of the great taoists – the Yellow emperor Huang-di and others. Of course, much of it was seriously obscure, but some of the formulations bewitched me with their refined absurdity:

When all in Celestial Empire learn that beautiful
                                        is beautiful then there is ugly.
When all learn that kind is kind then there is evil.
And therefore
what generates each other is life and non-existence,
what counterbalances each other is heavy and easy,
what limits each other is long and short,
what serves each other is high and low,
what echoes each other is a voice and a sound,
what follows one after another is last and coming,
                                        and so endlessly.

This is my favourite Lao Tzu. Think about this, and in these phrases all world order is described! But it is best of all to think about it after long meditation, purging your mind of busy thoughts …

To be serious, Lao Tzu said some other things, for example, here: 'Walking wins against cold; rest wins against heat.' 'Tranquility creates an order in the world'. It is true, it needs to be accepted, then go further.

But what further was there? Perhaps, the beginning of the war in Iraq. No, before the war there was a preparation. I remember how everywhere it was said that Saddam and his allies from Al-Qaeda were guilty of 9/11, that they killed thousands of innocent people, and now they were preparing for the slaughter of hundreds of thousands, maybe even millions, as they prepared to launch a war with weapons of mass destruction.

People argued about those Iraqi weapons of mass destruction anywhere and everywhere – at gas stations, in snackbars, in supermarkets, and even us at the Garage.

Then there was that well-known performance of Colin Powell at the UN Security Council when he showed the whole world a test tube with white powder and said:

'…We know that Saddam Hussein has what is called quote, 'a higher committee for monitoring the inspections teams,' unquote. Think about that. Iraq has a high-level committee to monitor the inspectors who were sent in to monitor Iraq's disarmament. Not to cooperate with them, not to assist them, but to spy on them and keep them from doing their jobs...

The committee reports directly to Saddam Hussein. It is headed by Iraq's vice president, Taha Yassin Ramadan. Its members include Saddam Hussein's son Qusay.

…We know that Saddam's son, Qusay, ordered the removal of all prohibited weapons from Saddam's numerous palace complexes. We know that Iraqi government officials, members of the ruling Baath Party and scientists have hidden prohibited items in their homes. Other key files from military and scientific establishments have been placed in cars that are being driven around the countryside by Iraqi intelligence agents to avoid detection...

...Let me now turn to those deadly weapons programs and describe why they are real and present dangers to the region and to the world. First, biological weapons. We have talked frequently here about biological weapons. By way of introduction and history, I think there are just three quick points I need to make.

First, you will recall that it took UNSCOM four long and frustrating years to pry--to pry--an admission out of Iraq that it had biological weapons.

Second, when Iraq finally admitted having these weapons in 1995, the quantities were vast. Less than a teaspoon of dry anthrax, a little bit about this amount--this is just about the amount of a teaspoon – less than a teaspoon full of dry anthrax in an envelope shutdown the United States Senate in the fall of 2001. This forced several hundred people to undergo emergency medical treatment and killed two postal workers just from an amount just about this quantity that was inside of an envelope. Iraq declared 8,500 liters of anthrax, but UNSCOM estimates that Saddam Hussein could have produced 25,000 liters. If concentrated into this dry form, this amount would be enough to fill tens upon tens upon tens of thousands of teaspoons. And Saddam Hussein has not verifiably accounted for even one teaspoon-full of this deadly material.

And that is my third point. And it is key. The Iraqis have never accounted for all of the biological weapons they admitted they had and we know they had. They have never accounted for all the organic material used to make them. And they have not accounted for many of the weapons filled with these agents such as there are 400 bombs. This is evidence, not conjecture. This is true. This is all well-documented.'

11:35 P.M.

"But the presence in Iraq of weapons of mass destruction wasn't proved," the Lawyer noted.

Kold nodded:

"Of course. The performance of Powell can be considered as a typical model of 'so-called lies', and although the world would like to believe them, and be guided by their good intentions, in the case of Iraq, the road down which we moved on this unfortunate country was paved with such intentions and, as you can see on the news everyday, it was a road to hell."

The Lawyer wanted to say something, but Kold interrupted him with a raised finger:

"But! Then, in the spring of the 2003, we didn't even guess anything. The war on terror had been declared two years earlier, and the enemy pure and simple wasn't pure and simple: the blue corner of the ring was empty. And suddenly condensed into it was the dark shadow of the bloody dictator, moustached and degenerate, ready to lay waste to the whole world with anthrax. The referee hardly had time to cry out 'Boxing!' as all America spoiled for the fight."

FILE 006.WAV

"On one not so fine day I came to the Garage and came across a half-naked Neolani and Pincher rolling under a cover on the stove bench in Central Station. I didn't know if they'd done anything or not, but boy was I mad. I completely lost it. I kicked over a plastic barrel full of paint, smashed a bunch of bottles and made one hell of a mess.

I think neither of them knew I could be that crazy. I didn't even know it myself.

Finally, my rage spent, I asked Neo:

'Are you with him or with me?'

She just smiled. Pincher stretched and lowered his lean hairy legs on to the dirty floor.

'What's up, Joshua-boy?' he asked lazily. 'Property rights on people were cancelled by Honest Abe. She is a free person. If she wants to sleep with you, she can. If she wants, she can sleep with me. And if she wants, she can sleep with Sparki.'

Sparki was the mangy dog that lived in thickets near the Garage. We fed him up and sometimes for fun we added magic mushrooms to the pieces of pizza or hamburgers we gave him.

Sparki had a bad trip and howled long and terribly. I imagined Neo on all fours, behind the twitching, howling Sparki, and I felt totally revolted.

'Why are you silent?' I asked Neolani.

She continued to smile. Still smiling, she rolled on her back, and I couldn't see her face behind Pincher's thin torso. He also smiled his usual wry douchebag smile, ready at any moment to stab you in the back.

'Have a rest, Joshua-boy,' Pincher said. 'Go, find yourself a girlfriend firing on fewer cylinders. Little Liu is always ready, and she has a redhot uterus. And live in the present! There is no past, you forget. That's my advice for you.'

'I don't need the advice of a motherfucking kid like you,' I replied. He burst out laughing and thrust up his middle finger.

I left Central Station, determined to leave the Garage forever. But I hardly managed to reach the door before Neolani caught me up wrapped in the cover like a toga. She silently grasped me by the hand, turned me and embraced me, then stuck a kiss on my lips. But as she did the cover fell. She was completely naked...

Of course, I survived, but something changed, broke up, cracked, and it wasn't the same any more. I sat down at the computer, and plunged into cryptographic programs. Enciphering data by transfer to networks began to interest me wildly. Indeed, I was hooked on it as strongly as I had been on the Garage. Once, we had discussed the freedom problem on the internet there and someone – Black Rick, I think, he always was nuts about such affairs –made this short speech:

'The internet should have a program or special plug-ins that makes every user anonymous automatically. You need to prevent a targeted registration with data computation. This is the only way the internet can become a truly free territory, a place where no one owes anything to anybody and no one is afraid of anybody.'

Of course, what he spoke about was impossible. But maybe you could encrypt data to hide it all from the government, from hackers, and from the ubiquitous businessmen. That was a real possibility, and I became deeply engaged in it, partly to fill the vacuum left by Neolani's treachery.

I visited Mr. Thewlis's club too. At first it was interesting there, but soon I hit a ceiling. Mr. Thewlis and the college computers just couldn't go where I wanted to go. And so my studies there came to an end, even though in theory I had another two years to go.

One day I talked to Mr. Thewlis about it. He took off his glasses, chewed a handle, looked at me thoughtfully and said:

'As a teacher, I hate to hear this, but as a scientist I am flattered that you, Mr. Kold, were my disciple. You will go far, I assure you, and I … I will do my best to promote it.'

'How?' I didn't understand.

'You see, one person, the representative of a very reputable corporation engaged in developing products of the same kind as you, has asked me to acquaint him with prospective candidates. Do you think, Mr. Kold, that you would be interested in making such an acquaintance?'

As you probably guessed, I'm a bit of a sociopath and reluctant to meet strangers. They frighten me – not by their appearance, of course, but the potential threat introduced into my life. The threat alone was enough. Besides, after the break up with Neo I didn't want to communicate with anybody at all, especially a stranger.

'Thanks, Mr. Thewlis,' I said. 'But no need. Goodbye.'

We said goodbye, and I went to the hostel. I probably would have forgotten this conversation as I forgot many other things. But the next day as I was walking along the Ring Road by the Humanities campus building, a big, black Mercedes stopped right next to me. I glanced towards it – good car, powerful and beautiful, though made in Europe – and walked on. But the Mercedes began to glide along beside me. It was a wet day, and little drops of rain shivered on the tinted glass of the passenger door then started to trickle down.

'Maybe he's lost and wants to ask the way,' I thought, stopping, though standing in the rain wasn't much fun. 'Number's not local'.

From the leather belly of the car I heard my name:

'Mr. Kold! Would you be so kind as to give me a shred of your attention, dear sir?'

Nobody had ever yet called me 'dear sir', and I, of course, stopped, bent down and glanced in the window. A white man of forty years had one hand on the wheel. He had a friendly face, a short crewcut of fair hair, the reddish weather-beaten skin of a yachtsman and cheerful eyes the color of summer sky.

'Are you talking to me?' I asked a little foolishly, trying to guess what he wanted from me.

'Yes, Mr. Kold. My name is Jenkins. Ed Jenkins, at your service,' he smiled kindly. 'I represent … However why are you getting wet in the rain? Get into the car. It is very comfortable.'

I looked around. It was broad daylight, people were going, cars were going. Of course, since we were children we've been told not to get into the cars of strangers, but… I haven't been a child for a long time! Besides, this Jenkins doesn't seem like someone who even in the long term could threaten my safety. Of course, the circumstances were a little strange, but …

Curiosity, as we know, killed the cat. I opened the door and got in.

Jenkins pressed my hand. He had a strong handshake, mannish, like my Pa's. 'Of course!' I suddenly realized. Pa! 'This is one of his acquaintances, a friend or a colleague. That's where he knows me from, why he has weather-beaten skin.'

'Mr. Kold, you are undoubtedly surprised, and possibly having other, not very positive feelings toward the stranger who stopped you on the street. So to quickly establish a rapport between us, I will not beat about the bush.' Jenkins sat half-turned to me and said, still smiling. 'I'm not a Baptist preacher, nor a salesman, and not an army recruiter. I've been told about you by your teacher, Mr. Thewlis …'

I sighed with disappointment. So that's what was going on!

"I see that my explanation hasn't met your expectations,' he smiled even more broadly. 'But believe me, my proposal won't leave you indifferent, and in a positive sense.'

He spoke very softly, modulating his voice at the end of each phrase. His way of talking was full, pleasant and gave you no desire to interrupt him.

'Your researches in the field of cryptography and encryption of information messages when sending them to the network made a favorable impression on our staff.'

'On your – who are they?' For the first time since I got into the car, I stared open mouthed.

'Speaking simply, Josh' he changed his tone and at once turned into a simple guy 'I want to offer you a collaboration. A job, you know? Not so very complex and skilled at first; you have a lot to learn. But later...

'Who is the employer?' I asked.

He came straight out with it:

'The government.'

I laughed. The situation reminded me of a cheap HBO series.

'Sorry, Mr. Jenkins, but I won't work for the government. It contradicts my beliefs.'

He laughed, but when he started talking, his voice became serious.

'Beliefs? You are a joker, Mr. Kold! What beliefs are you talking about? You grew up in a good American family, your father is a respectable person and it is not his fault that your parents broke up. When I say the government, I mean the United States. The values practiced in your family are the values of the United States.'

'I haven't lived with my family for a long time!' I said challengingly, even though that 'for a long time' was a very small part of my life.

'So be it,' he didn't argue. 'Beliefs are not socks, you can't change them every day. Do you agree?'

I shrugged. To agree meant to recognize his correctness – and what psychologists call 'youthful maximalism' was boiling in me. I very much wanted to prove to this Mr. Jenkins that the main thing in life was freedom and...

'The main thing in life is freedom,' he said, and I shrank my head back in fear.

Had he read my mind? Who was he, damnit?!

'I love baseball very much,' Mr. Jenkins continued. 'But what attracts me is not the beauty of a blow or the flight of a ball, nor the account of matches, nor the passion of the fan or even the odds at the bookmaker. No, Joshua, what I appreciate in baseball is the teamwork. They focus on a result, they work in tandem, and win victory because they understand each other well. Tell me, is there the same understanding between us?'

I shrugged my shoulders again, not knowing what to answer. He nodded.

'Well, I will continue. Freedom is the basic value of our society. Or, speaking simply, it is for freedom's sake that thousands, tens of thousands, hundreds of thousands of Americans gave their lives. Do you remember the text of the Declaration of Independence, Joshua?

'Well, in general…'

He closed his eyes and loudly recited by heart:

"We hold these truths to be self-evident, that all men are created equal, that they are endowed by their Creator with certain unalienable rights, that among these are life, liberty and the pursuit of happiness. That to secure these rights, governments are instituted among men, deriving their just powers from the consent of the governed. That whenever any form of government becomes destructive to these ends, it is the right of the people to alter or to abolish it, and to institute a new government, laying its foundation on such principles and organizing its powers in such form, as to them shall seem most likely to effect their safety and happiness. Prudence, indeed, will dictate that governments long established should not be changed for light and transient causes; and accordingly all experience hath shown that mankind are more disposed to suffer, while evils are sufferable, than to right themselves by abolishing the forms to which they are accustomed. But when a long train of abuses and usurpations, pursuing invariably the same object evinces a design to reduce them under absolute despotism, it is their right, it is their duty, to throw off such government, and to provide new guards for their future security.' This fragment is exactly about freedom, Joshua. Do you understand me?'

"'Yes, but I…'

'You are in an unenviable position, boy. On the one hand, you have such abilities and talent that you will decorate any team. On the other hand, your life path is under threat,' Mr. Jenkins said softly. 'I wouldn't like to look like a mentor, but the people you communicate with now won't lead you to success, but the opposite…'

'And how do you know who I talk to?!' I felt anger boiling in me. 'You spoke absolutely correctly about freedom. So who allows you to tell me, a free person in a free country, damnit, what I do and who I talk to?!'

'Knowing is part of my work,' he answered, without changing tone. 'As for freedom of choice … You probably know that the freest beings in the ocean are dolphins. But after the birth of a dolphin baby, the other dolphins surround it and don't let it swim to the side or too deep, pushing it to the surface with their noses so it takes a sip of air and begins to breathe. Of course, they could give him freedom to choose and where to move, but there is a 75% chance the baby dolphin will die. You're not going to argue that nature is stupid, are you?'

'No…'

'Every freedom has its symbols and traditions. One of the main symbols of our freedom is the national flag. You need considerable courage, Joshua, not just to know that it is a piece of fabric with strips and stars, but to defend its honour in very difficult circumstances. Our platoon sergeant, a veteran of the Korean War, often used to say: 'Eddie, remember, it is always easier to spit, than to clean spittle up, but look around and you will see that our world is not spittle.' Do you still want to say something?

'N-no… s-sir,' I really was a little confused. This Mr. Jenkins somehow easily and simply turns everything upside down – or, maybe, puts everything in place?

'Then let's postpone our conversation; I can see that you need to think.'

'Yes, yes…' I jumped out of the car and almost ran away, feeling like a hedgehog or a porcupine which has lost all its needles.

I went to the Garage because I didn't know else to do. On the one hand, everything Mr. Jenkins told me was true. On the other hand, isn't this just what the garagers were fighting, and didn't all of us mock it?

I say 'us' but was it them? I, Joshua Kold, who am I, when it comes down to it? Which of the camps do I belong to? All my life, except for the last one and a half years, I had passed on the other side of a fence. My father was one hundred per cent American, ready to die for the sake of our country. And my sister and I grew in his civil paradigm, we were the same and didn't even imagine otherwise – until a certain time.

And here for the first time I thought, what is America for me? No, it is clear that there is a set of ideological clichés, some 'hallmarks' of the country, both for external, and internal, consumption.

There is a history, there is culture and celebrated persons. There are The Golden Age and 'the American dream'. There are, damnit, Longfellow, Hawthorne, Fitzgerald, Hemingway, Updike, Charlie Chaplin, Paul Newman, Clint Eastwood, and Tarantino. There are Frank Sinatra, Amstrong, Elvis, Janis Joplin, Bee-Bee King and hundreds more, and even thousands of people who are known by the whole world, and all of them are America!

But how one is connected with another? Pincher, wiping his bum with the American flag and the same flag on a soldier's coffin brought by plane from Somalia or Libya. What is more important here: to have the freedom to wipe with a symbol of the country or the freedom to die for it?

I was overflowing with feelings and thoughts, My hands shivered like an old man's. I suddenly felt like a freak, an abnormal turncoat, a troubled teenager throwing dirt on the newly washed windows of the Sunday school just because of an uncontrollable feeling of contradiction.

I will tell you frankly Mr. Jenkins had been able to prise open my soul and heart, to sew seeds of doubt about how I live, and had done it with mastery. In the language of the game that he had praised highly, Mr. Jenkins had delivered the ball precisely for the catcher's trap and earned a strike, and the hapless batter flailed his bat in the air.

Reaching the Garage, I tapped in the code on the entrance door, went to lock it carefully (the first rule!), but came face to face with Frisbee, and the door remained half-closed.

Frisbee was sitting on the floor of the Waiting room and drawing on pieces of wet cardboard with a paint brush. She drew very well, probably better than all the garagers. I could not help staring at her quick, precise strokes, but I couldn't understand the plot of her picture at all.

Bach came in with more pieces of cardboard, watered them and spread them out to dry.

'What are you doing?' I asked, coming closer.

"Unknown' paintings by Andy Warhol,' Frisbee said cheerfully without turning around. "Pincher had the cool idea of selling pictures through online auctions. You hang a lot out, set the starting price, write in comments that you found this picture in the attic in your beloved grandmother's house. Grandma was a journalist in her youth, lived in the Big Apple and was on friendly terms with mad Andy. So, he gave her this masterpiece. And that's it, after that you sit on your bum and wait for suckers around the world to throw you green stuff.'

'But the painting isn't real!'

'And where did we write that it is real?' Frisbee grinned. 'This not our problem, but the young journalist's, Lord rest her guilty soul. Let them learn the ropes.'

'Pincher is a genius!' Bach said with conviction.

'And how many have you done so far?'

'Over there, have a look in the Vernissage.

I pulled back a curtain and saw three 'pictures' on a long table – and on one of them there was the notorious can of Campbell's soup, only instead of 'Tomato soup' Frisbee had written 'Yamato soup', with a circle in the center to represent the Japanese flag, and instead of vignettes at the bottom, skulls in army helmets.

The next cloth represented Marilyn Monroe sucking the dick of President Kennedy with a target on his breast.

The last was a sobbing Statue of Liberty from which the toga had been torn off. It looked at me, as she tried cover herself with her torch.

'So, how is it?' Frisbee was standing with a brush in her hands behind her back. 'The real Warhol, no kidding!'

'But...' I tried to find the words, but I could only think of educational terms which were wrong here in the Garage. 'It's... mean!'

"What do you mean 'mean'?" Frisbee was struck dumb.

'All of these. It's not right.'

'Du-ude!' Frisbee relaxed, grinning broadly. 'Understand: there are no rules; there is no boredom!'

'Are you sure that boredom is the main thing you need to fight against in life?' I asked.

'What else? With enemies?' Bach came in to the Vernissage and shrugged his shoulders. 'Do you have lots of enemies?'

'Me personally – no. But our country has enemies.'

They laughed as if they had just smoked Mexican. They just began to neigh like horses.

'So you're a patriot, Joshua-boy! Frisbee mocked. 'Sing the anthem, boy, and we will salute you! Right down to the ground! How do you prefer to gain somebody's honour – orally, anally or vaginally?'

Finally, I spat on these clowns and went to the Dispatching Office, from where I could hear music. I was hoping to find Neolani there. I made my way past pyramids of old boxes, bypassed racks of dusty old spares for plane and boat motors, faltered over old tyres... and, as I approached my target, the music – in the R'n'B style, such sad music – was overlain by a hoarse female voice – and then another voice joined that voice, a woman's too, very familiar, and it was moaning, sighing, rhythmically, with unfeigned pleasure.

I knew very well when, and under what circumstances, Neolani groaned that way. Yet for some reason I went to see with my own eyes…

They were doing it on a sofa, in the doggy position, with Pincher thrusting his fingers into Neolani's mouth and pulling her lips back. It seemed disgusting to me, though, probably they thought differently.

Both of them saw me and didn't really react in any way, continuing unabashed. With us in the Garage, things were pretty free, and anyone could fuck with someone in full public view, although people tried to go behind curtains, behind boxes, to secluded corners…

'Hi!' Pincher winked at me, continuing to move his bum rhythmically.

'Jo-o-osh' Neolani moaned and hoarsely laughed in the tone of the singer. 'Come join u-us…'

For a second I imagined, wondered how it would be – Neo, Pincher and me – and I nearly threw up.

And then I did something I did not expect of myself. I slapped a palm on the table so hard the player jumped up and became silent.

'Hey!' I told them 'Separate. I'm on business.'

Silence hung. Pincher slid out of Neolani and flopped on the sofa. She stretched out nearby, brazenly staring at me through bleary, half-drunk eyes.

'Killjoy,' Pincher muttered.

'I'm leaving,' I said, trying not to look at Neolani. 'Altogether.'

'Where?' Pincher asked yawning. 'Come on, dude, what happened, happened. There is no past, you forgot? If it is because of Neo, she wanted it. She has the right.'

'Jo-o-osh!' Neolani drawled. 'Are you jealous, you little fool? Well, I simply… I just wanted, but you weren't near, understand? We drank some whiskey with Tina and I…'

'I'm leaving for good,' I interrupted. 'The Garage has turned into garbage. And into a whorehouse. I don't fit in here.'

There was dead silence. Neolani pursed her lips.

'Well get out, you rat!' Pincher exploded. He went deep red, jumped up and began to hastily yank his jeans on. 'Get out of here, sucker, neatnik, nerd, shitass!'

'Neo, will you come with me?' I had to ask this question though I already knew the answer.

'Jo-o-osh… Well why are you so-o complica-ated?' Neolani sang, rolling up her eyes.

I turned and spat on the floor. I don't know why. I never spit, even on the street when nobody's looking, but here I spat. Perhaps, in my subconscious the words of Mr. Jenkins emerged, well, about the Baseball player, about the spat world. Or I was just pissed off.

Pincher rose up at once:

'Stop, asshole! Wipe this fucking spittle with your fucking muzzle!'

I looked at him already absolutely quiet. Out of the corner of my eye, I could see that Neolani was wrapped in that same red tarp that she had once caught up with me in.

Pincher rushed at me, swinging his hands. He was certainly much more skilled in such affairs, In fact I'd never fought, except as a little child, in the sandbox, in the Galaxy Star cargo space ship with the Makflinov brothers.

But Pincher was furious, and I – no, Lao Tzu – said knowingly: 'You are controlled by someone who makes you angry.'

So I quietly waited for the moment when he ran up to me and punched him in the bare stomach. He gasped and fell to his knees, his eyes bulging, his face becoming even redder. Neolani screamed, huddled on a corner of the sofa.

There was a clatter in the Control Room. Bach and Frisbee fell in.

'What happened?'

'Grab him...!' Pincher croaked, jabbing his thumb at me. 'Quickly... if he runs away!'

Bach immediately grabbed me by the elbow.

'Back off.' I told him. 'Back off, or else...'

'Or else what?' Bach said between narrowing his eyes and wringing my hand.

I hit him in the face with my free hand, somewhere on his thick cheek, but it really hurt my hand.

Bach jumped away from me, snarled and, raising his fists, advanced to attack. Frisbee stupidly jumped aside and shouted something. Neolani screamed. Pincher tried to rise from his knees.

I tried to dodge but Bach struck my jaw, and then my chest, knocking all the air from my lungs. It became clear that it was time to get out, and reeling, I staggered to the door, feebly waving away the punches of my former friends. But Pincher finally got up and decided a different approach. He launched himself on my back and clung to me like a tick, pulling me to the floor. Then Frisbee kicked me in the face...

Maybe they would have killed me if Sparky hadn't appeared – for the not-locked door played a dirty trick on the garagers. With a wild bark, the dog flew into the Control Room and began to bite all and sundry, probably maddened by hallucinogens again. Guys were rushing in every direction, beating off the enraged dog, and in the chaos I managed to get out of the Garage.

With a broken face dripping with blood, I went down the street past the neat American lodges of respectable American families with American values who would reject all we created in the Garage.

You could call what occurred that day a fight for these values. I had battled for the Homeland against people who ate its garbage and tried to spoil everything they could reach.

They identified rats all around, and actually they were rats themselves – pathetic, greedy, stupid rats whose whole life revolved around satisfying their desire to have a good time by all available methods.

They lived at the expense of society – and spoiled society.

They spat on everything: on morals, on tradition, on the country which had given them the chance to do things, which had brought them up and presented them with the chance to live as they wanted.

They were asked little – to become worthy citizens of this country. Instead they preferred to live as animals – to guzzle drugs, copulate and crawl in their own sewage, feebly forgetting in the morning, according to the hollow 'there is no past' doctrine, their yesterday's shame.

You remember, I spoke about rats at the beginning? In the Garage I nearly became one of them…

I didn't win, but I also didn't lose. Now I had no friends, no girlfriend, but there was my Homeland…

'Hey, guy!' some man called to me. 'Is everything all right? Do you need any help?'

My heart warmed at once. If the garagers had seen a guy on the street with a bloodstained face, at best they would have mocked the poor fellow.

I wanted to scream with delight 'Do I need help, of course. I do!' I was so made up I wanted to cry – to ask a stranger on the street if he needs help – that is our, real, primordial America, we are strong with it, we are strong with the fact that we are together…

And for this reason I turned to him slow and dignified, and saw the elderly lieutenant with his veteran stripes and medals, and shook my head:

'No, sir, I'm ok. Everything is all right. I just squabbled a little with some scum.'

'What was the dispute?' he asked without a suggestion of a smile.

'They don't love our country,' I answered honestly.

'Then, sir, you protected the United States. What is your name, and how old are you?'

I answered. He gave me his hand.

'Joshua Kold, I have the honour to invite you into the armed forces of the USA! Such guys as you are very necessary to us. Here is my business card, the address of the recruiting point in Arnold is specified there. Have a good time!'

I saluted him and started wandering further, and the one and only thought which seemed to solve everything sat down firmly in my head: Army!.

…So I had lost what always attracted me to the Garage. More precisely, I had lost the one – Neolani. And without her the entire purpose of going into that hell-hole had gone. Maybe I could reconcile with Bach, Frisbee and even with that douchebag Pincher, but with Neolani there could be no reconciliation. This became the grain of sand that started an avalanche.

I had passed the Rubicon and wasn't going to change my decision. The Army was exactly the place for me to forget about everything. And if someone has to protect our country, why shouldn't this someone be me?

When I declared at home that I was going to go to serve, and in the marines, Pa sat down silently for a long time. When he started talking, his voice trembled strangely.

'You know,' he said. 'As a man I will shake your hand. But as a father…'

Mr. Jenkins met me once again, just approaching me as I sat on a bench in the park, looking through the papers they gave me at the recruiting point.

'It's a small world!' he said with such sincere joy that for a moment I truly believed we were meeting accidentally.

I asked him to sit down out of, well, elementary politeness, no more, and he took seat, crossed his legs and began to talk about baseball. The Baltimore Orioles had lost their last game. Everything was down to the fact that they had to 'pull' their rivals, but the Orioles messed up, and now they've lost the champion's title.'

I nodded, glancing over pages of the recruitment papers because I had no idea how to keep that going.

'Joining the army?' Mr. Jenkins unexpectedly asked.

'Something like that.'

'You are running from problems, right?' he stared at me like a cat at a mouse. 'Squabbled with your mad friends at the Garage, huh?'

'I am not running anywhere!' I became angry. 'Just now there is war occurring and I… I have to be there!'

'Ah really?!' again he appeared sincerely surprised. 'So it turns out you are a good guy, Joshua Kold! A real American, huh? Well, I am glad that we are familiar, only...'

'Only what?' I muttered.

'Are you sure that you will bring any benefit to the war?' he narrowed his eyes like a snake. He often did so, as if looking into your soul. 'What do you know about war, boy?'

'No less than you!' I became angry. 'It's clear that people kill there and so on. But if no one will fight, these freaks, like those that blew up the twin towers in New York, will appear here with increasing frequency, and then settle here and begin to kill everyone.

'All this is so,' Mr. Jenkins inclined his head. 'But this is not war in any way. This is a war on terror, you know. The other side of the same coin so to speak. And war... This is not a spectacular raid, not firing at enemies from behind a beautiful and reliable rock, nor forced marches and not even pulling your wounded commander out from under enemy fire. War, first of all is a very dirty and, I would even say, smelly life in such disgusting conditions that it'd give you one hundred points in your Garage. There's a lot of hard manual labour. Real marines or G-I's are like camels always carrying a burden: weapons, munitions, products, equipment ... And all this under a scorching fifty-five degrees Celsius sun and however many it will be in Fahrenheit, Joshua. You'd better not know if you want to sleep peacefully today. There are no toilets, no proper food, or normal water, and there is no mobile communication and television – just nothing at all! And in all this time you may never see the enemy for your entire round of combat operations, or ever shoot from an M-16, or ever have the magic feeling of satisfaction of a day well lived. Not once, for all your time of service, you understand me, boy?

'Everyone has his own experience,' I muttered under my breath.

'Scepticism is peculiar to youth,' he parried, hitting me with this phrase. 'But to become a hero, you don't have to go into the army and march to the end of the world. You can protect your country here. Remember, Joshua: the front is everywhere. Do you understand what I'm talking about?'

I silently shook my head, getting a grasp of the contract in mind. This Mr. Jenkins was little by little beginning to irritate me with his mentoring, cheesy metaphors and vague hints.

'You are a very promising boy as regards computers, an ace,' he was switching back into the role of Baseball player again. 'We need people like you!'

'Do you – to whom am I promising?' I asked, barely restraining myself from telling him where to get off.

'To us – the organization that protects the United States,' he became serious. 'We don't shoot from rifles and machine guns, we don't fly fighters. But our contribution to state security is no less, and maybe more, powerful than the armed forces or navy.

"So you're FBI!' I turned my head to him, interested. 'Did I guess?'

Mr. Jenkins smiled.

'The FBI, Joshua are only our journeymen. Look higher.'

'CIA?'

'Even higher!'

This time I smiled:

'And what's above? The State Department?'

'The State Department often follows our guidance and recommendations.'

I was already amused. Mr. Jenkins, it seemed, was a commonplace schizophrenic, living in his own invented world.

'So who are you? Mossad? KGB? MI6?'

'National Security Agency,' he said simply.

'Ah, No Such Agency!' I continued to laugh. 'Never Say Anything... Mister Jenkins, I have to go. All the best.'"

11:56 P.M.

The food ordered by Kold was delivered, and he took a break, shoveling down pizza and salad from a plastic container with unexpected enthusiasm. The Lawyer ate a salmon sandwich, and, as he drank coffee, asked:

"Mr. Kold, you told me about your patriotic feelings just now. Doesn't it seem to you that your picture of the world is a little… idealistic?'

Kold wiped his oily lips with a napkin and nodded as if to say, I got your question. But he took his time with the answer. Five long minutes passed before finally he said:

"Idealism is a kind of protective reaction. That's why so many teenagers are idealists. Cynicism comes with life experience."

"The dispute between the physicist and the lyric poet ended with the victory of cynics," the Lawyer smiled sadly.

"What?" Kold didn't understand.

"Don't pay any attention. It is our Russian, or to be exact, Soviet meme. If everything goes well, you will have time to study this and many other similar inventions of national folklore."

"I'm ready to go on," Kold told.

FILE 007.WAV

On the bus taking new recruits to the base, we at first exchanged glances, then began to scoff.

A Latino by the nickname of El Gato, a big guy in a green shirt, reported to all the bus in broken English that the writing was on the wall: Saddam had it coming and it's now all over.

A guy in a sleeveless leather jacket, a typical redneck, antsy and angry, lisped through his broken tooth something about a steak up the ass, and a couple of blacks, brothers I think, gave an impromptu rap on an army topic, with the refrain: 'All day long you'll be guzzlin' dirt; at night you'll be scrubbin' the toilets!' On the whole, it was cheerful, and the accompanying sergeant with a plastic hand had the most fun.

At last, the bus drove in through the gate of the Parris Island military base where I would have three months military training to achieve the proud rank of private 1st class and be deployed to Iraq as part of a brigade of US marines to restore democracy and justice there.

Parris Island, also called the 'recruiting depot' brought together all recruits from areas to the east of Mississippi, while those from the west trained at the base in San Diego, California.

The bus rolled on for some time through the base past mesh fences, army barracks and inscriptions: 'Warning! Restricted area! Sentries will open fire without warning!!'.

The bus came to a halt, the doors opened, and we were ordered to leave. For some reason, the bus had stopped not by the barracks or headquarters, but in the middle of a huge puddle in a yard. Several officers and sergeants in raincoats and gumboots began to yank us skilfully from the bus and shove us face-down towards the dirt. The one-armed corporal was laughing crazily in the front seat. Then we were forced to do push ups so that our faces dipped into the dirty water. While we were doing push ups, we were given a lecture about discipline in the American military, whether we have rights (no!) and what will happen to us if we're disobedient (everything, up to the death penalty).

Then there was a communal shower and a hair salon where we were cut under the cobbles. In the dining room, we were given ten minutes to push down puttylike porridge, beans and potatoes, and sent back out to the yard to do push ups. So my first day in the military began.

In the evening, after the command 'Hit the sack', I dropped on to my bed and fell into a dream and if anyone had asked at that moment how to ping a computer into a local area network from another subnet, I would send his ass to hell – according to the local lexicon.

We were allowed to sleep for three hours, then roused, of course, with curses and kicks, then driven up the hill behind the base and forced to run under the moon and stars on a dusty road until dawn.

Two of us were ill and the redneck that had been hysterical on the bus – his name was Ken – threw up bile.

In the morning, exhausted and hungry, we talked with the chaplain. He was a captain, already elderly, with grey temples and rows of medals.

The chaplain told us that we are all now private-recruits and will be up to the end of the initial training course. If we have problems, complaints or claims, we have to address him and only him. Exceptions are cases when a soldier feels a threat to health. In this case you go to the physicians – the medical block is to the right of the gate.

The chaplain also explained that the sergeants' and officers' job is to turn us civil marshmallows into hardtack. They have the right to shout at us and call us any word, but for curses connected with sexual and racial identity. Sergeants are allowed to touch military personnel, but only in strictly defined places (here someone even found strength to laugh), and only during the training process.

The chaplain once again summarized our duties and what is forbidden in the military. We were required to submit to sergeants and officers in everything. Anything else, including unnecessary questions, was simply forbidden.

A fight between recruits, the chaplain emphasized, would be punished by imprisonment for up to ten years. And the sergeant in whose division there was a fight would also be punished – if his soldiers have the strength to fight, he has trained them badly.

'From now on and for the next three months, the sergeants headed by Master Sergeant Westerhausen will become for your parents, older brothers, teachers, mentors and all other people who are above you,' the chaplain said and added: 'I have already spoken about claims, but I think I should tell you it has not been in the glorious traditions of our base to complain since the landing on Omaha Beach. Wimps and whiners have no place in the US marines!'

…Master Sergeant Abraham Westerhausen was six foot seven inches tall, and weighed no less than a hundred kilos. Add in Boris Karlov's physiognomy, a closely shaven skull with the tattoo of a hornet, and pack all this into camouflage and heavy combat boots – and you get 'Devil Hornet', the scourge and damnation of all newcomers to the military base …

Our day began with his ear-splitting: 'Get up, bastards! Time to air your shitty asses!', and came to an end with at least as loud: 'Hit the sack, shit-tards! And make it so silent that when Rear Admiral Bird farts in Fort Knox, I can hear it here!"

Why the long deceased Admiral Bird passed gas, and in Fort Knox, none of us knew, but naturally nobody ventured to ask Sergeant Hornet, as we called Westerhausen.

His favourite entertainment was to order a recruit to: 'Turn around! Attention!' and then kick just under their tailbone as they tried to turn on the spot. The pain is so excruciating that the recruit begins to hop. So Hornet shouts: 'Attention!' – and how can he stand to attention when he's writhing and hopping? So he doesn't obey an order from a senior and collects a punishment in which Hornet was a master. Washing toilet bowls or cleaning wheels on combat vehicles is just child's play compared with Hornet's favourite: 'Hunting for a dollar'.

The hunt was like this: the master sergeant threw a dollar coin into a ten-foot deep cement pool located near the obstacle course. The guilty recruit had to dive into the pool with a compressed air hose clamped to his teeth, then come up with the dollar in his hand. That was bad enough in clean water but the pool was filled with sewage.

Altogether, I remember six guys from our platoon 'hunting'. Three ended up in the hospital with intestinal infections and were transferred to other divisions on the base because their preparation term was increased. And two made complaints to the chaplain and were moved away altogether, and as they went to the bus with their bags they could hardly walk – the chaplain hadn't said for nothing that they don't love complainers in Parris Island.

Well, the sixth who went 'hunting for a dollar' was that fine big man El Gato who had threatened Saddam Hussein. He couldn't find the coin in the pool and when Hornet pushed him into the shit with his foot for the third time, El Gato grabbed the master sergeant by the boot and dragged him in too.

There was a big trial, the military police came, and El Gato was convicted of attacking the master sergeant, and sent to prison in Fort Leavenworth for a year. After bathing in shit the Hornet went absolutely mad, and at every chance he told us what the jailers in Leavenworth would do with El Gato.

'He'll become a girl on the first evening. In a week his asshole will so be fucking big he can sit down on a bottle of apple cider and not squeal. Understood, bastards?!' shouted Hornet before lights out.

For all that, I wouldn't say service was difficult for me or that I felt some serious discomfort. Of course, it was heavy physically, but morally I had a rest because the shouting of the sergeants and their flow of words was so primitive and plain that it provoked no emotional reaction – some ethnographic interest, but no more.

And I also really liked the fact that in the military you don't need to think of the future at all. It is entirely predetermined for years ahead according to the contract. Here, others think for me, following rank.

Of course, it is also interesting to any man to try cunning stuff and accessories not in the normal arsenal of a civilian.

Once we were familiar with everything we had a right to use during military operations, I remember, being rather confused when it turned out that besides field and parade uniforms there was also daily and special 'evening' kit. The same was true of the arsenal. I understood that marines have machine guns, grenades, pistols and bayonets, but why do only police officers have a bludgeon and non-lethal weapons such as rubber bullets, stun grenades with CS tear gas or Dazzlers?

But these questions were rhetorical. The military doesn't like curiosity and if I ask a sergeant about the bludgeon or CS, he'd just reply 'You'd have it if you needed it' or 'Fifty push-ups in the pigsty.' That was the hunting pool by the obstacle course.

What else do I remember from that time? My relations with my companions never changed – because I never had any. We came from very different layers in our society. You know that more than fifty percent of American marines weren't born in the USA? And the fact that half of them can't take the hardships and privations of military service means they break off the contract and join the ranks of criminals simply because they have no place else to go? But this is just statistics, and in general those in my platoon were the typical dregs of society, human garbage, slag and scum.

On the whole, they saw the military as a chance to escape from the 'nomadic city' from smelly trailers and equally smelly farms, and from the colored suburbs where human life doesn't cost a cent and people, normal people I mean, don't want to live.

The military gave them the chance to earn money, buy status and citizenship, and after contract completion collect a pension or maybe go on to a military career – to pass exams in a non-commissioned officer's school, for example.

I wanted to serve our great country because I saw in it the meaning of life for each normal citizen. Ok, I understand that this sounds a little pompous, but at that time, after college and my encounter with the guys from the Garage, this is how I really felt and I was ready to go to any spot on the globe to assert the right of people for true democracy and freedom.

By the way, my relationship with weapons never really developed. At home, there were several cases of guns and rifles, since Pa liked to do some shooting – all his friends too. Both Mom and Judith, by the way, quite often went with them to the National Rifle Association training ground and fired at targets or just bottles.

Twice was enough for me. The first time I went the rifle bounced off my shoulder because I didn't hold the butt firmly enough, and so the bullet hit a light. The second time, I was bitten by a dog, and Pa had to take me to hospital.

In the military, I shot badly, and was very slow at assembling and disassembling the Colt M4A1 automatic, and so regularly collected punishments from Hornet and threats to send me 'hunting for a dollar'.

Meanwhile, our guys in Iraq had already taken Baghdad, but Saddam went on the run and his soldiers adopted guerrilla tactics. Our training came to an end. One day I saw a civilian car on the parade ground in front of headquarters – the same car as that Mr. Jenkins who gave a ride to me and spoke about heroism on a bench in the park. The occupant went inside and Master Sergeant Westerhausen was called so urgently he practically ran across the parade-ground.

We were cleaning weapons under the canopy, next to headquarters, and we had a clear view of the goings on. The guys began to speculate at once what the civilian cone was doing here and why our Devil-Hornet needed him.

I stood up to see better if it was the Baseball player or not, but Sergeant Gross, whose breath stank like an old drain, shouted that he would drive a ramrod up my ass if I didn't get back to the table and clean my gun at once.

So I didn't learn who it was for certain. Soon the unexpected guest left, and the sergeant returned and for some reason looked at me as if I had become a dead man then recovered and lunged to strangle him.

The day ended without further incident. We were driven up the hill. There was training with inflatable landing boats, then dinner, an hour of hand-to-hand combat which I successfully shirked, having gone to clean car racks, then a further hour of personal time, then lights out.

But we weren't going to get any sleep that night. At one fifteen, Hornet and other sergeants roused us sharply. The task was simple: going through the Big Jack obstacle course in full gear.

What does that mean? Only that you put on all your ammunition, a bullet-proof vest, harness, a helmet, loaded weapons, means of chemical protection, and a machine gun – and then you run through ditches filled with dirt and stinking water, along booms and bars, climb the Destroyed Ladder, the Serpent and the Monkey ladder, you clamber over stone and wooden walls of various heights, you slither under an electric wire, you jump over ditches with shit in the bottom, you go down tunnels, you shoot at targets, you run through dirt, you fall down on command, you stand up, you put on a gas mask, you run again, and all this under fire of military weapons, in flame and smoke.

At the end of Big Jack, you're sweating madly, your boots are squelching, your hands and legs are quivering, and your heart is beating over one hundred and twenty beats per minute. But nobody will let you rest because you need to clean your weapon, get your ammunition in shape, and get ready for the morning parade.

To say that we didn't love Big Jack means to say nothing. We didn't even hate it. If there was a word for a stronger emotion, maybe, but I don't know it.

And so they kicked us out of the barracks, mustered us and sent us running to the strip. There was already a sheer hell of burning, smoking and blowing up.

Master Sergeant Hornet raised a hand and shouted:

'Get on with it, you bastards! Faster. Faster! Remember: slackers will envy the dead!'

And we ran…

Somewhere in the Serpent, only a third way through Big Jack, I realized I had no strength left any more. It felt as if my boots were lead, and I had a couple of twenty-kilogram pancakes on my back.

I crept under the wire on my last legs. But I couldn't jump off in the tunnel, and fell down like a limp sack. There, in the dark, I got my breath back, but the guys following me were already banging their soles on the steel crown of my helmet and I had to twist like a worm in the wet cement pipe to get out upward, then shoot, pull myself on to the Horizontal Rope and take the Destroyed Ladder with a running start to jump in a ditch and get away up the slippery cliff.

The Swing came next. It is something like the Destroyed Ladder, only all the beams are at one height and suspended on chains. In principle, the Swing wasn't thought of as a difficult element. The main thing here was that your leg didn't slide off – and if it did, you had to grasp the beam to avoid a fall on to the concrete blocks piled below. They were only four feet down, but they are not heaps of sand, like under the Destroyed Ladder, so no one wanted to fall from the Swing.

I jumped onto the first 'swing' and found to my surprise that my weakness had gone. My legs and body seemed to obey me, and the ringing in my ears was not mind-numbing fatigue, but the thunderclaps of explosions.

I remember thinking that this was the notorious 'second wind', and I began to scamper along the beams like a squirrel, rejoicing that at last I was becoming a real marine.

Whether in euphoria, or through congenital carelessness, I noticed Sergeant Hornet too late. He emerged from the smoky haze like a demon of evil punishing the 'sleep of reason'. He glared at me and stuck out a bamboo pole towards the beam on which I was going to land in a fraction of a second. The beam swayed aside, the chains rung out and as though from the outside, I saw my right boot with its ribbed sock sliding from the beam and falling into emptiness. Then afterwards, waving his hands ridiculously, all the rest of private-recruit Joshua Kold followed...

I fell very badly. It is hard to imagine a worse fall. The height I fell from was just enough to ensure I twisted in the air so that I fell at a sharp angle onto the filthy concrete slab. My helmeted head struck first, then my left shoulder, then my hand and then all the rest. Finally, my legs jerked to the lowest point of fall and my shins twisted above my boots in the wrong order on the slab.

Wild pain lashed me like a bicycle chain. My mouth went dry, and my eyes darkened. I became deaf and went blind, lost orientation in space and, like a dying animal, began to twitch desperately. I tried to get up. The doctor in the hospital told me that was a big mistake and seriously worsened my condition.

The pain that shot through me at this attempt was so intense I fainted from shock and only came round in the military hospital in Charleston.

The diagnosis was unfavourable: fracture of both legs with an offset. In the first day several officers from our unit led by the chaplain visited me. They were accompanied by two lawyers.

I was told that it was an accident, and that I should sign a paper agreeing that I had no claims on the powers that be. I was assured that I would receive an insurance payment to cover all expenses for transportation by helicopter and for treatment. I would get compensation and everything would be great.

I hadn't recovered fully from the effect of the anaesthetics and the comforting medicines I was being drip-fed so I was not really thinking clearly. I managed to mumble something about a pole in the hands of the Sergeant Westerhausen, but no more than that. In reply, the chaplain assured me that it was standard procedure when passing the Swing and that the Master Sergeant fulfilled his duty and naturally, without malice – especially as I had never had any conflict with him during service.

The last argument finished me off. It was airtight, and so I signed their devil's papers and dropped off. When I woke up next morning, it became clear that in addition I had signed the official report with a request to resign for health reasons.

Lying in the hospital with broken legs, I had suddenly turned from a gallant marine into a helpless being with a urine bag. I thought a great deal about those guys I'd trained with who were now off to Iraq without me.

It was dangerous there. Scorching winds whip across the desert, and marines with machine guns peer from under their helmets in the military convoys that bump along the roads in clouds of dust – squinting into the yellow haze, and every second expecting from somewhere a rocket fired by the mobile Soviet RPG-7 launcher which in Russian slang goes by the unpronounceable name *granatomiot*. This rocket could come at any time from any direction and pierce the armour of their Humvees. It will burst clean through the emblem representing the globe and anchor over which the fearsome American eagle spreads its wings, and the hot jet stream, hot as the inside of a star, will burn through the metal and reach the ammunition. Then 'bang!' and the heavy Humvee will flip over and rip open in the explosion like a can of sardines.

In such a scenario, we were told, the best chance of survival is to be the one manning the machine gun. The chance is scant, but there had been cases were the gunner was blown away from the car by the blast wave to land in the dunes and suffer only a spinal compression fracture.

When I thought about it, looking at the white hospital ceiling and the round lamps with their opaque plafonds, it made me angry. It was such a shame that it made me want to cry. Those guys from my platoon, those rather stupid, uneducated, loutish rednecks and Latinos, black and white, had gone to protect their homeland and were ready to give their lives for it.

Maybe they didn't even think about it, never thought about it... yet they did it, and deeds will always mean more than words. Words meant nothing. People were judged by what they did, and it turned out that I, Joshua Kold, the one who had signed his contract consciously and joined the military with a point to prove... I wanted to prove first to myself that all are equal in the fight for freedom and democracy, and that in a free country there is no 'gun meat', there is no payment in blood for citizenship, there is no caste on national and social grounds... Well …

The result was clear. While my platoon is fighting in the Iraqi deserts against the saddamites... me, the big intellectual, white collar Joshua, I'm lying on a white bedsheet and looking at a white ceiling.

I had proved nothing to anybody. Life had taken me by the scruff of the neck and killed my idea in the form of Master Sergeant Westerhausen. He'd aimed at the head, got my legs – but what's the difference, the result was achieved.

The first days I was obsessed with the injustice and my own bad luck, constantly, and even at night I couldn't drive the thoughts from my head. In the special ward for patients with heavy leg injuries where I was lying, there were three more beds, but all empty because no one was interested in breaking their limbs but me.

And so I lay, gritting my teeth with rage and powerlessness, hesitating to press the call key for the nurse because in the afternoon it was a young girl, a mixed race girl with very beautiful lips and eyes like a cat's.

And so I suffered on, with ringing ears, gripes in my stomach and only when it became absolutely unbearable and spots were whirling in front of eyes did I press the damned button. She came with an astounding dancing gait and undulating hips, and at once said with a deep chest voice, 'Hi!', dexterously handed me the urine bag, then delicately turned away to the window to chat on the phone to some Nick. It was meaningless chat, small talk between lovers whiling away the day until the evening when they would merge later in one being groaning with passion and pleasure.

To me, that Nick was for some reason the sergeant from our base – a strong, stately black demigod who'd been through a couple of wars, was confident in himself and what he did.

The nurse – her name was Kelly – was proud for certain that she had such a boyfriend, a white-toothed athlete never at a loss for words, capable of beating off two or three Puerto-Rican addicts/robbers on the street, and as good as a stallion in bed.

I narrowed my eyes, urinated into the urine bag, and listened as Kelly sang into her phone: 'Da-arling, my honey …', she cooed, and my face reddened, and my ears reddened, and even my dick seemed to become red, because of the burning shame, rage and offense – for myself, for the world, for the damned Iraqis and Russians, for the redneck Ken and the other guys from my platoon which already was not mine, for that unknown Nick and the beautiful Kelly whose intelligence was probably not much higher than of a monkey's in a zoo. In a word, for the whole world!

I envied them all! I envied them because it turned out that I, educated and possessing huge knowledge of computers and hacking, in my mature years lie like a helpless doll with broken legs in a hospital while life passes by. And all of them, insignificant small fry whose existence doesn't make any more sense than the existence of amoebas or cockroaches makes sense, live and feel pleasure, and even bring benefit.

It's they who fight for democracy, freedom and justice, fuckit, and do what I had dreamed of since that moment I left the damned Garage!

When Kelly carried the urine bag away, I usually fell asleep, but those thoughts remained with me even in my dreams. They were transformed into fancy images, into some whirling dance of cleavers and ridiculous but extraordinary charming beings cheerfully hopping along a wide road through green fields to mountains over which the sun shines. In those dreams I looked like a reptile, a creeping reptile, or even some pathetic worm or caterpillar crawling in the dirt-filled ditch beside the road.

Pa came to see me a few times. He brought a wall TV, a computer and a hi from sister. I asked him whether Mom knew I was in hospital. Pa, in his usual way, answered quickly and directly:

'There's no need for her to know. She has no relation to our family.'

But Mom, of course, found a way to meet me, and regularly came with delicious food, but always cautiously, as if I wasn't in hospital, but in prison and she was doing something illegal.

I set up several news channels on the TV and watched them day and night. And online it was forums and chats where our soldiers in Iraq communicated among themselves. They usually posted photos against a background of the desert or urban landscapes, or looked for acquaintances or told stories, not often funny but terrible in their realness.

Sometimes there are garage rabble – pacifists and anarchists, or just trolls, psychopaths and perverts who derive pleasure from slinging mud at something precious to others.

Those who swore straight off were banned at once, but there were others planting propaganda and talking of the injustice done by ours marines and GIs. Some said that Iraq was a peaceful and even prosperous country, and Saddam Hussein was its legitimate head. Those little fools made me laugh, and I always got deeply involved in discussions and posted the materials about the chemical attacks of saddamites on civilians, and data on weapons of mass destruction in Iraq and the methods of killing dissidents in the jails of Iraqi counterintelligence.

Some people agreed – there are still some smart people in the world. Someone were dead opposed, saying, I believe in his innocence, and that my arguments are unconvincing. I was very much amused by those who said 'I believe' as though it was a question of religion.

But there were also those who didn't just argue, but tried to prove me wrong. They posted statistical calculations, translations from Arab or even Russian media, but we – me and those real Americans who hang out on forums – understood that all this is blatant propaganda in the spirit of the Cold War, which wasn't over for these people.

My legs gradually ceased to hurt and began to itch terribly under the plaster. Doctor Gilbert, a fat, grey-haired man with a colonial moustache, told me that this was very good because it meant that the process of healing had started.

'Josh, my boy,' he said, as he puffed against his moustache, 'My grandma always said: if it itches it doesn't hurt and will heal soon.'

The words of Dr. Gilbert's grandma helped, of course, but I would have preferred him to base his data on modern medical devices and magnetic resonance tomography.

Still, time passed, and it worked for me, in a sense, and my legs. And everything else went on – the war in which our guys perished, the chat online and the skirmishes with pacifists and anti-Americanists.

And then someone with the username Passerby joined the forum. He wrote little, just short captions. But he posted photos. Lots of them, lots of photos. Of Iraqi settlements and villages, cities. Streets, houses. And corpses. There were a lot, a lot of killed people. Not soldiers, not military. Mostly not men. In Passerby's photos it was mostly women, old men, children… They were poorly dressed, sprinkled with dust or partially covered by brick crumb and pieces of concrete from blown-up houses. They had perished from the bombings, from the bullets and shells released from our weapons.

They were unplanned losses, but judging by the photos, there was too much. I don't know if Passerby took those pictures, or someone sent them to him, but one thing was clear – firstly, they were not fake, nor staged, and secondly, something in that war had gone wrong.

Dead children – grey faces with cheeks pierced by splinters, half-closed eyes, blood clotted hair, crooked fingers – it was awful. Shock and, yes, exactly shock – that was the word for what I experienced.

In a war with soldiers, men have to perish; it is their work and their debt, so my old man always said so and I always thought.

When soldiers meet face to face – even if one goes in Humvee armour, while the other is skulking behind a wall with an RPG-7 – it is fair and correct. But when you try to destroy a group of fighters you suppose are in the middle of a residential block in Basra with three hundred 'saddamitovs' – no, not marines or GI, but large-calibre shells... they destroy the entire block, leaving a heap of ruins, a concrete medley and bent fittings. It is wrong, unfair...and reminds me of the methods of the Nazis in World War II.

Passerby also posted photos of captured Iraqis – pathetic, ragged men with sallow faces, rather like illegal Mexican immigrants. They huddled close to each other in fear, and our soldiers towered over them. In their bullet-proof vests and helmets, wielding their high-tech weapons, our soldiers looked like mythical Atlases rounding up savages.

But in some photos our Atlases behaved bestially. They kicked the legs of prisoners lying on the ground. They spat on them. They even urinated on them. It was disgusting, mean, but, alas, they weren't staged either. I recalled Ken at once and he easily could have done this. And many other guys from our platoon too.

Many on the forum tried to ban Passerby from uploading all these photos and complained to the moderators, but when the question was put to a vote, I, surprising myself, wrote that if we ban the publication of Passerby's photos, then we ourselves are like Saddam and any other dictators – Hitler, Stalin, Mao Zedong, Kim Jong-il – and will stop being citizens of a democratic state.

People grumbled a little, but nobody wished to speak against democracy, since that's why we were fighting a war in Iraq.

But my conviction in my own correctness and the correctness of my country was especially badly shaken the day when Passerby uploaded the next set of photos – a small one, just a few frames. In them were hundreds, if not thousands, of Iraqi women, dressed in black scarves.

They were going down a street in a big city against a background of partially destroyed houses. Many of the women were carrying placards in the Arab language and portraits of Saddam Hussein. The laconic caption said:

'Iraqi women who have lost loved ones during the fighting stage a peaceful demonstration against the American invasion. An inscription on the poster reads: Americans, why are you killing our people?'

In the following pictures, I saw appalling things. Marines smashed into the women, my marines. I could not be mistaken. I had served two months and could not confuse regimentals and details of equipment. Clad in camouflage armor, the marines beat the protesters with rifle butts, bludgeons, fists and boots – protestors who were mostly old women, old enough to be the soldiers' Moms.

I looked at the pictures, I looked at the blood-stained women's faces distorted by pain and anger. I looked at the guys from our platoon laughing, dragging a grey-haired old woman through the dirt by the hair, at the bludgeons raised in the air, at the women tangled in hems of black dresses, trying to protect themselves with thin hands from the blows…

Several minutes later I removed my account from the forum and closed the computer. Chaos danced in my head, and my thoughts were tossed like autumn leaves on the wind. Gradually the realization came: we did something wrong. And maybe to some this realization came earlier – it wasn't for nothing that there were so many opponents of war around the world. Not supporters of Hussein, as I began to understand now, but opponents of war because war is terrible, it is death and pain. It is ruin. It is diseases. It is hunger. And again death.

Yes, Iraq, probably, was a totalitarian state, aggressive and dangerous to the whole world. Probably… but I am not sure of anything at all. And… again, probably… the people of Iraq lived in servitude, under the heel of a cruel dictator, in perpetual fear, and everyone, including the most high-ranking officials, was afraid for their lives daily. How else do you explain that many Iraqi statesmen came over to our side as soon as the opportunity was presented? Or is it the truth that a donkey loaded with gold is the best battering ram against the castle gate?

Anyway, when we brought democracy to Iraq, it had to become an important, even a great event, for all Iraqis.

But it turned out that Iraqis thought differently. Perhaps, they would have been happier with some other form of help, but not bombings and retaliatory raids. But the main thing was not even that.

To establish democracy, we agreed that for some time we would forget about it. Yes, yes, it was a very dangerous paradox: to establish democracy you forget about democracy! And if there is no democracy, everything is possible: killing, raping, urinating on prisoners, dragging old women by the hair…

And suddenly I was delighted that I had broken those fucking legs. And that in a semi-conscious state I had signed those papers palmed off on me by the chaplain. I was delighted because if not for the accident and the hospital, I would now be there, in Baghdad, Basra or El-Nadzhaf, and I would be shooting at children and thrashing old women with a bludgeon.

My broken legs preserved my honour and delivered a wake-up call to my brain – that's what I understood in the hospital. And from now on my life will go differently."

00:17 A.M.

Kold raised his eyes to the ceiling and thought. The Lawyer switched off the recording, took a folder out of the briefcase and slid a few pieces of paper joined together from it.

"I think you'll find this interesting. Someone called Andrew Liebman – do you know him? – has published an article about you in the *Los Angeles Times*. I printed it out."

"Liebman…" Kold said. "I think he worked as a deputy for the head of the National Anti-Terrorism Committee for some time. He is a member of the CIA. I wonder what he's written, especially considering it's the *LA Times* – that's almost a tabloid. He's probably cursing me in it…"

"Not quite," The Lawyer moved pieces of paper towards Kold who picked them up and began to read out loud:

"'Joshua Kold, in all likelihood, is stuck in some country house as he agonisingly ponders what kind of surprises the next stage of his young life will bring him.

Having worked for 30 years in the intelligence services, I truly hope that his food is sickening, the winter is fierce and his access to the internet is awful. But I'm not so much worried about what will happen to this young man as the damage which Kold has caused and is still capable of causing to the long-term ability of America to find an optimal balance between the protection of private life and the security of the country.'"

"Bastard!"

"Well, one can understand him as well – he is still on the other side of the barrier and has to show loyalty," the Lawyer noted.

Kold snorted as he continued reading: "'Kold was working on contract with the NSA, and from the moment he made public top-secret materials about the surveillance programmes, he and the government of the USA have pursued a fierce debate about the essence of these programmes.

Those who follow Kold's epic should understand two main postulates. The first one is the fact that in the modern world, filled with dangers, many things must be kept secret. The line between 'secret' and 'not secret' is quite blurred, and if we prioritise security, then we should better 'sin' towards even higher secrecy than go in the other direction. Secondly, despite the complaints of Kold and his admirers, the government of the USA has made sustained efforts not to violate the right to privacy and not just because it respects the right to a private life (although it does respect this right) but also because the government simply doesn't have time to read meaningless electronic messages or listen to conversations, which have no bearing on any potential plots against American citizens.

Cases like Kold's put many of my colleagues from the intelligence community in a difficult situation. Indeed, the official explanations in regard to data collection programmes can look unconvincing, or they can be regarded as an attempt of self-justification. But they are the truth. I know first-hand that General Keith Alexander, the director of the NSA, tells the truth when he claims that many plots have been uncovered and terrorist attacks prevented thanks to information acquired by his agency. I know this because I used to work there, because I had access to the secret information and I took part in many of the operations he's talking about.

I have spent years among those who worked at detection and discovery of attacks by Al-Qaeda. We were working in secrecy not because we were ashamed of something. We were working this way because it was necessary. Al-Qaeda and its allies are studying our actions. They learn from our mistakes. America has become safer because we made it our goal to study their methods better than they did ours.

I understand that a certain balance is necessary here. But the intelligence community hides the information from American people not because it doesn't trust the people. The fact is, as soon as important information in connection to security becomes public, anybody can use it to their advantage, including those who want to harm us.

That is why I find the contradictions which Kold's case revealed so discouraging. I understand that many Americans don't trust their government. I would've liked to be able to change it. I would've liked to be able to tell people about the astonishing things I have witnessed during the 30 years of my work in the CIA. About the fact that I have never before seen people like this who would be prepared to work so hard and so selflessly. Such long hours and for such small pay. People who were prepared for their smallest mistakes to be subjected to the most thorough analysis and for their successes not to be noticed. But I have enough experience to affirm that the deeply rooted distrust towards the government cannot be shaken by the stories of people like me. Fans of conspiracy theories never stop making cries of protest at the thought that the government may find out how long they spent talking on the phone to their favourite auntie.

Let me explain the situation tactfully. The government is not interested in the least in your conversations to your auntie, unless of course she's the head of a terrorist organisation. Last year each day more than 100 billion electronic messages were sent – 100 billion! In this huge mass are concealed some small pebbles which have immediate interest, amid masses of waste rock, which has no value whatsoever. Unfortunately, the metadata (phone numbers, length of the conversations and the like, but not the content of the conversation) in relation to your phone call to a member of your family can get into the same large basket, in which the data about a planned terrorist attack is contained. As Jeremy Bash, the former head of the CIA, once said, 'if you are looking for a needle in haystack, you first to need to find the haystack'.

Unfortunately, in covering Kold's case, much of the mass media has spent more time looking at how the government can misuse the information to which it has access, rather than focusing on the efforts the intelligence community is making to protect the right to privacy. We have spent a lot of time establishing how to separate the few 'pearl seeds' of valuable information from the huge 'dunghill' of useless data.

It is done with tough and well thought-through limitations. I had an opportunity to personally observe the consequences of the incursion into private life in an organization I was working for – the National Counter Terrorism Center. As deputy of the director of that center I had to fire employees, good employees, or dismiss them from their posts, for breaking rules for acquiring and use of information. It didn't happen often and the matters were never in relation to malicious attempts to collect personal information. We had mandatory training courses and special employees who made sure that the rules relating to privacy are followed. We used our precious resources to hire lawyers and experts in the field of civil rights, who monitored our efforts. And on those few occasions when we made mistakes, the punishments were severe and would follow immediately.

Yes, some information now classified as secret may not have been in the past. Such 'super secrecy' can undermine the public trust in us and weaken our ability to protect the data, which requires protection. Kold hasn't given any proof of mass errors in our policies. It's more that he took upon himself a right to judge which instruments the intelligence community can use to provide security for our citizens. Unfortunately, Kold has attracted the public's attention and the government's reaction now seems too weak, too late and too self-justifying. But the intelligence community, *a priori* a less attractive character than a self-proclaimed informer, has a lot to say about how the government ensures the integrity of the private life. And we have to say it."

Kold grinned, put the printout to the side and said thoughtfully:

"You were right, what you said about the barricades. And if I had stayed in America I would, in all likelihood, be thinking the same as Liebman."

FILE 008.WAV

"Mr. Jenkins, well, the Baseball player, came to my ward with a bouquet of wisteria and a book by Tom Clancy. I think it was the novel *The Cardinal of the Kremlin*, although I may be mistaken.

He took the bull by the horns straight away:

'The English people sing "God save the queen"! The anthem for our agency should be: "God save the creator of the internet, electronic mail and social networks!"'

'What does this have to do with social networks?' I asked.

'Aha, that's where the dog is hidden!' The Baseball player raised his finger triumphantly: 'The information that the special services used to spend years and years of painstaking work to acquire can now be collected in seconds, thanks to the internet! Just think about it, Joshua – in seconds! And one of our main helpers in this task are social media.

We now control time and therefore we can now prevent crimes and terrorist attacks before innocent people are killed. Children, old people, women – they all stay alive and the criminals get what they deserve. It's an incredible breakthrough in the international fight for security, it's the future! My boy, don't shake your head, just listen to me and weigh all the pros and cons.'

'No, I won't work for the government,' I said firmly. 'Let's end this conversation. I am ill, tired and I want to sleep.'

'You're as healthy as a bull!' the Baseball player roared, then retreated straight away. 'OK, Josh, I won't pressure you. At the end of the day, it's your life – so it's your choice. Just listen to me, alright? I'll say a few things which are very important for me – and I think for you as well.'

I continued to be obstinate. I even said:

'You just think so.'

But in the end I agreed to give him a last chance – it was painful to see how upset he was getting. Later I often reproached myself for not finding the strength to avoid that conversation but now, rethinking my life, I may even be grateful to Mr. Jenkins. He gave me the opportunity to get everything I have today. He could even be called my Godfather, although in the documents he is named by a much more boring word: 'curator'.

Back then in the hospital, after my nod, he paused for a few seconds, then sat on the chair more comfortably, drew himself up, and began to talk. At first he was looking me in the eye but then he got carried away like a schoolboy reciting a poem learned by heart, and began to look over me, somewhere into the distance, even though behind me there was just a white hospital wall.

'When computers first appeared, Josh, I considered them to be useless toys unworthy of attention of a real man,' Mr. Jenkins was saying, moving his right hand monotonously as if he was winding an invisible rope on his palm. 'In those distant years I was a strong, athletic boy. I played my beloved baseball. I was known in my class as the main instigator when it came to fights. And every morning I chopped wood in the back yard. We lived in small town Chester, not far Saint Louis on the Mississippi. It's very beautiful there, exactly the way Mark Twain described it in his books about Huckleberry Finn, only a bridge has been built over the river. People say that in the past the steamships going down the Mississippi used to always stop at our town – and those who had died during the voyage were buried, and they would also restock on food, water and castor oil – which in that time it was used for the lubrication of mechanisms.

And the artist Elzie Crisler Segar, who created Popeye, was born and lived there. Don't smile, Josh, it's true – we have a bronze monument to Popeye and the Segar Memorial Center. The residents of Chester are very proud of it and every year they organise a big Popeye festival and the woods by the bridge have now been turned into a Popeye theme park.

But I wanted to tell you about something else – about my childhood. We would spend whole days on the river or race on bicycles or play in the forest – building wigwams, making bows and tomahawks and would fry bacon stolen from home on the fire. In summer, just like all my friends, I'd go home only to eat and sleep. And none of us ever thought that instead of swimming, racing on bicycles or fighting with the boys from Kaskaskia Street one could spend hours sitting in front of a computer screen, staring at moving pictures or clicking a mouse.

Do you know, Josh, when I realised that computers are the future for the first time? In 1970 an oxygen cylinder exploded on board Apollo 13 on the way to the Moon and the lives of the astronauts were in danger. Back then, briefings from NASA were shown on TV every hour and we, with the whole class, watched how out there in space they were trying to correct the trajectory of the ship without a computer, because it had been switched off to save energy. We had a computer in school, it was a huge electronic computer which occupied the whole hall. So, while the lads inside the metal box of Apollo 13 were struggling with calculations, our math teacher Mr. Fincher went and calculated everything in half an hour. Then he rang NASA and passed his calculations on to them. They thanked him and said that they, of course, had also carried out the calculations, but Mr. Fincher's calculations were more precise because he took into consideration key parameters and used algorithms. So when the crew of Apollo 13 safely returned to Earth, Mr. Fincher was invited to work in the Center for Space Research. For me, it was like thunder in the clear sky. I always thought that there are only two worthy occupations a man could pursue to make himself rich and successful – sports and military service. But it turned out that science, this computer stuff, could also be a spring board, capable of throwing even such a jerk as Mr. Fincher – and he was a true jerk, a useless weakling, even though he was a teacher – into NASA!

Of course, I didn't make it as a computer technician – I still chose the military and then when the United States needed my services as an agent, I moved to the service in Fort Meade. But I ended up being right when after the rescue of Apollo 13 I said to my friends: 'Hey, lads, the time will come when people like Mr. Fincher will rule the destinies of the world and we big boobies will be bringing them coffee and guarding their peace, while they are fighting the enemies of the USA.'

I understand, you probably find it unpleasant me talking about jerks and so on, but God created us all different – some with strong muscles, and some with strong minds. And, to be honest, I was deeply touched and astonished by your desire to serve the United Stated in the marines. It's hard, dirty and sometimes nasty, and most importantly very dangerous work, but you chose it like a real man. Of course, it's not your fault that the log on the obstacle course turned out to be harder than your bones, but I see the hand of providence in it. Joshua, your strength is in something else! There are always plenty of those who want to run with an assault rifle, parachute from a helicopter and stuff canned food, especially because you get money and status for doing it. Give the opportunity to the lads with a green card to earn an American future for themselves. The country is expecting something else from you, my boy. Don't frown – there are things which cannot be said without using words so pompous, as you consider them.

The modern world – is the world of computers and information systems, the world of the internet, hacker attacks and invisible fights which take place in virtual reality. That's where the front line is. Tense work is going down there. People are working through the night there, hammering their hatred for the enemy into the keyboard. We don't have enough fighters because, as it turns out, you can't just train good specialists from anybody, it's not like the marines or G.Is. A true IT specialist is God's gift. It's a talent like the talent of a musician, artist or writer. You – you're a creative person, that's why in your time you were attracted to the Garage, and we didn't impede you, understanding that you needed to discover the world of bohemia, that you have to taste of this fruit and get poisoned in order to recover afterwards. You are a chosen one, Joshua; there are very a few people like you. That's why you have to think properly before wasting yourself for nothing.

But most importantly, Joshua, I envy you! I envy you and I'm not ashamed of it even if God told us that envy is a sin. In essence, who am I? I am an ordinary clerk with a narrow range of skills and professional abilities. I'll never be able to fight on the virtual front. I won't be able to stop the main threat heading this way. I won't be able to serve my country behind the computer monitor. But you – you will easily replace me. All you need to do is attend a half-year course. America needs you, son. Islamists, China, Russia, Koreans, drug mafia, leftists, anarchists and anti-globalists – all our enemies mastered cyberspace long ago. They are mobilising all their human resources. It's not a secret that the best hackers nowadays are not Americans, that the best warriors in data fights aren't from our country. It's not a secret that we are losing our position in the virtual world precisely because we don't have enough people. A version of the most far-reaching and super-modern program which will allow us to change the balance of power is being prepared for launch now. Joshua Kold, sir, America needs your talent, your knowledge and your hot heart of a patriot!'

I said:

'No.'

And he stood up and left.

I was discharged three days later. And a week after that I was working in Fort Meade in the department with the bleak name of 'information processing'.

Why did I decide to do it? Fuck knows… I don't think the Baseball player's words, his flattery or hints convinced me. It's more likely something else: he offered me an alternative to the dead end into which I had driven myself.

And I found that alternative quite attractive!

I can't and don't want to and I will not tell you in detail what the essence of my job was –what I consider necessary has already been published in the newspapers. Also, my frankness can harm America and

I promised, you know to whom, that no matter what the circumstances are, I won't do it.

Anyway we'll come back to the BRISM programme later, and the internal kitchen of NSA is not for a stranger's eyes. At the end of the day I am not a defector, spy or double agent. I am only an whistleblower and beyond that I really want to kill the octopus which has smothered the whole of my country – and the whole world – with its tentacles."

00:47 A.M.

Kold's story was now interrupted by yet another phone call. The Lawyer apologised and picked up the phone. It was his office. His secretary informed him that she has received copies of the documents for temporary asylum. The originals were kept in the Russian Federal migration service.

"That's a good sign," the Lawyer told Kold. "It's already late at night but if this – what is called a document circulation – is taking place it means that people are not sleeping but working on your case."

"I understand nothing of Russian realities," Kold responded. "So I can only hope that your words prove to be prophetic."

"I would like the same. But of course it's a bit naïve to think so."

"I think that naivety is a sister of ignorance." Kold said seriously. "If we go back to my story, then I can tell you that only now everybody rushed to seek the octopus' tentacles and discover where he had flung them. Here, have a look…"

Kold passed the Lawyer a tablet with an open page showing one of the popular internet news sites. A large heading caught the eye: 'The National Security Agency has kept Americans under its eye for half a century.'

"Interesting…" the Lawyer murmured, reading.

"The National Security Agency of the USA was invading the private lives of Americans half a century ago, carrying out not very reputable and even completely illegal actions, according to the news agency France Press. The agency refers to declassified documents published by George Washington university.

The documents reveal that in the period between 1967 and 1973 the NSA carried out the Minaret program, in which it bugged the international conversations of 1650 American citizens. Among those who happened to be under the eye were the preacher Martin Luther King, the boxer Muhammad Ali, and Art Buchwald, the famous journalist from *The Washington Post*.

So the NSA provided presidents Lyndon Johnson and then Richard Nixon with information about the overseas contacts of human rights defenders and opponents of the Vietnam War.

Also, it transpires from the documents, that two influential legislators – Democrat Senator Frank Church of Idaho and Republican Howard Baker of Tennessee – were under surveillance. The first one was a Johnson supporter and voted for American intervention in Vietnam but gradually became 'more critical' towards American policies there.

Baker on the other hand opposed Johnson's politics but then supported Nixon's Vietnamese strategy, while still being wiretapped. The news agency guesses that probably Nixon wanted to know what Baker was saying about him.

Remarkably, a few years later Senator Church was actively supporting an initiative for the creation of a secret department (the Foreign Intelligence Surveillance Court), intended to control the NSA's activity in regards to its legality."

After waiting for the Lawyer to finish reading, Kold grumbled:

"You see, now everybody tries to become an unmasker.

The Lawyer thought he heard the notes of envy in Kold's voice but decided it was best not to say anything.

FILE 009.WAV

"I found out about the octopus's existence in Pretoria. I think it was in 2008, towards the end of the year. Yes, that's right – I ended up in South Africa at the beginning of the winter during the rainy season. To be more precise, it was winter for the US, but there, in the Southern Hemisphere, this time of the year was summer.

In our embassy in Pretoria there was a technical checkpoint, and I was sent there to check the condition of the computers and equipment installed there. Actually, I should start in the correct order, because this trip had a strong influence on me and every detail is important.

The plane landed in Pretoria, one of the three capitals of SAR. The executive powers of the country are located here, while the judicial and legislative powers are located in Cape Town and Bloemfontein.

While our Boeing was circling over the city and its suburbs, waiting for its turn for landing, I was looking through the window at the green plains and hills gradually becoming small mountains covered in forest. From the air, South Africa gave the impression if not of paradise on earth, then at least of a land no worse than California and I was already anticipating that this routine trip might turn out to be a good vacation, regardless of the rains.

Our attaché Dick Walker was meeting me at the airport. He was a pleasant black-skinned man with a dazzling smile, a native of New Orleans. He shook my hand, picked up my bag and walked me through the crowds of the main terminal of Pretoria Vander Boom to the car outside.

'First time here?'

I nodded:

'Yes, first time. The only thing I know about Africa is that giraffes and hippos live here.'

'And also Americans, Mongrels, Playboys, Naughty Boys, Hard Livings, Junkie Funkies and Corner Boys…' the smile on his face faded.

'What are those? If those are the names of the local sports clubs it sounds a bit high school.'

'These are the names of the black gangs, which terrorize the country. Although organised crime is not the worst evil in the SAR.

Our car left the airport territory and dashed past the green hills, attractively overgrown by clumps of trees. Long bands of clouds floated along the sky, and the sun would appear then disappear behind them again. Dick turned the car at the cross roads and I saw a city in the distance – an angular line of building silhouettes, a lot of greenery and the skyscrapers, melting in the haze.

'Pretoria,' Dick said. 'The safest city in this damn country. And really its only safe business zone.'

'Is everything really that bad here?' I was surprised, trying to recall everything I had ever read about South Africa.

I could remember a little about the Anglo-Boer War, the separation of the white minority and the black majority under apartheid, the fighter for freedom and democracy Nelson Mandela, the revolution of 1993 and… and that's it.

'Do you really know nothing?' Dick sped up.

The road crossed ploughed fields. Here and there some buildings flashed past – maybe barns or garages. A few people appeared by the roadside. They were waving their arms, shouting something. One even lay down on the asphalt across the road.

'Do you see these boys?' Dick asked, then without waiting for a response, closed all the windows in the car and locked the doors. 'If I stop, they'll break the windows, pull us out, rob us and beat us up and then steal the car.'

He swerved sharply, making a risky turn, and drove around the black lad stretched on the asphalt. Luckily for us, no cars were coming the opposite way.

'After the apartheid system was broken, it all became chaos here,' Dick hissed through clenched teeth, looking in front of him. 'Now one third of the population of this country doesn't have a job. The crime level here is the highest in the world. You'll be told all about it during your briefing, but for now remember this: never ever leave the business district of the city. Never! And even there try not to go anywhere by yourself. Don't talk with unknown black people!'

'How so?' I allowed myself to smile since Dick himself was black.

'You can smile in the morgue!' he snarled. 'When your liver gets cut out on the street.'

'What for?' I blurted out.

'To eat the liver of a white man means to get his luck.'

'Are you serious?' I felt my heart beating much faster than usual.

'I couldn't be more serious,' Dick began to smoke and lowered the window. We were approaching the city. Fences and warehouses stretched along either side of the road. 'Sorry for talking about the morgue, but newcomers need to get a bit of a cold shower or they don't believe. Later you will also be shown videos and photos. If you have a weak stomach – I'd advise you not to have a big lunch.'

'What on earth is going on here?!' I raised my voice.

Dick threw the cigarette butt out of the window and wound up the window again – it looked like he was doing it all automatically.

'The South African Republic takes first place in the world by the number of crimes and especially serious crimes per capita,' he began in the tedious voice of a professional lecturer. 'And there are fifty murders per day and the same number of attempted murders. Here on the streets, robbery happens like this – first you get hit on the back of your head with an iron pipe or get shot in the temple and only then do they check if you've got anything in your wallet or if you've got a wallet at all. Here for a woman, born in SAR, the probability of becoming a victim of rape is higher than the probability of learning how to read. We carried out secret research – more than a quarter of the local men admitted they had committed rape, and every second one of those admitted he had raped a few people. Half a million of rapes take place each year here, Joshua.'

'Does it have something to do with the peculiarities of local food?' I asked carefully.

'It has something to do with peculiarities of local heads.' Dick answered firmly. 'The majority of locals are Christians of various types, but only on paper. All blacks are really pagans who believe in crazy prejudices and superstitions. I am not saying this for effect – three years ago our attaché for agriculture Mr. Bronk, who was collecting information about local cults, went truly crazy. He put on a white sheet, took a cross and headed for Alexandria. That's one of the most dangerous districts (in a criminal sense) of the biggest city in the country, Johannesburg. Basically... basically no one has ever seen him since.'

'Cults, pagans,' I nodded with a knowledgeable air. 'Voodoo...'

'Damn voodoo!' Dick shouted. 'Get all that Hollywood stuff out of your head. There's no voodoo here! Here people believe that if you copulate with a virgin, you'll get cured from AIDS, and every fifth man here has AIDS. That is why there are so many rapes, especially of children! They rape even eight months old babies, do you understand? The most important thing is that it's a virgin. And you're talking about voodoo...'

We carried on for sometime in silence, then he said in a calmer voice:

'Also people here believe that a woman's love for another woman is an illness and that she can be cured if she receives the satisfaction of copulating with a man. That is why there is such thing as 'corrective rape'. Have you ever heard this term?

I shook my head silently. I was beginning to feel sick from South African realities.

'Usually it's initiated by the relatives of the poor lesbian – grandfather, father, older brother. They hire a few people, a strong well-equipped man, and after kidnapping the victim, they rape her until she, in their opinion, doesn't reach an orgasm. Almost always such procedures end up with damage to internal organs and maybe the death of the victim. And don't think that it's only relevant to the people from slums! In April, a local celebrity, the captain of the women's national football team Eudy Simelane, a very popular woman in the country, was killed. She was killed because she was a lesbian, lived with her girlfriend as a family and fought for the rights of sexual minorities. Eudi was caught on the street, beaten up, then raped multiple times, then stabbed in the head, body and legs twenty-five time before her corpse was thrown in a brook in the outskirts of the town. A rape takes place here every twenty-six seconds. After the murder of Eudy Simelane, Dr Sonnet Ehlers has invented a 'condom against rape', called a 'rapecs'. It's a silicone inset into the vagina covered with barbs, which damage the penis at the moment of the exit...'

'Enough!' I begged. 'Tell me more about why the police, government – all of them – why don't they sort it out?'

Dick's surprise was genuine.

'Why would they?' he asked. 'Here the only things that are done are those that bring money. And when did the fight against crime and prejudice ever bring any income? It's a troublesome and thankless job. Apart from that, the corruption in SAR is as bad as a anywhere in the world. Half of all police forces are completely bought, like in our Chicago in the thirties.'

'And what kind of future awaits this country?'

'Why would I care?' Dick responded with a question again. 'Probably SAR will become a classic corporate state. There are plenty of natural resources here. The areas of extraction and business centers will be safe zones and the rest of the country will return to its primitive state, but instead of clubs and arrows the local savages will be using pistols and machine guns. Why am I saying 'will be'? They already use them.'

'But wasn't it always like this?'

'No, the situation was different before apartheid. The black lived in Bantustans and did what their ancestors used to do for hundreds and hundreds of years – they worked the land and raised livestock. There was order in the country. This system was destroyed during Leclerc's time. And then the chaos began…'

I said quietly:

'I think you approve of the old orders.'

'Of course!' Dick smiled. 'You don't know many things and we don't have much time, that's why I'll simply say: freedom is like a drug. In small portions it's a medicine, but in big doses – it's poison. One should be ready for freedom, otherwise it'll kill you.'

We stopped by the checkpoint. The policemen checked the documents, noted the car on their computers and we entered the city.

'Here's Pretoria,' Dick said. 'Do you know what this word means?'

I shrugged my shoulders, although I was happy that he had changed the subject.

'It's the Romans' word for the place in a military camp where you find the tent of a commander, legate, consul or emperor. It later became the name for a concentration of power and the warriors guarding the emperor were called the Praetorian Guard. By the way, Pontius Pilate questioned Christ in the Jerusalem Pretoria. And from there he was taken to execution. But the funniest thing is,' he chuckled, 'that originally this city was called Pretoria Philadelphia – in other words 'The place of the power of the brotherhood of love'. And it was named this after Martinus Wessel Pretorius, the first president of Transvaal. There's his monument.'

We drove past the monument – the bronze founder of this odd state looked at me grimly from the height of his pedestal. He somehow resembled Churchill. Soon we pulled up at the hotel.

'This is 'Sheraton Pretoria Hotel,' Dick said and gave me his business card. 'It's safe here but remember what I told you about. Check in, have some rest and then give me a call. I'll come myself or send a driver to pick you up. At fourteen hours local time you have a briefing, and at fifteen a meeting with the chief.

I got out of the car, slung the bag over my shoulder, and bent down to the open door.

'Thank you, Dick.'

He smiled.

'Get me a drink and we're even.'

He drove off and I was left alone by the doors of the hotel – a big Victorian building in colonial style, decorated with columns. The shaggy palm trees by the entrance looked to me like severed heads of rastafarians impaled on the curved stakes of the tree trunks.

The flight, the sleepless night, the conversation with Dick – they had all knocked me off my balance. Not that I was exceptionally tired. I could just feel a constant desire to lie down both, during the briefing, which, contrary to my fears, had not had much effect on me, and during my conversation with the chief – the head of the local department of the NSA.

Then I headed to the basement where the equipment was located. The job turned out to be not fairly simple, strictly speaking, just like it always is when it comes to servicing equipment.

I ran tests through the system, checked the versions of the programs and the protective modules – all of which took a few hours. All that time I was thinking about the residents of this unfortunate country, about how they see life, history and what future awaits them, and if everything really was really that bad – I couldn't believe that Dick hadn't exaggerated a bit.

Looking at the columns of numbers running across the screens, I suddenly thought that if all of our clever machinery installed here was connected to local communication lines, there is a very simple and easy way to check what is going on in this country.

I entered my access code, and got into the database, where the records of the telephone conversations of individuals under surveillance were located. They were all listed under pseudonyms and numbers. I put the headphones on and randomly clicked on one of the files recorded last year.

The interlocutors were speaking English in a strong local accent and used many words I didn't know but I got the gist of the conversation. Someone called Ngodila was reporting to an unnamed superior about negotiations with Russians about a purchase of helicopters. I was astonished that the local bandits – and what else could Ngodila and his boss be? – are so rich they can use helicopters as a means of transport, and I won't even mention the unscrupulousness of Russians, prepared to trade with all kind of scum.

After doing all I had to do in the embassy, I asked the secretary about Dick – I still owed him a drink – but it turned out he had gone away on business. So I went back to the hotel in the company of a taciturn driver, a boy with a square jaw and transparent eyes.

It began to rain. When I got to my room, I headed for a shower straight away, then lay in bed and turned on the TV to see the local news. It was a way of learning more about the country, its inhabitants and seeing the truth of what Dick had told me.

I didn't pay much attention to the international news, just continuous chatter about economic crisis. But then the news of the South African Republic began – the chronicles of political life, the president's speech on some national occasion, and preparation for the upcoming football world cup.

Right at the end the broadcaster, a pleasant black woman, announced in a boring voice that the Ministry of Transport of the republic had signed a contract with the American Sikorsky Aircraft corporation for the supply of helicopters to replace the outdated French-made choppers. The delay with the signing of the contract, already discussed a year ago, was linked to former minister Ngodila who used to lobby interests in third world countries to the prejudice of the economic interests of the republic. Ngodila had been dismissed and a criminal case had been opened against him.

A few Sea Kings painted in camouflage colors flew across the screen, then the credits came and an advertisement began.

My sleepiness had vanished. I stood up and saw in the mirror, hanging opposite me, the reflection of a very surprised man…

The second day failed to bring the answers I was looking for. On the contrary, there were even more questions. No, I did spend half a day fiddling with the servers, but curiosity gnawed at me from the inside, like the larvae of the parasitoid wasp eats the caterpillar. I brewed myself some coffee and got into the databases – for the first time ever using my level of access for something that was not work.

I got really interested in the whole story of the helicopters. If I understood it all correctly, there was an ugly scheme showing up. It seemed the agency had been tracking private information about a specific commercial deal in order to use it in the interests of a large American company.

I won't say my guesses were confirmed one hundred per cent, but after studying the tagged documents it became clear that the NSA doesn't only work on issues of national security but regularly acquires purely commercial information – in other words commercial espionage.

At the same time, I discovered that our programs are constantly holding at gunpoint the governments of a number of states and this surveillance has been taking place for decades.

Among the countries in which leaders, politicians, ministers, establishments and even ordinary citizens were under permanent wiretapping were Brazil, India, and the UAE, not to mention America's bugbear countries Russia, China and Iran.

The agency also spied on allies of the United States, including the UK and Germany and Saudi Arabia and Israel. This has come as a shocking revelation for many European politicians, but I remember that back then it didn't touch me in the least – since nobody had repealed the principle of 'trust but verify'.

In the case of Russia and China, though not everything was going entirely smoothly. Here in cyberspace, real battles were booming soundlessly. Our programmers had managed, for example, to listen in on the temporary Russian president when he was at the G20 summit in London, while the transcripts of telephone calls and files of electronic correspondence of the Chinese prime minister occupied an archive of folders to a total volume of thirty-six gigabytes.

I tried to look at the contents of some files. At that moment I was motivated purely by curiosity. I was simply interested, for example, in what information the leaders of India and Iran exchanged on 11th September 2001. But a bitter disappointment awaited me. All I could see was a general catalogue. To gain access to the documents themselves or to the media, I had to send a request to the main office in Fort Meade. The data was collated on the server in Pretoria, each quarter was archived and sent to the central database.

This bureaucratised system had one very important up-side, that it completely eliminated the possibility of data leaks – unless of course the members of the head office wanted to organise this leak themselves.

After spending a few hours digging into the databases, I eventually gave up and started the program for cleaning the registry, sat in the armchair and dozed off to the barely audible humming of the cooling systems for the server.

The octopus came to me in my dream. It was huge, faceless and almighty. Its invisible tentacles were spreading across the world, entering every house, every room. They were no thicker than a thread, but inside those threads powerful streams of data were pulsating, feeding this horrible creature.

The octopus never moved, but from time to time new tentacles emerged from the disgusting bag, replacing its head and body, and crawled out along the surface of the planet in search of prey. In utter silence, it slithered into another house in which there was a computer connected to the internet, another person who had just bought a mobile phone or a tablet. It would attach itself to the gadget and soon start pulsating, draining out gigabytes of data. From that moment, the person didn't belong to himself anymore, but had become part of a huge information organism, a food source which can be completely sucked out to leave only an empty skin.

I woke with a stiff neck and a feeling of brokenness through my whole body, I went through a few unpleasant minutes of psychological self-flagellation, After all I had just committed an official misconduct and maybe even a crime by exceeding my official duties and sticking my nose somewhere I should not have. Apart from that, the helicopter case clearly showed me that the NSA treats such concepts as 'honour' and 'duty' quite freely, which was a direct contradiction to the Baseball player's belief.

But then the bright sun outside the window, the singing of African birds, the rustling of the trees and the aroma of freshly baked bread, which came up through the slightly opened window from the café on the ground floor, reconciled me with reality.

'Josh, people don't come to the baseball field with their own rules' I told myself. In the grand scheme of things, the supply of our helicopters to SAR in itself is quite a positive fact. The Russians were left holding the bag – there's nothing so special about it, it's business!

And then, direct assault is not always the best way to take over a fortress. If you remember Iraq, a donkey loaded with gold breaks the gates much more effectively, more cheaply and more safely.

'Do what you must – and come what may', I said out loud.

And the wheel of my service went on rolling."

01:21 A.M.

"Tell me, Mr. Kold," the Lawyer stirred his coffee and took a sip. "It is believed that the action of Private Banning, who passed a huge amount of secret information for publication to Cassandzhi, had a big influence on you. Is that true?

Kold thought. The Lawyer noticed that he didn't have an unequivocal answer to this question. Silence went on for quite a long time. Finally Kold began to talk:

"You know, I'll say it's both: yes and no. The thing is, in the United States itself, there's no clear position towards Banning's actions. You see, from the point of view of the law, he is a criminal, a traitor, and because of his actions and the information which he helped make public, people have died. And society doesn't see a hero in him. As for my point of view, I pay tribute to him, of course, as a man who managed to force himself to cross the fatal line. I'll say more about Banning, but it's not a simple subject, so I need to think about it first. I just don't want to talk about it now. I'll tell you now about the 'honey trap' in Zurich – which had much more influence over my decision than Banning's actions."

FILE 010.WAV

"The Baseball player told me about a trip to Europe. I was sitting in the cafeteria on the sixth floor, drinking coffee and looking out the window, thinking about all sorts of things – like fishing, for example. My father and I had been planning for a while on going to the coast and staying in a camping lodge to fish, grill what we caught, drink wine and just chat. To be honest, last time we had something like this was when I was still at school.

Of course, I doubted that my father, despite his promises, would indeed be able to leave all his stuff and take a week-long holiday. And I too had issues with spare time – at that time we were testing yet another version of our latest cryptographic program and I often had to stay at work as late as two o'clock in the morning.

Anyway, I was drinking my coffee and looking at clouds floating by in the faded late summer sky. It was lunch time, the cafeteria was booming with a melee of voices, people were walking around my table, the waiters were scurrying past with trays, and it all smelt of fried bread, sausages, vanilla, coffee and boiled milk.

The Baseball player appeared suddenly, just like he always did – just materialised from thin air. He was all positive in his impeccable suit and his sportyhaircut and classic American smile.

He began the conversation without any preparatory etiquette about how I'm doing or my health. He just came flat out with it:

'Tell me, Joshua, have you ever been to Europe?'

I shook my head. No, I'd never been to the Old World. I'd been to Asia a few times. As a schoolboy, I went on an exchange trip to Sendai in Japan, and then we went with the whole family to Thailand on holiday. I've also been to South America – to Brazil and Peru. And you know about Africa. Though Australia was also beyond the world I happened to see, but, to be frank, I didn't want to go there. What is Australia? Deserts, kangaroos, eucalyptus and koalas. And to sit for nine hours in the plane for that – no, thanks.

Old Lady Europe is completely different! You don't need to be a genius to understand that our whole modern civilization was born there and any person who carries a passport in a pocket of his trousers wants to return to the basics, to perform a kind of pilgrimage and go to London or Paris.

All the same, I must admit that we Americans do treat Europe with some scepticism. In essence we are a part of it but we Americans broke free from the geographic and social-historical shackles that poor Europeans are forced to still live by – you can put it this way – in crowded living conditions, constantly wary of the rock of Russia hanging over their heads.

Still, of course, I was fascinated to visit Europe, and the Baseball player guessed at once that he could pull me in on a hook, like a marlin.

But he needed a hundred per cent result; people like him never rely on chance, so he asked me another question:

'And what do you, my boy, think about gnomes?'

I can't stand it when people call me 'my boy' and other words like this, but this time I ignored it because the word 'gnomes' awoke many more emotions. I even asked Mr. Jenkins, whether I had heard him correctly. He said, yes, and smiled.

What did I know about gnomes? First of all, the books by Professor JRR Tolkien and the films made from them by Peter Jackson, of course. I had watched a couple – they are quite tolerable gum for the brain, pure escapism. They probably have hoardes of fans who run around in homemade tin armour, fake beards and duralumin swords.

But gnomes themselves, or rather the word, was invented, I think, by Paracelsus, who got it from the Latin *gnomus,* which means 'knowledge'. The alchemist thought that each natural element in this world has its own spirits-protectors, and he called them gnomes.

In reality of course, gnomes are bearded dwarfs, the owners of countless treasures. Different nations call them differently: 'dvergi', ' cvergi ', 'dwarves', 'nibelungs', 'krasnolyudki', 'svartalvy', 'kobolds', 'leprechauns' and many other names.

By their character, gnomes are mean and miserable, but they are also workaholics, and in their free time they like nothing better than to drink beer, eat, sing, and rampage with their fellow gnomes.

That's pretty much what I told the Baseball player, and then asked; has our agency decided to take over a fantasy race? He, as usual, didn't answer my question but said:

'The German Swiss from the Zurich canton have an ancient legend about how two shepherd brothers found their way into an underground kingdom of gnomes. They saw there untold riches – even the poorest miners were wearing boots with golden buckles and ate from silver bowls. The brothers were astonished by the fact that the columns and beams of the houses were made out of gold, the signposts on the walls of the grottoes were decorated with precious stones and the handrails of bridges and balconies were made out of silver. The brothers bent double and wrapped themselves in their cloaks and pretended to be gnomes to find out where the mines that the gnomes got their precious metals and gems, were. But every time they reached an underground lake, beyond which the entrances to the mines were located, an unknown force would turn them back. So then the brothers decided to use a trick. They gave the gnomes a barrel of beer and, of course, the gnomes really liked a drink. So they began to ask for more and the brothers offered them a deal – they would fill the barrel with beer in return for the same barrel filled with gold. That's how two poor shepherds soon became rich and left their sheep to build themselves houses on the banks of the Limmat River. And Zurich, one of the world's largest banking centers, is now located there. But people say that gnomes, eager for beer, still live in the depths of the surrounding mountains and in the city itself – and the descendants of the legendary brothers, in accordance with the ancient agreement, still swap beer for gold.'

'It's a good legend,' I said. 'Europeans are generally quite good at making up fairy tales and myths.'

'That's true,' the Baseball player laughed, but then he became serious: 'The embassy in Zurich needs a man from our department. The work is the usual – check the technical condition of the equipment, and standard maintenance of the software according to the project. And the local boys need some help; they've got problems with the local network. And, Joshua, you are the best candidate…

"I'm in!' I finished my coffee and put the cup down with a slam. 'Switzerland – is it somewhere north?'

'Sweden is in the north,' the Baseball player got up. 'You have one day to brush up on your geography and other subjects. Tickets, passport and visa you can get in the transport office, and you get your briefing from Heidi after four o'clock. Good luck!'

…In the plane I was reading all I'd downloaded the day before about Europe in general, about Switzerland and specifically Zurich, but for some reason I couldn't find the legend about the shepherd brothers.

But among the serious files, stuffed with historic data, statistics and geographic maps, I came across a funny text about what Americans associate with various European countries:

Romania – vampires, Dracula and internet brides.

Bulgaria – isn't it a part of Russia?

Greece – gyro (national dish), the country on the verge of bankruptcy.

Albania, Bosnia and Herzegovina, Kosovo, Macedonia, Montenegro and Croatia – a lot of organised crime, constantly at war.

Hungary – no thanks, I've already eaten.

Italy – mafia, pizza, spaghetti and the film *Gladiator*.

Vatican – the Pope, child molestation, and the book *The Da Vinci Code*.

Slovenia – isn't that a manufacture of equipment?

Austria – a small Germany, with a lot of mountains and classical music.

Czech – beer! Cheap prostitutes… Beer!!!

Poland – jokes and anecdotes about poles, not very clever people.

Sweden – socialism, Pirate Bay site.

Norway – Vikings have become fishermen.

Denmark – makers of 'Lego', everybody wears wooden clogs.

Holland – drugs, prostitutes and prostitute-drug addicts.

Germany – beer, porno, Nazis, sauerkraut (sour cabbage), rubbish food.

Switzerland – rich and secretive people, Alps, banks.

Monaco – Grace Kelly, casinos.

France – wine snobs, bread (baguettes), could not win the war, short rulers.

Spain – bulls, hot girls.

Portugal – isn't it Spain?

Belgium – chocolate, 'Manneken Pis'.

England – fish and chips (national dish), bad teeth, James Bond, Harry Potter, haven't managed to keep a single colony.

Ireland – ginger, alcoholics, potatoes, band U2.

Scotland – film *Braveheart*, everybody wears kilts, haggis, golf.

Iceland – volcanos, odd language, hot and sexy blonds.

Russia – communism, hackers, vodka, Anna Kournikova.

Estonia, Lithuania, Latvia, Belarus, Slovakia – are these actually countries?

Ukraine – Chernobyl, everybody is rude.

Moldova – it doesn't exist, never heard of it.

All Europeans are crazy about soccer.

I smiled, and for my smile I got an unfriendly look from my neighbor on the seat next to me – an unshaven man with bushy eyebrows, clearly European. Then I thought, well, that's pretty much how things are: we, Americans, indeed form some vague ideas about European nations and treat them accordingly.

The French for us are cold and calculating grumblers. The Swedish are crazy, rather infantile, sexually obsessed eternal teens. The Germans – aggressive pedantic workaholics. Spanish – lazy psychos who love dancing. Italians – sentimental artists-killers. Irish – goofy brawlers and drunks. English – arrogant snobs, convinced they know better than anyone else what to do and how to do it, but constantly missing the mark. Turks – modest traders, who count every single cent. Although stop, Turks – I think they are not a part of Europe?

I didn't manage to put the Swiss in this scheme because I realized that French, Germans, Austrians and Italians live there and there are five official languages.

I liked Zurich. It was exactly how I imagined that good old Europe, with medieval stone houses a few storeys high under pointed tiled roofs, towers with high spires, and gothic cathedrals overlooking the light waters of the river Limmat and Lake Zürich. Yes, and above all of this urban cosiness tower, the white peaks of the Alps. Basically, it's a country of gnomes, no less.

But I've also read that in the Middle Ages Swiss gnomes with long pikes defeated the armour-clad knights of almost all European countries and then became mercenaries protecting French kings and the Pope and were generally known as desperate thugs, but that was a long time ago. Having fought long enough, the Swiss decided to become pacifists, and even during the Second World War their little country managed to stay neutral, which provided an opportunity for hundreds of thousands of refugees from Germany and European countries occupied by Hitler to escape.

The technical center in the Zurich consulate turned out to be much smaller than the South African one, but the consulate itself, on the contrary, was almost vibrating from the hidden activity which always accompanies the guys from Langley.

In the past they were called 'knights of cloak and dagger', but today this definition has become outdated. I would've called the modern spies 'adepts of the mobile phone'. Or 'warriors of the tablet'. But to blend all these features into one, then in the Zurich consulate they are 'paladins of the smartphone'.

With these gadgets they collected information published on open source internet. Based on this, they drew some conclusions, then called people who were in any way connected to this information to arrange a meeting.

Of course, it was a secret to me what they were doing during those meetings, but judging by the troubled faces of the consulate staff working under cover, things were not going that well for them.

In my opinion, just one analyst from our department sitting on the information streams would easily outdo all these 'paladins'.

The nerves of espionage were almost ringing in Zurich and sometimes I even thought I could hear it ringing!

The octopus was moving its tentacles, groping about in the darkness of the Swiss night in search of victims, but I was ok. Everything being done here and in other corners of the world, was done first of all for the benefit of my country and its citizens, and so 'he saw that it was good'.

But I probably shouldn't slander these guys. Outside work they were quite friendly, even though wearily arrogant as if it was 1982 and they had only just returned from the Soviet Union from some top-secret assignment, where they had to escape the clutches of the terrible and insidious KGB.

A couple of times during the fortnight I spent in Zurich, we went for beers in an authentic German beer house called the Elephant, which overlooked Lake Zürich. From their conversation, I realised that the main problem for the local residency was recruiting people in some way connected to the Swiss banking communities.

Zurich is one of the banking capitals of the world. Major offices for almost all the large banks, of which there are more than a hundred, are located there, and it looks like half of the town's population works in them. Zurich, at least during the day, is a town of business suits and strict hairstyles. Of course, it's a little bit boring, but at least everything's calm. Yes, there is a kind of nightlife – I saw a few night clubs with quite unusual names: Abart Music Club, Alte Börse or Basilica. But not a lot.

Two days before my departure I visited one of these clubs, perhaps the most unusual one. It was in response to a request from one of my Zurich colleagues, Stephen Mallers, an economic adviser to the council.

I guess he was the one I got closest to – we used to chat, sit in the Elephant, bantered about other paladins. And so Steve asked me to go to a night club called Adagio to have some beers, relax and keep an eye on a certain German, Herr Hagen, he'd be talking to.

We had been sitting in my hotel room and I was tinkering with his tablet – there were some issues with the wi-fi module – when Steve began to talk about a favour.

'Josh, help me out. You've seen James Bond movies, haven't you? How about you make yourself a super agent!' he began to laugh but his eyes remained serious. 'Actually we don't have enough people. The task in itself is nothing, a trifle, you won't need any special training for it. You just need to go to a club, stay there, listen to the music – some good groups perform there – and at the same time look who he's talking to, what he orders, how he acts. And then just tell me everything – and that's it.'

"And that's it?'

"Of course. Did you think you had to film him on a camera installed in a button, or prick him on a bridge with a poisonous umbrella? Ha-ha, Josh, our work is not like a movie!'

'But I hope he's a world terrorist. An emissary of Al-Qaeda, no less?'

'Of course,' Steve reassured me. 'He's a major banking exec – a top dog at Deutsche Bank.'

'And does he finance international terrorism?'

'Something of the kind, yes. Well, you agree? I'll give you seven hundred euros – you can spend it all in Adagio.

I shrugged my shoulders.

'Excellent,' Steve rejoiced. 'I knew I could rely on you. So one wolf won't gnaw off a tail of another wolf, we are doing the same job!'

To be honest, I wanted to refuse – I just couldn't be bothered to go anywhere. But after his phrase about the same job I felt I just couldn't refuse.

By the evening, it was raining in Zurich – heavy clouds the color of hardened steel drifted over the snow-white peaks and crawled down onto the town's roofs, like slugs creeping down grape leaves. The clouds brought with them the cold breath of ice, fog and darkness. The light of the street lamps blurred into orange splashes, and passers-by pulled their heads into their shoulders and raised their collars, and the raindrops streamed down the windows of my taxi. My mood was rapidly getting worse. I was tired after a day of work and the prospect of going to bed at who knows what time was looming ahead.

And I was also very nervous. After all, it's not very often I have to be a secret agent and conduct surveillance on someone. Of course, I'm slightly exaggerating – there was not supposed to be any real surveillance, but still I felt severely uncomfortable.

Adagio, contrary to my expectations, turned out to be a decent place, finished in the style of a medieval castle with solid furniture, a ceiling painted in the Baroque style, a huge fireplace with a pile of logs, a bar with forged hooks and a quite intelligent clientele.

I chose a high stool by the bar to one side. Steve had said it was the best place to watch the entrance. I sat half-turned and ordered a double martini with vodka and ice.

I'm not the biggest admirer of this drink and have a generally negative attitude towards alcohol.

First of all, I don't like being drunk, when you don't belong to yourself anymore. It's like the feelings drugs awake, but that's acid in the brain experiencing the influence of a complex chemical compound, when in the case of alcohol you're controlled by the waste product of billions of yeast fungi. To be controlled by fungus is quite humiliating, to say the least.

Secondly, I simply didn't like the taste of alcohol drinks. Vodka, rum, tequila, cognac –just a burning, nauseating poison. After champagne, I get a headache almost straight away, probably because of the carbon dioxide. Beer is bitter, while dry wines are too sour for my taste. I guess the only alcohol drink I can consume and, of course, in small portions only, is martini with a little vodka. 'Shaken, but not stirred', yes…

I watched people entering the club. A motley crowd was gathering, from bank clerks in black suits to some complete etoiles in retro outfits. People were talking, laughing, drinking, and some guests were moving freely across the space. No one paid me any attention and I gradually relaxed.

Herr Hagen came in after about half an hour. By that time, there were quite a lot of people in the club, because some Austrian group I'd never heard of called Camo & Krooked was performing. They played in the fashionable drum'n'base style and it was strange to hear African-Australian rhythms in the medieval interior. Camo & Krooked and their energetic frontman were obviously popular with locals – the crowd was jumping as soon as they started.

Herr Hagen was tall and dark-haired, no older than thirty. He came alone but very soon two beauties in flowery dresses were draped at his table and even from my seat it was easy to see how carnivorous Herr Hagen's look was becoming as he gazed into revealing décolletés.

Judging by the number of beer glasses and plates with sausages and fried potatoes, my ward clearly didn't have any inclination for temperance. If someone asked me my opinion about him, I would've said that he is a typical representative of the target group which swallows the contents of entertainment internet portals where there are articles about new cars, photographs of beauties in negligees, and anecdotes and forums with private chat rooms for virtual sex.

People grazing portals like that usually sit in an office for five days a week and because their job is so boring, they use every spare second to entertain themselves. If the internet was taken from them, they would spend more time in cafés, rest rooms, smoking rooms – in a word, anywhere they could socialise with their own kind without leaving work for long.

The golden time for fellows like this is the weekend. It begins on Friday after lunch and ends on Sunday evening. On Monday morning our hero, clean-shaven and clean-shirted, will arrive at his office with only dark shadows under his eyes and the light tremor of his fingers to betray his tempestuous weekend.

The interests of the layer of people to which Herr Hagen belonged can be usually placed in the following triangle: new women – new cars – new movies. But at least they are a credit humus, a feeding ground for numerous finance companies. All of their belongings are brought on credit – house, car, furniture, household appliances, even clothes and shoes. It's the greatest invention of our economic system – which, I believe, is the future – to create a class of people-conductors, people-pipes. They get money in their account from their employer, then straight away, without taking any cash out, transfer it as payment for their credits. Sometimes the employer and creditor is the same organization. In this way, the natural circulation of money continues and these 'Herr Hagens' are an important part of this circulation.

In the States, by the way, there's plenty of people like this, and I wouldn't say they are exactly condemned by society. Quite the opposite. To become one of these white collars is as prestigious, and it's tough to get into this caste from a farm in the Midwest or from the ethnic districts of a megalopolis. The social life is social because it doesn't stop on all the floors of a building.

Sometimes I get a kind of fascist idea that if people like this didn't exist, nobody would notice it – apart from the banks and, of course, their relatives.

Why this creature was of any interest to the NSA, I'm afraid, even Buddha may not know. And why would I care – I just complied with Steve's request.

In the meantime, Herr Hagen was getting wild. He was either laughing his nuts off, throwing his head back and displaying his whitened teeth, or squeezing the girls, who, by the way, didn't object at all. Or he would suddenly jump up, inviting the girls to dance. By that time there was a totally unrestrained atmosphere in the club with everyone shaking and grinding, By the small stage where the musicians were performing, bras and tops of excited fans were already flying through the air.

After an hour, there was no sign of Herr Hagen slowing down. After beer, he moved on to tequila, and he sprinkled salt onto the palm of one of the two laughing glamourpusses, and after drinking sucked a slice of lemon from the breast of the other one.

I began to count how much he had drunk but I lost count after the tenth.

The evening was rolling down its habitually orchestrated rails. The musicians had left and a DJ of unclear gender and nationality took their place.

Distracted by the DJ, I only noticed Herr Hagen walking towards me when he was two steps away. My heart dropped to the bottom of my stomach and my palms became suddenly sweaty. The music moved to the distance and rang in my ears as it always does when I get really scared.

He's seen through me! He's done it so easily because I am green and probably staring at him too openly. And all my conclusions about a typical representative of office plankton are in reality worthless. He is a spy – a professional, probably – and a murderer, trained in Al-Qaeda camps. Damn, he even looks like an Arab! He will now approach me, discreetly stab me with a poisoned stiletto and carry on as if nothing has happened.

I was in uncontrolled fear. I was paralysed and only my teeth were knocking the resounding beat. Herr Hagen came right up to me. I had a faint hope he wanted something from the bar, even though I saw that he walked past the barman shaking a drink.

The moment of truth came.

'Hello, mate!' Herr Hagen said in English with an awful accent. 'How are you doing?'

I could only manage a nod – meaning, 'I'm good'.

'Where are you from?'

All I could manage to squeeze out was an unclear head movement and a muffled:

'From… from there.'

'Are you already drunk, er?' Herr Hagen began to laugh. 'Dweeb! C'mon, let's have tequila, it'll sober you up. Although you'll have a headache in the morning it doesn't matter. Would you like to come to my table?'

I was silently blinking, not able to force out a single word. Streams of cold sweat were running down my back. The first time in my life that had ever happened.

He put his hand into his jacket. My legs went rigid as if I had just stepped in ice-cold water. Now he'll get his stiletto out…

Instead of a stiletto Herr Hagen pulled out a five-euro note, waved it in the air and shouted over the DJ.

'Hey, barman! Two tequilas for me and my friend!'

I drank the tequila as if it was water, without noticing its flavor or smell.

'What about lemon and salt!?' Herr Hagen raised his arms sorrowfully. 'What are you doing, friend... Hey, man, looks like you already had enough. You better go home otherwise you may cork off here – then there'll be no end of trouble. Do you hear me?'

I nodded, struggling to realize that he hadn't cracked me but just approached me because I was the only guy in the club alone. I needed to play along and pretend that I was indeed very drunk.

'Maybe I should call you a taxi?' he was hanging over me like a pruned tree. 'Where do you live, mate?'

I somehow managed to explain that I'm a visitor and that a friend is waiting for me in the car outside. I paid for the martini, got off the stool and trudged towards the exit. The last thing I heard was Herr Hagen telling his laughing girlfriends loudly:

'American. They just can't drink.'

After leaving the club, I turned a corner, straightened up, stopped and called Steve.

'That's it, I had to leave.'

'Why?' my friend was surprised.

'He began to talk to me, got me a drink and then decided that I am too drunk and began to offer help.'

'But you are sober!' Steve surprised.

'It just happened…'

'Did he approach you himself?'

"Yes.'

"Do you know why?'

I had to confess:

'Probably because I was sitting there alone…'

He grunted.

'I see. So, what can you tell me about our friend?'

'He's a typical white collar not burdened by excessive intelligence,' I was getting my own back on Herr Hagan for the fright he gave me. 'He picked up two whores and pumped them up so much that in the end they were only capable of laughing. He likes to drink and eat but keeps well. After beer, he drinks tequila and claims it can sober you up. People say that's a sign of an early stage of alcoholism…'

'Josh, mate, let us come up with the conclusions,' Steve interrupted me. 'Thanks for your work. I owe you.'

…I probably would've forgotten about the event if there hadn't been a follow-up. It so happened that I got delayed in Zurich. I can't tell you all the details, but I'll just say that it had something to do with my job, with part of it which I have no intention of divulging under any circumstances.

These were lonely, miserable days. It rained non-stop. The wind bent the bushes right over on the waterfront, rattled the signs and tore shreds of clouds, which looked black, across the grey sky. The Paladins had for various reasons all suddenly left. Some had gone to Geneva. Some had even left Switzerland. So there was nobody left in the consulate except for security and a couple of diplomats.

The dreariest time was in the evenings when streams of vehicles crawled through the gloomy wet streets. Zurich residents were hurrying to their homes, to their families and pets, and here I was dawdling, stepping over puddles, back to the dull hotel where crap coffee and a cold bed were waiting for me.

One evening, I think it was Thursday, I felt so lousy I decided to go out for a warming drink, like mulled wine.

The Elephant was closed by then, and the only other place I knew was Adagio. So I decided to risk another visit to the medieval palace. Hey, even if I come across Herr Hagen again, it won't effect anything – after all, I'm not doing anything reprehensible.

Everything inside was the same. The barman with a shaker and the fireplace. Only the band performing on the stage was different and there were fewer people than that Friday night.

Obeying some inexplicable impulse, I sat on the same stool by the bar. The barman brewed some mulled wine for me and offered me a glass of Kirsch, the local cherry vodka, but when I refused he left me and attended to other clients.

I was drinking mulled wine, thinking I'll soon be back in America, when I suddenly saw Steve. He was sitting half-turned towards me at the table in the corner by the fireplace – and opposite him grinning with his white teeth and with a cup of beer in his hand was... Herr Hagen! The third person at the table was a small blonde with a large sensual mouth.

I guessed straight away that there's something odd about this. An angel on my left shoulder said to me: 'Joshua, my boy, finish your mulled wine, pay and go home to your uncomfortable cold, but peaceful bed'.

But at once a demon appeared on my right shoulder, who began to laugh mischievously: 'Finally something interesting happened! You'd be a complete fool to leave at this crucial moment and go to sleep like an old man.'

Do I need to say which one I listened to? Although in this case I am completely unoriginal in this sense, for some reason people always listen to the one who speaks into the right ear.

So I decided to stay, ordered coffee and relocated to the far end of the bar under a fake shield with the emblem of some ancient knightly family. From there I could watch the trio while remaining unnoticed. Steve kept telling Herr Hagen and the girl some stories, accompanying his words with soft gestures that made it look like he was conducting an invisible orchestra. The girl was laughing like hell and bent so far forward her breasts could be easily be seen through the neck of her dress. Herr Hagen also was laughing and downing beer. Then he rang someone. Steve ordered a bottle of kirsch, and by the time the German had finished his telephone conversation there was already a full glass in front of him.

It looked to me as if Herr Hagen tried to refuse but Steve was insistent and the blonde also joined in the persuasion. They had one drink, then another and another…

Herr Hagen suddenly looked heavy. His lower lip dropped, his eyes glazed and his moves became large and coarse.

He tried to dance with the girl but kept bumping into other people and tripped over the legs of the bar stools. He began to attract attention. Two club security guards started watching Hagen as he staggered over the dance floor.

Steve, to his credit, came to help out his friend and for some reason I had no doubt of the fact that they were friends, although there was still an unanswered question – why had Steve asked me to watch the banker?

After sitting Herr Hagen at the table with aid of the blonde, Steve gestured for a waiter, kept explaining something for a long time. Finally, the waiter brought them a tray with two glasses of tequila and the bill in a crystal dish. Traditionally, visitors would be putting tips into such dishes if they liked the service, but now it was more of a tribute to tradition, because for a long time in Europe tips were included in the final bill.

After paying and knocking back that last drink, Steve helped Herr Hagen get up and they headed for the door accompanied by the girl, while the German kept trying to bow to every passer-by. In order not to lose sight, I also paid and hurried to the exit. Mulled wine and coffee were warming me up from the inside and my curiosity led me there, where in theory I really shouldn't be. However, I decided at once: if Steve notices me I'll simply pretend I ended up there by chance.

I pushed the heavy door open and I breathed in the damp Zurich air, filled with a mix of petrol, female perfume, rancid oil from the nearest fast food and the distant Alpine snow. Steve, the blond, and Herr Hagen were looming ahead like three characters from the Irish song 'What will you do with the drunken sailor?'

I followed them with my hands in my pockets and smiled to the darkness, imagining how Steve's face will look when he finds out that he, the 'paladin' and super agent, was tracked by an ordinary IT worker without any special qualification or operative training.

After walking along the narrow pavement next to the pale wall of an old house, they stopped under a streetlight and Herr Hagen tried to light a cigarette. I hadn't seen him with a cigarette until now and I think people in Europe smoke much less – anti-tobacco propaganda and high cigarette prices seem to be working. So the fact that Herr Hagen was trying to smoke highlighted how drunk he was.

But he failed to light his cigarette and flung it carelessly on the wet asphalt. A short German curse reached me. The blonde burst out laughing, waving her handbag. She had a stunning figure and slim legs, but her voice and manners betrayed her lack of class.

All that time, I was getting closer to them. It was late, so there were hardly any other people on the street – just these three and an elderly couple, returning from a late promenade.

As I came up to Steve, the girl and Herr Hagen, they were walking a few steps towards a big white Opel. Then something unimaginable happened.

'You're drunk!' Steve said, addressing his drinking companion. 'So I'll drive.'

'N-no!' Herr Hagen banged his fist on the roof of the car. 'Thi-is is my car! I will dr... drive it... myself!'

'Teddy-bear!' the blonde laughed. 'The teddy-bear will drive us!'

'No-n!' Steve objected. 'You had too much to drink, mate. We'll crash into a lamppost and...'

'Your American politeness insults my German pride!' Herr Hagen said with sudden assurance and, pushing Steve aside, climbed in behind the steering wheel.

Steve snorted, spread his arms, and walked around the car to sit in the front passenger seat while the blonde giggled in the back. I was standing five steps away by a downpipe from which water was gushing, and I had the impression it was all just a hoax.

Will they really drive in a state like this? Will Steve really allow the banker to…?

I rushed to the car intending to stop them, but the Opel had pulled off sharply, swerved, raced past the married couple who huddled against the wall in horror. Its headlights swept the dark windows of a neighboring building as it shot onto the big road leading to the center of town.

I sighed as I realized that the performance was over and I was left only to hope that everything would end well for its main characters.

Walking slowly along the pavement, I soon forgot Steve and Herr Hagen. I was thinking about the next day, more humming servers and cold coffee and about whether I'll manage to finish my work or have to stay here longer…

But a surprise was waiting for me around the corner!

Across the road under the orange street lights a blue and white car of the Swiss road police slewed at an angle with its lights flashing. Herr Hagen's Opel had its nose right up against the police car's wing. Two policemen were talking intensely to Steve while the Opel's owner, watched by another policeman, was standing on one leg with his arms spread, desperately trying to balance – presumably trying to prove he was sober. The blonde, waving her handbag, was walking in the distance smoking nervously.

To be honest, if I can avoid meeting the police I always do. Of course, European police are not the same as ours. Here they quite often carry out the role of government clerks who give out fines.

I have to admit we have higher levels of crime and the potential threat is higher. After all, in a country where people in every other house has guns, the policemen have to be tough. And what else do you want with the Second Amendment to the Constitution – you have to pay for it. That's why if there's an altercation on a road and a policeman suddenly tells you: 'Be quiet, put your hands up and put them on the bonnet!', everybody obeys. If they continue to wrangle, the office can consider it defiance and get a gun out. In the USA, for your information, if a policeman gets a gun out, then he will definitely fire it – so better not tempt fate.

Why am I talking about this now? Well, because Steve himself would not have behaved like that with policemen who effectively caught Herr Hagen at the crime scene. Back in America both of them would've been taken to a police station – and that's it. But the local policemen here are liberal guys, and for some reason they were trying to prove to Steve that his mate is guilty.

As I was standing there watching, another two police cars arrived. Now Herr Hagen and the blonde were sitting in one of the cars and a policewoman, a pretty plump woman with brown hair, sat in the Opel. Steve was free to go and at once, suspiciously quickly, stopped a taxi and left. Then the policemen left too. I was left on the street by myself again.

I didn't manage to leave Zurich the next day, nor the day after. The program was playing up, time was running out and I even had to work at night to get results.

I saw Herr Hagen again when I arrived at the consulate to get in touch with the agency. A door into one of the offices was opened and I noticed the banker sitting in there in an armchair by the table. I couldn't see who was sitting opposite him and the voice was unfamiliar.

Herr Hagen looked depressed and confused. I lingered by the door listening to the conversation.

'You're not in a very good position, Herr Hagen,' the invisible interlocutor was telling the German. 'Drink-driving is a serious offence.'

'My friend wanted to help me,'Herr Hagen mumbled. 'Steve, he tried… tried to take my place and drive the car. Oh, my damn stubbornness! I already paid the fine and a fee for the medical examination and a fee for the tests… it came out at almost five thousand francs! And now I've received a subpoena and this is threatening my career – according to internal policies of the bank, someone up for prosecution doesn't have a right to occupy certain positions… High positions, do you understand? Steve said back then, when the policemen have arrived, he said that there's an opportunity…'

'There is indeed an opportunity,' the voice of the man sitting at the table sounded very convincing. He was now talking slowly, pausing between the words. 'The court will hear your case tomorrow. But unfortunately, Steve has left and won't be able to help you personally...'

'Oh!' Herr Hagen exclaimed sorrowfully.

'But he's asked me to make all possible efforts to get you out of this unpleasant situation. The only thing, Herr Hagen – we'll need a favour from you.'

'A favour? Anything you want!' the German exclaimed.

'Great!' the voice sounded satisfied. 'So, sign this paper. Here and here.'

'What is it?' Some papers rustled.

'It's a commitment, Herr Hagen, just a commitment. A document confirming our agreement.'

'It says here that I... that I'll have to pass...'

'...information that, let's put it this way, has importance for our service,' the voice finished for him. 'But note from now on every month you will receive the sum shown below on a secret account. And any prosecution in regards to your drink-driving will be stopped.'

'This is... This is recruitment!' Herr Hagen suddenly shouted.

'Why so harsh,' the voice scolded him gently. 'It's just an offer of cooperation, which, I'd like to note, comes to you not from enemies, but friends! Aren't our countries the closest allies and partners? Are you not fighting side by side against international terrorism and crime?'

'Yes, but you're trying to force me to commit crimes! No, I refuse. I don't give a damn about the driving license or reputation. Goodbye!'

'Sit down!' the voice immediately filled with steel and clanked like a shutter. 'Your management may be upset to lose someone like you but in the end they'll get used to it. But your wife – she has a heart condition if I'm not mistaken? – and may not survive a view of one quite interesting video. Would you like to have a look?'

'I... I...' Herr Hagen suddenly bleated.

A hissing came from the office, characteristic of a recording where the microphone cuts out unwanted noises. Then a familiar woman's voice said loudly:

'But, teddy-bear, I don't want it like this… You go on your back! And I will be an Amazon, darling! Let's ride!'

After that the sound of the bed and the long moans of a woman, receiving pleasure, could be heard. Then the record stopped.

'Give me the disc!' Herr Hagen shouted with a breaking voice.

In response, an unexpectedly sincere – although at the same time mocking – laughter sounded. The man, talking to the banker, laughed heartily, but not for long. I heard the sound of a falling chair, quick steps, then some noise – and the sharp voice of the paladin:

'Sit down! You forget, I am a diplomat, and to attack me…'

Herr Hagen, breathing heavily, croaked:

'You bastard…'

'These are just emotions.'

'God will punish you…'

Laughter sounded again in the agent's voice.

'Until now he was mostly punishing others!'

'That's because the devil helps you!'

'Herr Hagen, let's put demagogy aside. Here's the paper. You need to sign all three pages. You can refuse. You can walk out of this building; You can even kill yourself. It will all be the same as you refusing to cooperate with us, because when all of this…' a pause followed, during which the paladin probably pointed at the screen, 'will come into, so to speak, the public domain, your life will loose its meaning. Your wife, if she survives your infidelity, will divorce you, your children will forget about their father and I won't even mention your career – no one will take you to the banking system even as a member of security team.'

Silence descended – and I suddenly heard cries.

I knew very well what a 'honey trap' was. One of the oldest methods of recruiting agents. A charming girl – people say you need to establish a man's preferences to ensure a hundred per cent hit! – or a young man would be sent to the man, whatever he prefers. Then after the fun in bed, a banal rough blackmail comes along: you either work for us, or everyone, beginning with your wife and ending with your boss, will find out about your adultery.

'Honey traps' were frequently used in the past by the special forces. I read the files about the history of intelligence service where this method of recruitment was maybe the most popular. The girls doing the dirtiest part of the job were called quite romantically 'swallows'. The first 'swallow' was the biblical Delilah, a treacherous Philistine who seduced and dragged into bed the Jewish strongman Samson. And in the breaks between fun, she discovered Samson's incredible power lay in his long curly hair. Everyone knows what happened afterwards. One thing excuses Delilah – that she went into coitus with Samson not for money but for patriotic reasons, like those French whores, who were going to infect the whole German army with syphilis when the Kaiser's troops came to Paris.

Maybe Homer's Helen of Troy wasn't a victim of Paris either but a swallow like Delilah. After all, it was she who convinced the Trojans to draw the infamous horse into the city.

Later 'swallows' were generally ordinary representatives of the oldest profession. I saw photos of the legendary Mata Hari on the net. She was a fat brunette with short legs, a rotund figure and a bloated face. But she was working for a fee for three intelligence services at the same time – and in the end paid for it, as she was shot.

Representatives of totalitarian countries, where the state controls all areas of a citizen's life, often became victims of honey traps. Swallows were apparently used to recruit the Russian military intelligence GRU Filatov, who was working in the consulate in Algeria, the Russian spy Ogorodnikov in Columbia and even UN Deputy Secretary General Shevchenko. As far as I'm aware, in the latter case the 'swallow' was sent by the FBI, which is not surprising – these guys have no moral principles and sometimes I think they are prepared to do anything to achieve a result.

And now Steve… I suddenly felt as disgusted as if I had stepped on a toad with bare feet. Herr Hagen was lured into a honey trap like a bull into mating. Bulls are given a special aphrodisiac, a so-called bovine exciter, which gets them going. With Herr Hagen, it was plain alcohol that was the aphrodisiac.

The trap into which the German fell was the stepped one – first the rigged accident then the honey trap. If the victim managed to get out of the first one, just as Herr Hagen tried to, then the second one would be triggered.

The sappers and demo men call it a 'second fuse'. It's hidden in the depth of the infernal machine and waits its time. When disarming a mine, the specialist snips the necessary wires, takes off the tension from the contacts, inserts the circuit breakers in their place and then when he is finally convinced his job is done and the mine is defused, suddenly there's a big boom and the sapper disappears in a cloud of hot plasma.

Herr Hagen had no chances. The octopus needed him – and the octopus got him.

'Al-alright…' he pronounced barely audibly, sobbing and sniffing like a child. 'I will sign it all. But I…'

'Well done!' the paladin said contentedly. 'You chose the right side, and got the winning ticket. A big and successful future awaits you, Herr Hagen. Congratulations!'

'Leave it… Stop!' the German exclaimed with pain in his voice. 'You… You…'

'Emotions,' the agent reminded. 'These are just emotions, dear partner. Alright, I understand. You're tired… go, get some rest, have a drink, relax. When your services are needed, someone will contact you. Most likely, it'll be an offer to meet under an innocent pretext, so remember to check your emails. And remember the code phrase: 'Rumpelstiltskin can spin straw into gold'. And now go!

I shied away from the door on tiptoe, trying to make as little noise as possible, walked away, hiding around the corner of the corridor. Luckily, there were no surveillance cameras in the internal areas of the consulate, to save any information leaks, and nobody saw me.

A little more than a day later I left Zurich."

01:49 A.M.

"Methods which the special services employ are always considered dirty," the Lawyer noted. "A lot of books, movies and stories in the press are dedicated to this subject, but when you come across them in reality, everything you saw or read before fades away."

"Tell me, did you have a similar experience?" Kold asked.

"Yes," the Lawyer admitted. "For example I had to defend one diplomat, also a writer of horror novels, who was accused of working for the MI6. What's more, the prosecution claimed that to contact the British 'james bonds' he used some incredibly complicated equipment which not even every professional IT worker would know how to use. The thing is, he was, how to put it, not all there – or to be more precise, he suffered a serious mental illness. It was so severe that when he was abroad, he would sometimes spend hours wandering across town, unable to find his own house. Once, tired and lost, he went into a park, bought himself a hamburger, sat on the grass and began to eat it. Then a dog came up and grabbed the hamburger from his hands, ate it and run away. So he bought himself a Swiss knife, spent a few days tracking down the dog then caught and dismembered it. How a man like this could work for the Russian MFA (the Ministry of Foreign Affairs) – I have no idea. As a result I had to enter into polemics on the pages of mass media with representatives of our counterintelligence who were very proud that they had caught such a scary 'super agent'. And the English also did well with the story – they could report that they had recruited a 'prominent Russian diplomat'.

In the end, he was recognised as mentally ill and sent for compulsory treatment. For some reason our counterintelligence weren't too upset with me. I am even a member of the Public Council of the FSB – that's the public control on the special services…

But Mr. Kold, if I begin to tell you about it in detail now, we will have to swap our seats – you'll take the Dictaphone and I will start on my memories."

"Who knows," Kold smiled, "Maybe one day it will happen. But you're right – everybody should do their own job, so I'll get back to my story…"

FILE 011.WAV

"I was really ill when I came back from Zurich – maybe the Alps' icy breath did chill something in my body. So I was wrapped up in three blankets, shaking with fever, suffocating from a never ending cough and stuck for a few days in my bachelor flat without food or internet. The thing is, while I was still in Europe I had contacted my seniors and asked for a few days off, as compensation for all that overtime. Nobody objected and that's why nobody was looking for me now.

I was so tired I didn't even turn the lights on in the evenings, making my way to the toilet by feeling along the wall. I had no pets, lover, or friends. In short, I didn't have anybody who could've remembered about me.

The illness only strengthened that odd and scary emptiness which had appeared inside me back in Zurich and was getting more and more overwhelming with each hour, with each day.

For the first two days I was convinced I would die and I accepted it with gratitude. Death for me was karmic retribution for the wrong I had done in Zurich helping Steve – that's why I didn't call anyone, completely surrendering to the will of providence.

I was lying in bed, looking into the ringing silence and whispering Buddhist mantras I learned back in the Garage:

'AUM-SHRI-GAIYA-ADI-SHIVA-GAIYA-ADI-KALI-GAIYA-ADI-KALA-BHAIRAVA-NAMAH-FORAM: in order to rid myself of addiction and leave this world pure;

REM-RAO-AUM: in order to destroy anything bad in me;

OM-MAHADEVAIYA-NAMAH: in order for the Great Absolute to accept me as I am.'

Sometimes it seemed to me that the demons were holding me and not letting me pass into the next world. But I read and learned by heart the Tibetan book of the dead *Bardo Thodol*, and its first stage Chikhai Bardo:

'The time of your departure from this Reality is drawing nearer. The signs of Death in feelings follow. The immersion of Earth into Cold Water; the earth is filled with Cold as it sinks; it chills and pours lead; Water becomes Fire; throes of hot and Cold; Fire becomes Air; Explosion and Disintegration with sparks fading into emptiness. These are the elements preparing us for the moment of death, by mutually swapping. When Fire scatters into the Emptiness of Air, it's time for you to enter Chikhai Bardo. Avoid absentmindedness, pull yourself together, look, listen... Pay attention. Try to recognise praeternal Trinity, Tri-Kaya.

Dharma-Kaya, the Law, is like a desert sky without Air, which is held only by light.

Sambhoga Kaya, Wisdom, is like a Rainbow in That Sky.

Nirmana-Kaya, Embodiment, is like a Nimbus of the holy ones in the vale of tears.

Soon you'll breath out your last breath and it will stop. Then you will see praeternal Pure Light. An incredible space will swing open before you, endless, like an Ocean without waves under the cloudless sky.

You will float freely like a fuzz, alone.

Don't get distracted, do not rejoice! Don't be afraid! This is the moment of your death! Use death, because it's a great opportunity. Keep your clarity of thought, don't cloud it even with compassion. May your love become dispassionate.

After the out-breath ends, it will be good if someone reads into your ear these words: You are now in the Primeval Light, try to stay in the state you're experiencing now.

If you see Glistening – this is the Glistening of the Primeval Light of Enlightened Reality. Know it. Your current Consciousness, which is not filled with impressions, sounds, pictures and smells, comprehends Itself, and this is the true reality.

Your own mind is no longer existential, it yawns with eternity, it's not emptiness or unconsciousness. Left only to Itself, it shines, flashes, and burns – it is your true purified Consciousness...'

I couldn't remember anything after that and that's why I recited this piece over and over again. My lips cracked and became covered with scabs. Black spots floated in front of my eyes. My ears were ringing and I could hear the voices of some people, maybe deceased relatives or friends or maybe my neighbors behind the wall. I would fall asleep as if I was falling into dark water. Each time I thought that I wouldn't wake up again, but death still didn't come.

So one evening I sank into the slumber which normally precedes sleep and may precede death, when suddenly a bright light flashed in front of my eyes, like the one which is mentioned in *Bardo Thodol*.

In my final dying (pre-dying) effort I clenched my fists… and saw the Baseball player. Well, Mr. Jenkins. He was standing in the middle of the room in his mac and cap and looking at me like a character out of some gangster movie.

'You look awful, Josh,' he said to me. 'Why didn't you call?'

I wheezed something in response.

'Alright, alright, we can talk later,' he took his hat off and hung it on the corner of the door. 'I'll call for some doctors. They'll patch you up, give you the necessary pills and you'll be like new. And then we can talk.'

'Then' happened about a week later. I was indeed patched up, although pills alone weren't enough and I had to have injections of antibiotics. Either way, by the time of my conversation with the Baseball player, I was pretty much healthy, though still quite weak.

'The psychiatrists have a term – 'escape into illness', the Baseball player said, when we ordered coffee in a café overlooking the black mass of the main building of Fort Meade. 'I get a feeling, Josh, that you had a bit of a nervous breakdown.'

'It's nothing to do with nerves,' I answered irritatedly. 'The weather in Zurich was just awful – rain, wind and also damned cold. Even Popeye would've caught a fever or something of the kind.'

'You know in Europe it'll always be like that,' Mr. Jenkins laughed for some reason. 'Global warming will bring them global cooling.'

'I think these are mutually exclusive,' I said, stirring my coffee.

'I think you're not familiar with the principle of work of our HAARP laboratories involved in complex ionospheric studies.'

'Is that the station in Alaska built during the Cold War?

'After, Josh, built after the Cold War.'

'Or are you talking about the super-cannons HARP, created by Gerald Bull for sending satellites into low orbit?'

'You're a bright lad!' the Baseball player blinded me with his smile. 'I see you don't waste your time on the internet. But whether it's HAARP or HARP, what I am saying is: you're simply tired, my boy. You've done your work very well. You helped the guys out even though you didn't have to. Your superiors value your work a great deal. By this evening, I've been told, there'll be something added to your bank account. Anyway, you should go on holiday. To Hawaii, say. And why not – it's an amazing place! Palm trees, the ocean, volcanoes, music, stars shining in the night sky as big as my fist… And the girls there – m-m-m… I am not an envious person, as you know, but I really envy you now. Hey, waiter! Bring me a fresh orange – I have nostalgia.'

Do I really have to say that after this recommendation from Mr. Jenkins I was soon off to Honolulu and from there to the base of the sleeping volcano Mauna Kea?

I ended up in a bungalow, rented for two weeks, lying in a recliner with a glass of Blue Hawaii on an open terrace with a mind-blowing view over the snowy dome of the volcano and the dark-blue ocean. And yet, for some reason, I felt exactly the same hopelessness and loneliness as I did during the first week in college.

The octopus was holding me tightly and I could not break free from its tenacious tentacles. To distract myself, I climbed again into the thickets of the internet, reading various cryptologic theories connected to HAARP. The Baseball player never mentions anything without a reason and so I knew something related to this installation, which can influence the ionosphere with high frequency rays, would somehow come into my life in the very near future.

The aerial fields of HAARP, the electro station and the research units are built in a remote area of Alaska near Gakona village. The mesh design antennas, incoherent radiation radar, and laser radars tower like aliens from the fantastic future amid dense taiga and wild mountains. Officially, HAARP is considered a scientific laboratory for studying the ionosphere. Unofficially, it's acknowledged that the installation has been constructed not just to study the nature of the ionosphere but also for the development of the systems of air and missile defense.

In particular, according to information from inside which I managed to discover, HAARP can be used to interfere with Russian stations tracking ballistic missile launches in the Northern Hemisphere. This is all gossip, but the gossip is in the zone of reason. And beyond this zone people say things about the station which would make our Hollywood scriptwriters cry with envy.

For example, idle reporters and crazy followers of the internet call HAARP the 'most modern weapon'. A few dozens documents have been published on the net in regards to this subject, in which it's described in detail how this installation creates devastating typhoons, brings Russian satellites down, stirs the psyche of whole nations into mass riots and civil wars, and even triggers artificial earthquakes which destroy whole cities.

It would've been quite funny if it weren't for the Baseball player. Why did he start talking about HAARP? At the moment, all I could see was a thick information curtain, like a smoke one, around this project. By the way, the Russians have similar installations but people don't write even a tenth as much as they do about HAARP. So people write that this means that someone for some reason needs this fog. And it seems that after my holiday this headache has every chance of becoming my headache.

To get distracted and give my brain a chance to switch on to something else, I renewed my memory of another project HARP, spelt with a single 'A'. This story dates to 1961, long before the construction of the aerial fields of the current HAARP in Alaska.

Everything began, as it often does, with the scientists. They constructed an experimental light-gas cannon with a barrel thirty metres long in order to track the behaviour of ballistic objects. But soon the military became interested in the cannon, and HARP received financial support and began to develop rapidly. It was assumed that the cannons will throw out small military satellites to heights of up to two hundred kilometres, the so-called low orbits. It was much cheaper and quicker than taking the devices into space by rocket.

From open sources, it became known that about ten cannons were built and located across the whole of North America – from Arizona to Quebec, and one cannon was located on Barbados, because it had the best conditions for ballistic launches. By the way, the calibre of the

Barbados cannon was 406 millimetres and the length of the barrel was forty metres, which was a record.

To achieve a launch speed of 3500 metres per second, the gun barrel was filled with an inert gas, and there were also other technical tricks but all was in vain. The cannons of HARP project could hurl their ballistic satellites only to heights of 180 kilometres, and that wasn't enough to enter low Earth orbit. The experimental ingots, weighing almost two hundred kilograms, fell into the ocean time after time.

In 1967, the project was closed, but it had a completely unexpected resurrection in the eighties. That's when Canadian engineer-artillerist Gerald Bull, one of the chief designers of HARP, got an invitation from Saddam Hussein himself.

There was a war between Iraq and Iran, and the Iraqi leaders, who'd failed in their plans for a quick seizure of the oil and gas province of Khuzestan, were in desperate need of a super-weapon to change the course of the war.

Bull's new project was called Babylon. It was estimated that the 1000 mm, multi-chamber cannon could blast a six-ton projectile a thousand kilometres up, powered by a nine-ton charge. With it, Iraq would've been able to bomb Tehran all the way from Bagdad. The super-cannon could also fire special reactive shell-rockets with a mass of up to two tons. Four weapons were supposed to be constructed.

Bull's first brainchild for Saddam was an experimental 350mm cannon – basically a copy of the cannons from the HARP project. It tested successfully and Iraq embarked on Big Babylon, which was supposed to change everything: the course of war, the balance of power in the region and the place of Iran on the world arena.

But Saddam's triumph was not meant to be. The special services of a few countries of the West and the foreign intelligence of USSR interfered, slowing down the development of the project. The Iran-Iraq war ended without bringing any noticeable dividends to either side. Parts of the super-cannon, manufactured in Europe, were confiscated on the way to Iraq, and no matter how hard the Iraqi government tried to prove that these were for oil refining, they never made it to Bagdad.

And then in March 1990 Bull was shot near his home in Brussels. The killers were never found but behind it were maybe Mossad, the CIA or the KGB – who knows?

The experimental super-cannon and the rest of the project were completely destroyed by special divisions of UN during Operation Desert Storm in 1991. That was the end of super cannons – although there are rumours the Russian army is armed with the self-propelling 20 metre monsters Oka and Kondensator, which can fire shells, nuclear ones, up to fifty kilometres.

Tired from all this military history, I made myself another glass of Blue Hawaii, although without the extra Curacao, and returned to the recliner.

It occurred to me that the fates of both projects – the old artillery HARP and our highly technological HAARP – are very similar. They both began as objects of purely scientific interest, both went through the stage when the military got seriously interested in them, and both have become (at least nominally) weapons and... The similarities ended there – unless you listen to conspiracy theories, because the HAARP with double A hasn't killed anyone yet.

Dozing off to the whisper of surf and the rustle of leaves, I suddenly saw myself as some kind of sea creature – a prawn or mollusc-nautilus – swimming in water pierced by shafts of sunlight.

I remember inexplicable delight from the sensation of weightlessness, the chill in the chest from the realization of how many kilometres of water there were beneath me, and a feeling of euphoria – which lasted until the moment when it appeared from the depth.

The octopus.

The disgusting creature noticed me at once and made a lunge. I felt that I cannot move, that I am shackled, my hands and feet are bound.

An octopus doesn't kill its victim straight away. It goes about its business gradually, as if following a scheme. First it wraps its prey with its tentacles. Then is grips it with its suckers and injects poison with its sharp chitin beak. Only when the fish, crustacean or mollusc finally falls still, does the octopus begin to feed, tearing pieces off its paralyzed prey and swallowing them.

It looks like I am in the second stage. I am entwined by the slippery tentacles of this creature so tightly I can't break free. Now the bite has come in and the poison is already entering my blood.

Waking up tangled in the blanket with a frantically beating heart and staring wildly, I grabbed the bottle of Curacao and gulped back almost the entire contents. Only then did the horror which took over me during my sleep ease off a little.

Sitting by the foot of Mauna Kea, breathing in humid and warm Hawaiian air, watching the sunset, the appearance of the stars and their falls into the dark endless ocean, I clearly realized – I have only one, last, chance.

The octopus's poison is a virulent liquid, a complex mixture of alkaloids. On most of inhabitants of the sea – fish, crabs, crayfish, prawns, molluscs – it has the same effect, causing paralysis of the central nervous system and death. For a human this poison is also very dangerous. Dozens of cases are known where fishermen and divers have died after being bitten by an octopus.

But there are creatures – the golden armatus of the south seas, for instance – on which the octopus's poison has a different effect. It stimulates their physiological processes, forcing their hearts to beat faster and their muscles to contract more powerfully. After an octopus' bite, an armatus struggles in the tentacles so forcefully that it very often manages to escape and survive.

I found a picture of an armatus on the internet. It's a not very big fish. It looks a bit like marlin but more yellow and with a flattened head. I don't look very similar at all – and anyway how could a *Homo sapiens* and a fish be similar?

Nevertheless, I made the first meaningful moves to free myself from the deadly grip of the octopus while I was in Hawaii – right after the poisonous information bite the octopus had struck me through the agency of the Baseball player.

Even now I don't know what project linked to HAARP I was supposed to join. Indeed, did such a project exist? But Lao Tzu says:

'You can mould clay into a vase, but it's the nothingness inside that is used. You can cut doors and windows in a house, but it is the nothingness in the house that is used.'

I was using what was given to me to change my life and my entire situation.

Later I completed an algorithm which I had begun to develop while in Hawaii.

Lao Tzu was my guru.

Orwell was my ideologist.

The octopus's poison bubbled in my blood.

Hawaiian stars were shining on me from the sky.

I remember a storm roaring. The electricity flickered, wet palm branches whipped against the roof of my bungalow. Gusts of wind hurled rain water against the glass door and a big puddle washed in under it, which oozed slowly towards me.

I was sitting on a mat reading *1984* again trying to find in this book the words to inspire me and give me the courage to act.

I read on and with each line, each paragraph, I was submerging deeper and deeper into Orwell's text – sinking into a swamp, a sticky quagmire, from which it was impossible to get out.

Images, characters and their actions engulfed me and the plot sucked me into its suffocating embrace. It was a delusion, a druglike effect, when that combination of chemical elements takes control of your mind and body so you are no longer your own master.

Orwell, like a Siberian shaman or Indian mahatma, plunged me into a trance and pumped my consciousness with surreal images, which turned out to be uncannily real.

The lights went out. The old palm tree behind the house fell with a crack. But I did not flinch. I was bending over the faintly glowing screen of the tablet, and repeating after the characters in the book:

'You are a flaw in the pattern, Winston. You are a stain that must be wiped out. Did I not tell you just now that we are different from the persecutors of the past? We are not content with negative obedience, nor even with the most abject submission. When finally you surrender to us, it must be of your own free will. We do not destroy the heretic because he resists us: so long as he resists us we never destroy him. We convert him, we capture his inner mind, we reshape him. We burn all evil and all illusion out of him; we bring him over to our side, not in appearance, but genuinely, heart and soul. We make him one of ourselves before we kill him. It is intolerable to us that an erroneous thought should exist anywhere in the world, however secret and powerless it may be. Even in the instant of death

we cannot permit any deviation. In the old days the heretic walked to the stake still a heretic, proclaiming his heresy, exulting in it. Even the victim of the Russian purges could carry rebellion locked up in his skull as he walked down the passage waiting for the bullet. But we make the brain perfect before we blow it out. The command of the old despotisms was "Thou shalt not". The command of the totalitarians was "Thou shalt". Our command is "Thou art". No one whom we bring to this place ever stands out against us. Everyone is washed clean. Even those three miserable traitors in whose innocence you once believed – Jones, Aaronson, and Rutherford – in the end we broke them down. I took part in their interrogation myself. I saw them gradually worn down, whimpering, grovelling, weeping – and in the end it was not with pain or fear, only with penitence. By the time we had finished with them they were only the shells of men. There was nothing left in them except sorrow for what they had done, and love of Big Brother. It was touching to see how they loved him. They begged to be shot quickly, so that they could die while their minds were still clean...'

The realization that everything written by Orwell is not just a great prophesy, but a truth of life that turned from fiction to reality, pressed on me like a slab of super dense lead. The fact that it was all written about the totalitarian regimes of the last century, rather than my country and my time made me squirm with powerlessness and humiliation.

I had been deceived – and millions, tens and millions of people had been deceived with me. We had been lead into a trap, like fish lead into a net, like herds of sheep and cattle go into a pen where they are cut, castrated, or killed by electrocution to skin them and cut their carcasses for meat.

Anything can be done to us. That was the main thought troubling me. Big Brother has decided everything for us. He is watching and watching our every our move.

And the Baseball player's words kept spinning in my head: 'to become a hero you don't have to join the military and travel to the other side of the world. You can protect your country right here. Remember Joshua – the front line is everywhere.'

02:28 A.M.

"And so then you decided make information about NSA surveillance of internet users public?" the Lawyer asked.

"Yes and no," Kold replied. "I simply realised that there's a war going on in the world, an undeclared, quiet but cruel war. It's a world war and it would be impossible to work out its scope because it has no end. Conflicts of interests of political, religious and economic groups in the end are embarked on a neverending fight of everybody against everybody. Nowadays, there are a number of conflicting sides. There are rich people who are interested only in increasing their wealth. There is the digital generation which doesn't want to live according to their fathers' covenants. There are lumpens who demand bread and entertainment and at the same time refuse to work. There are islamists, who are trying to create a World Caliphate. One quiet player, quite strong until recently by historical standards, left the stage and left very suddenly and unexpectedly."

"Are you talking about communism?" asked the Lawyer.

"Of course. So," Kold put his fingers to his forehead, "At first I asked who the octopus harms the most. In other words – who is its main enemy, Who should I pass the information to for it to work? But gradually it dawned on me – I mustn't choose a side, I mustn't become a player in the big game on the 'great chess board', especially because information can get classified and used to harm others. That is how I realised that I have no alias and lost heart – but it was Orwell who returned me courage.

FILE 012.WAV

"I think that one incident can play a colossal role in the life of every man. I mean accidents of history. If you think about it, the whole of history consists of such accidents.

If Frederick Barbarossa hadn't drowned during the Third Crusade then there wouldn't have been the Great Arabic caliphate.

If the Scottish king Alexander the Third hadn't broken his neck when he fell off his horse, Great Britain would not have existed.

If the beauty Thérésa Cabarrus, lover of the Commissioner of the National Convention Jean-Lambert Tallien, hadn't ended up in prison, then there wouldn't have been the coup of 9 Thermidor and the insidious tiger-cat Maximilian Robespierre would've sent his enemies to the guillotine again.

And if the *Mayflower* had hit the rocks by Cape Cod, the United States would not have existed, at least not in the way it does now.

Isaac Asimov described it all much better in his book *'The End of Eternity'*. But I am talking about something slightly different – an accident in the life of a particular ordinary man. For example, a man like me.

It happened – yes, it did happen! – after I came back from Europe but before I went to Hawaii. Well, as I said I wasn't going through the best time in my life. After the story with poor Herr Hagen I was questioning everything so seriously. Am I serving a good cause? So seriously I almost died, as I said before.

I'll elaborate. I wasn't doubting the rightfulness of protecting your country; it was the methods I was doubting.

From our early years, all Americans know: the good always act with 'clean hands'. Batman will never take hostages, Superman will never blackmail anyone, Spiderman will never hit someone from behind, even if it's his only chance.

Of course adult life and especially espionage and the intelligence service are not made up the adventures of the superheroes in Marvell cartoons, but…

The basic principles and methods of existence, damn them, can't be so radically different! That's why what my so-called colleagues in Zurich committed became like some giant crude humvee smashing through the fragile and colorful stained-glass window of my reasons for serving.

Now my soul was showered in their shards but nothing has appeared in their place and I had no idea who to talk to about it. The most logical thing would be to meet up with Baseball player. After all, he was a psychologist and a good one, but something held me back from talking to this man. Perhaps it was the fact that Mr. Jenkins was a true pro and able to dig into the darkness of someone else's souls. And I, as you've already gathered, was wary of the professionalism of my colleagues.

It was a clear. damp September morning. I was on my way to the Agency's headquarters in Fort Meade, not far from Baltimore. I was listening to the radio – old Bon Jovi songs were playing and drinking cold coffee from a plastic cup and singing along with John without any enthusiasm:

'It's My Life!'

Slowing down behind a big shiny tanker truck carrying chemicals, I turned my head and saw her on the other side of the road.

Neolani.

She was standing at the bus stop looking into the distance as she waited for a bus. There were a couple of teenagers nearby looking just like we did seven years ago. It was beginning to drizzle.

She hasn't changed at all. Only the piercing ring in her bottom lip and her bright make-up have gone. But I had seen her in many ways, including like this, homely. She hadn't put on any weight, hasn't changed her hairstyle or style of clothes. She was still the same Heavenly girl.

My first instinct was to lower the window and call her. But then the engine of the truck in front of me roared, and letting out a dark cloud of diesel exhaust from underneath its shiny chassis, the truck began to move.

I had to move to. There were a few cars behind me and some red Japanese pickup was already honking impatiently – displeased with the fact that I, in the opinion of its driver, was lingering.

I got to the nearest cross road – which was quite far away – turned round and raced my Nissan back, praying to God, the Universe and Mother Nature for the bus not to beat me.

I don't know why I was doing it, or what came over me then. I had been deeply angry with Neolani after what happened in the Garage. I had even wanted to kill her back then, to be honest. To take a knife or get a gun, go to the college and there right in front of everybody thrust the blade into that beige knitted top where it bulged with her chest. Or to fire a gun into her face from short range, but before doing it shouting, like in a movie: 'Die, you lying bitch!.'

But the offence and bitterness were forgotten, covered over by new events, and then there was the Recruiting depot, Master Sergeant Vesterhauzen and other things. Neolani's image faded and became an unclear silhouette, a bleak picture in a dull frame hanging on the back wall of my memory.

Then suddenly I had seen her! And everything came back to life, became bright, clear and etched in relief. The memories crashed back like ocean surf and my leg almost suffered a cramp as I tried to press the gas all the way down to get to that damn bus stop!

She hadn't left. She was still leaning with her shoulder against the post. And she was still wearing a similar top – knitted and beige. Flared trousers, handbag of hemp fiber, amber earrings, feathery hairstyle – damn, she really hasn't changed at all!

I stopped my car by the bus stop, leaned over and looked out of the passenger window and, just like Mr. Jenkins, said:

'Mrs. Neolani! Would you be nice enough to give me a little of your attention, dear lady?'

She turned her head at looked at me with perplexity and indifference. Then a shadow of irritation ran across her face and after it – a happy grimace of recognition and, straight after, a smile.

'Josh? It can't be you!'

'It can, Mrs. Neolani.'

'Actually Miss,' she began to flirt. I grinned and opened the car door.

"Would you like a lift? Get in.'

She nodded and got into the car.

'How are you?' I asked, pulling away.

'Everything is great!' she replied. A standard answer to a question like this but I suddenly cringed because that former, real Neolani, would have never replied like a classic housewife from the East Coast. She would've said: 'All is cool, dude!' or 'Things are ringing like bucks on the counter!" or, at very least: 'The case is in court, babe!'

But she replied the way she did and I felt sad thinking that I'd turned out to be a man who experienced the rightness of Heraclitus – one indeed cannot enter the same river twice…

'Where would you like me to take you?' I asked, trying to be polite.

'Home. Do you remember my parents' home?'

'On Aquaheart Road?'

She laughed.

''It's hard to forget a street like that,' I smiled.

Actually I had been going in a completely opposite direction – the Agency's headquarters were located halfway between Baltimore and Washington while Neolani's parents lived in Glen Bernie, much further to the east.

But because I didn't have set working hours and I had no meeting arranged in the Agency, I left the large Baltimore-Washington Parkway, turned on to the Paul Pitcher Memorial Highway and headed the Nissan towards Curtis Bay.

All the way there, we were chatting pleasantly, remembering old friends and funny events. But neither she nor I mentioned that wretched day or the names of the guys in the Garage back then.

I remembered the house where Neolani's parents lived very vaguely, and for some reason I thought it was a small two-storey cottage on the east coast.

In reality, the house turned out to be neglected, with a shabby door and dirty windows. Only one thing I was right about: it indeed was two-storey high.

The hall and rooms of the ground floor were littered with junk, old chairs, boxes and bags.

'Follow me!' Neolani called. 'I live upstairs.'

Her bare feet slapped on the wooden staircase – just like they did back then. I followed her, avoiding the dream-catchers hanging from the ceiling.

'Where are your parents, Neo?'

After a short pause, an indifferent reply came from upstairs:

'They died, Josh. Just like they lived – happily and on the same day. An overdose. I'm selling the house.'

Upstairs, I found myself in a bright room, flooded with pale autumn sun, with a big bed in the middle. Neolani was lying on it face down with her arms spread.

'You were almost right with Mrs,' she said hollowly. 'I am getting married.'

"Congratulations. Do I know him?

'You do. It's Bach.'

'Is it? And what…' I couldn't find what to say.

'And that's all!' she turned around sharply and sat up, pulling up her knees. 'The Garage burnt down five years ago together with a drunk Pincher. Studies finished and everyone went all over the place. I got hit by a car and spent two years in the hospital. The only person who visited me there was Bach. I'm not blaming anyone, and especially you. It's retribution, everything according to the laws of karma. I do know that I stand guilty before you, Joshua-boy, very-very guilty, that's true, but – and try to understand me – I will not be asking for forgiveness, because…

'It's My Life! It's my… your life…' I murmured the words of Bon Jovi song.

'So when's the wedding?

'We are free people. There's no future – have you forgotten?'

…Then we were lying, naked, and she was smoking and I was looking out of the window at the clouds floating by. A strange unexplainable emptiness rang inside me. Somewhere deep in the bottom of my soul, dark water was splashing – the water in which I had almost drowned a few weeks ago. I knew that if this water rose it would drown me from the inside, and I would die. But now I felt very content.

Neolani moved and touched my arm.

'Bach and I are moving to Cleveland after the wedding. He has relatives in Ohio and his father's brother has a medical clinic in the city. I'll work there.

'Doing what?' I asked for the sake of asking something.

'At first as administrator. While I was in the hospital after the accident I did a distance learning course for 'manager in a sphere of medicine.'

Everything went silent. Cars swept along the street outside. Somewhere in the distance some kind of juvenile country music was playing. A sleepy autumn fly crawled across the window.

'I should go,' I got up and began to get dressed. As I buttoned my shirt I heard Neolani crying.

'Don't comfort me!' she shouted as she saw me watching her. 'Go. Go away! Take something from downstairs as a souvenir – and goodbye, Joshua-boy! Goodbye forever!'

I went downstairs and walked through the hall. By the door, I tripped over a bag, some old books fell out – Huxley, Camus, Heinlein, Orwell… I picked up a volume with 'Animal Farm' and '1984', opened it and saw an inscription in red ink on the flyleaf: 'Neo, remember: if an object is no good for one purpose, it can be used for something else.' And a signature: 'Dad'.

I took the book and left this weird house. I sat in the car for a while looking at the porch – for some reason I thought that Neolani would jump, run out, wrapped in some ridiculous blanket, would run down the path to the gate…

A police car woke me out of my stupor – stopping next to me. I must've had a strange facial expression because the second officer shouted:

'Sir, is everything alright?'

I nodded.

'Everything's great!'

They left. I took Orwell and opened it at a random page. Running my eyes across the page, I read:

'The Party seeks power entirely for its own sake. We are not interested in the good of others; we are interested solely in power. Not wealth or luxury or long life or happiness: only power, pure power. What pure power means you will understand presently. We are different from all the oligarchies of the past, in that we know what we are doing. All the others, even those who resembled ourselves, were cowards and hypocrites. The German Nazis and the Russian Communists came very close to us in their methods, but they never had the courage to recognize their own motives. They pretended, perhaps they even believed, that they had seized power unwillingly and for a limited time, and that just round the corner there lay a paradise where human beings would be free and equal. We are not like that. We know that no one ever seizes power with the intention of relinquishing it. Power is not a means, it is an end. One does not establish a dictatorship in order to safeguard a revolution; one makes the revolution in order to establish the dictatorship. The object of persecution is persecution. The object of torture is torture. The object of power is power'.

Having flipped through a few pages, I came across an odd paragraph:

'The seven commandments:
1. Whatever goes upon two legs is an enemy.
2. Whatever goes upon four legs, or has wings, is a friend.
3. No animal shall wear clothes.
4. No animal shall sleep in a bed.
5. No animal shall drink alcohol.
6. No animal shall kill any other animal.
7. All animals are equal.'

This fragment discouraged me. I wanted some clear conclusion to the morning – and I carried on turning the Orwellian pages.

My attention got drawn to another fragment:

'He gazed up at the enormous face. Forty years it had taken him to learn what kind of smile was hidden beneath the dark moustache. O cruel, needless misunderstanding! O stubborn, self-willed exile from the loving breast! Two gin-scented tears trickled down the sides of his nose. But it was all right, everything was all right, the struggle was finished. He had won the victory over himself. He loved Big Brother.'

And suddenly I realised the name of the octopus from my dreams. And many things fell into place – as if some mysterious force, some real life magic, had lifted the broken pieces of the stained glass of my beliefs into the air, whirled them in an enchanting dance and then joined them together into a complete image.

But it was a very different picture from before. Orwell had become the catalyst that had triggered a complex bio-chemical reaction in my brain. I felt I had gained vision and became blind at the same time. And all because I met Neolani. Or in other words, thanks to a chance…

Of course, I took Orwell to Hawaii. And there – in many ways thanks to Orwell – my transformation happened, or to be more precise, reached completion."

02:53 A.M.

"When I read Orwell's '1984' for the first time," the Lawyer noted, "Somewhere in the early 90s, I thought that the totalitarian model he described is a far-gone past and in our time, luckily, not relevant, especially in the West. Especially because it was thanks to the West it was defeated. To understand what's happening in the USA and in the countries of Western Europe, other types of thinker are needed. Maybe we don't know them yet."

"I've read many philosophers and politicians," Kold interrupted him. "The problem is that it was Orwell's artistic interpretation that turned out to be the most effective in my mind. It's like fuel for an internal combustion engine. It will work very poorly on kerosene. It'll work a little bit better on poor quality gasoline. But it'll achieve full power only if you fill the tank with AKI-97. Does that make sense to you?"

"Sort of," the Lawyer agreed politely.

"Reading various Orwell texts," Kold went on, "I understood more sharply and clearly what I had to do. In this sense, Orwell has become for me something like a Scripture and instructions at the same time. He very precisely indicated what I had to do:

'I know that the English intelligentsia have plenty of reason for their timidity and dishonesty. Indeed, I know by heart the arguments by which they justify themselves. But at least let us have no more nonsense about defending liberty against Fascism. If liberty means anything at all it means the right to tell people what they do not want to hear. The common people still vaguely subscribe to that doctrine and act on it. In our country – it is not the same in all countries: it was not so in republican France, and it is not so in the USA today – it is the liberals who fear liberty and the intellectuals who want to do the dirt on the intellect.'

'It is the liberals who fear liberty' It was a bullseye. The octopus has entangled us all with its tentacle. It has latched on to every head. It is pushing the tiny shoots of its prolegs with their greedy suckers through the soft spot in the crowns of our children.

The octopus is everywhere!

Of course, there are people who resist. There are even those who have managed to fight off the tentacles and live inside their own small worlds. But the octopus is so powerful and omnipresent that such exceptions only prove the old rule, formulated by Orwell: 'Big Brother is watching you'. This thesis has been joined by a new one, given life by the scientific and technological explosion of the new millennium: 'Big Brother is inside you.'"

FILE 013.WAV

I should really say a few words about how BRISM works. What is the essence of the octopus' existence?

Boytras and Greyvold have contributed to publications about BRISM, Tembora and other systems, and the world community has a rough idea about these octopus' organs, but they are still quite far from the nub of it.

Virtual tentacles are sent into all major social nets, communication programs and electronic mail. This is appalling. It's a complete destruction of concepts such as 'privacy of correspondence' and 'private life'. Hundreds of millions of internet users across the world for years unknowingly provided a nursery, compost in which the octopus grew and matured.

Surveillance programs, especially BRISM, are made in such way that even a child can work with the interface. That's so that any member of a consulate or embassy – and the data-mining terminals are usually located in places like that – could quickly get all the information he needs. For example, a diplomat, working undercover or a military man from the limited contingent of UN peacekeepers.

The program monitors data for a number of parameters. I don't want to overload you with specialist terminology, but I'll just explain what is meant by 'on fingers'. If you need to track a man's contacts, let's call him John Smith, then you need to know the bare minimum.

This minimum can include either his email address or mobile phone number, or name, surname and geographic address (and it doesn't have to be a full address), or just the number of his driving licence, his passport or his insurance.

BRISM will be able to find the John Smith you need using any of these criteria, sifting out thousands of other John Smiths. Then the operator enters into the program the required level of data gathering – tracking of electronic correspondence, his phone calls, his movements, his visits to internet resources, his contacts in social networks, forums and websites. All of this information is gathered, analysed by various parameters and issued in the form of reports.

BRISM and other similar programs are certainly a miraculous invention, a huge breakthrough in surveillance and espionage. Programs like this allow gathering of information about many people at the same time in all corners of the world with very little effort.

After the acts of terrorism which destroyed the towers of the World Trade Center, the creation of such system has become a necessity. Do you remember what president George Bush Jr. was saying on the evening of September 11th?

'...America was targeted for attack because we're the brightest beacon for freedom and opportunity in the world. And no one will keep that light from shining. Today, our nation saw evil, 'the very worst of human nature', and we responded with the best of America. With the daring of our rescue workers, with the caring for strangers and neighbors who came to give blood and help in any way they could... The search is underway for those who were behind these evil acts. I have directed the full resources of our intelligence and law enforcement communities to find those responsible and to bring them to justice. We will make no distinction between the terrorists who committed these acts and those who harbor them... Tonight, I ask for your prayers for all those who grieve, for the children whose worlds have been shattered, for all whose sense of safety and security has been threatened. And I pray they will be comforted by a Power greater than any of us, spoken through the ages in Psalm 23: 'Even though I walk through the valley of the shadow of death, I fear no evil

for you are with me'. This is a day when all Americans from every walk of life unite in our resolve for justice and peace. America has stood down enemies before, and we will do so this time. None of us will ever forget this day, yet we go forward to defend freedom and all that is good and just in our world. Thank you. Good night. And God bless America!'

And so the 'full resources of our intelligence' created BRISM and other systems like it. It was a good thing because it allowed us to trace, find and destroy many terrorists who were preparing to kill people.

But it turns out that even in the 21st century, the path to Hell is the same as it was in the Middle Ages – paved with good intentions. To destroy the termites eating away the walls of a house, you don't burn the whole house down. That's just pointless.

But in our case that is exactly how it happened. The war on terror has not only turned into bloody wars, in which our brave marines didn't fight so much against Al-Qaeda as peaceful civilians, but it also resulted in the coming of the octopus, omniscient and omnipotent.

Now the whole world knows that companies like Microsoft (Hotmail), Google (Google Mail), Yahoo!, Facebook, YouTube, Skype, AOL, Apple and Paltalk, basically everything computer-related and the whole of the internet community, are working with BRISM.

At the same time, the coming of the octopus has marked a new era, in which the words of Ecclesiastes are not relevant anymore. From now own there's a lot of power in a lot of knowledge.

I could say a lot more about programs like BRISM, about subchannel information and metadata, which contains not just information about our John Smith but also the opportunity to control him and his actions, his career and his personal life. In other words, everything I was doing to poor Herr Hagen as an agent, BRISM conducts in a moment, simply by analysing the contents of the messages, the essence of correspondence, conversations and even the likes and emoticons of the object of surveillance.

Gathering metadata about a person is not just an invasion of privacy but something much more sinister. I am not a religious man, as unreligious as a true American can be, but when I studied BRISM

I realized the deep essence of the program and I must confess, I felt deeply uneasy. I recalled the words from the Revelation of St. John the Evangelist:

"Then I saw another angel coming up from the east, having the seal of the living God. He called out in a loud voice to the four angels who had been given power to harm the land and the sea: do not harm the land or the sea or the trees until we put a seal on the foreheads of the servants of our God.
Then I heard the number of those who were sealed: 144,000 from all the tribes of Israel.
From the tribe of Judah 12,000 were sealed, from the tribe of Reuben 12,000, from the tribe of Gad 12,000.
From the tribe of Asher 12,000, from the tribe of Naphtali 12,000, from the tribe of Manasseh 12,000.
From the tribe of Simeon 12,000, from the tribe of Levi 12,000, from the tribe of Issachar 12,000.
From the tribe of Zebulun 12,000, from the tribe of Joseph 12,000, from the tribe of Benjamin 12,000.
After this I looked, and there before me was a great multitude that no one could count, from every nation, tribe, people and language, standing before the throne and before the Lamb. They were wearing white robes and were holding palm branches in their hands".
(Revelation 7:2 – 7:9.)

BRISM has become that angel which 'put a seal' on the foreheads of the 'pure' and has begun to count the 'impure'. Its creators are convinced that they are doing a good thing, but I knew for sure what will happen next:

'When he opened the seventh seal, there was silence in heaven for about half an hour. And I saw the seven angels who stand before God, and seven trumpets were given to them.
Another angel, who had a golden censer, came and stood at the altar. He was given much incense to offer, with the prayers of all God's people, on the golden altar in front of the throne.
The smoke of the incense, together with the prayers of God's people, went up before God from the angel's hand.

Then the angel took the censer, filled it with fire from the altar, and hurled it on the earth; and there came peals of thunder, rumblings, flashes of lightning and an earthquake.

Then the seven angels who had the seven trumpets prepared to sound them.

The first angel sounded his trumpet, and there came hail and fire mixed with blood, and it was hurled down on the earth. A third of the earth was burned up, a third of the trees were burned up, and all the green grass was burned up.

The second angel sounded his trumpet, and something like a huge mountain, all ablaze, was thrown into the sea. A third of the sea turned into blood, a third of the living creatures in the sea died, and a third of the ships were destroyed.

The third angel sounded his trumpet, and a great star, blazing like a torch, fell from the sky on a third of the rivers and on the springs of water.

The name of the star is Wormwood. A third of the waters turned bitter, and many people died from the waters that had become bitter". (Revelation 8:1-8:11)

I won't quote anymore from St John, although I do know his 'Revelations' well. Nobody but God and his prophets can foresee what the future will be like.

But the octopus has another hypostasis, the most vile and disgusting. He grants to a few the power over many, quite often raising most ordinary nobodies over the crowd.

Even at the testing stage in Fort Meade a few programmers used BRISM to track their husbands, wives and lovers.

It's not hard to guess that the octopus' tentacles are now present almost in all bedrooms in the world. Maybe only African natives, the inhabitants of New Guinea, the Indians in the Amazon jungle and the nomads of north Russia are still truly free people. Everyone else is carefully watched by the octopus, whose ethic is dictated by the ethics of the people sitting at the computer monitors as they control the program.

I remember back when I started working for the agency, the Baseball player and I had a very long conversation on this subject, at the end of which he brought up one of the well-known parables of King Solomon:

'Once a man came to Solomon, while he was furtively watching
children play, and asked:
'King, help me! I live in abundance, have a big house and many
slaves, but I see that my thoughts are directed towards shallow and
transient things rather than towards the eternal and virtuous things.
Then the king asked:
'But what is the virtue?'
The man replied without thinking:
'Virtue – is a way to get to the high while passing the low, to
understand the most important while ignoring insignificant.
The king frowned:
'And I ask you again, what is virtue?'
The supplicant replied:
'Virtue is a way to reach heaven.'
The king frowned even more:
'Answer me for a third time: what is virtue?'
The supplicant replied again:
'Virtue – is something that makes your soul purer and lighter.'
Solomon spoke:
'I've asked you three times and each time you, who spend all your
days thinking about virtue, couldn't give me a clear answer. You want
to reach high while passing low, but how can one reach the top step of
a staircase without walking the low ones first? You want to reach the
sky but is it right to go somewhere without knowing what will await
you there? You want to become lighter, but what is light without
darkness? A night is replaced by day and neither darkness nor light is
eternal. Would we have known what day is without knowing the night?
In the same way, pure thoughts go hand in hand with impure deeds.

A person who thinks himself virtuous can do the most horrible things. So should a noble man think about virtue just for the sake of it? You should love your wives, your slaves and your neighbors, be an example for everyone, and every evening, when going to sleep, ask yourself two questions: what have I done today in order to become happier, and have I not taken too much happiness at the cost of others? Only then your life won't be wasted and only then after your death you'll be called virtuous.'

At the time, I was satisfied with this answer. Indeed, to find a cure for a horrid illness, one has to dissect the bodies of the deceased and study their innards. To catch a criminal one has to communicate with the lowest type of people, the dregs of society. In other words, you can't fry an egg without breaking it first and you can't mould a clay pot without getting your hands dirty.

Gradually I began to be convinced that systems like BRISM are far too dangerous weapons for dirty hands.

And when I got a proof of it – the situation with the helicopters in South Africa wasn't the only one. When I realized the agency was conducting wiretapping and data gathering in Europe, Brazil, the countries of the Maghreb and the Levant, China and Russia, not to mention the United States itself – I was horrified. Because behind a virtual curtain and classifications such as 'Top Secret' I could see a real Overworld government, able to intervene in the internal affairs of any country, able to change not just the course of commercial deals but the course of history.

And that Overworld government was not the leadership of the Federal Reserve System, as some cryptologists like to portray it, nor the clans of Rothschilds and Rockefellers, nor a secret bunch of Zionists, nor hawk generals sitting in a secret bunker, no!

The octopus was ruling the world. The programs IT workers were ruling, without even being aware of it, through a few hundred eggheaded half-autists spending whole days behind computers. They were deciding the course of history and for now they were just carrying out the orders of their bosses, although now I'm not even sure that it's not the other way around.

If you really know everything about a man – what will stop you from pressing a right 'sore spot' or activating a 'pleasure center' to make him to do what you want?

Who knows, maybe the whole administration of the National Security Agency and maybe even the administration in Washington has long been controlled by the operators of BRISM and other programs?

Moreover, I do not rule out that what I have done might also have been initiated from outside. But one thing comforts me: if it is indeed the truth then the octopus has taken us over and we really do live inside the Matrix like in the movies of the Wachowski brothers.

Of course at the beginning I didn't think about fighting the octopus at all. I just wanted to get out, to go into the shadows, to step aside. I had no plan – I just tendered my resignation due to poor health. Why did I do that instead of just resigning? You need to know that you can't just leave the agency or any intelligence structure in any country of the world really. You need a valid reason for them to leave you alone and in this situation my unsuitability for work due to poor health seemed to me the best argument.

In the depths of the internet, I found an instruction for prisoners about how to simulate an epileptic fit and during the medical check, which I started myself by complaining on constant headaches, I fainted and imitated a tonic-clonic seizure.

Epilepsy is one of the most mysterious illnesses. Nobody really knows what causes it, how to treat it or why for some it lasts for tens of years, coming back regularly, while others just have one seizure in their whole life.

Apart from everything else, it is thought that a seizure can be provoked by a combination of sounds and light flashes on TV or a computer screen. In any case, epileptics shouldn't use these gadgets or tablets and smartphones.

It's not hard to simulate epilepsy. You just need to approach it seriously and not to spare yourself. If you fall down, then you fall properly. And if you have convulsions go for it hog wild.

Before your 'fit' you drip atropine into your eyes so that the pupils don't react to light and you have to tense the muscles around the eyes. It is also an important sign of 'true' epilepsy.

The hardest part was foam in the mouth. There were a few recipes given on a site for prison-malingerers but all of them were awful – soap foam, cocaine, dried belladonna… I had a much better recipe: a pinch of soda and a few crystals of citric acid. Putting this mixture in my mouth a few seconds before falling off the chair, I achieved quite natural authentic foam...

Basically, I really scared the doctors. I beat the back of my head on the floor. I smashed my knee on the chair leg. I arched, howled and wheezed, and bit through my tongue so that eerily bloody foam was oozing through my clenched teeth.

In the end, I was sent for many checks, which, of course, found all sorts of issues in various organs. That is why medics always joke that there are no healthy people, only 'underexamined' ones.

And that is what my tactic aimed at – not a single boss in his right mind would want to keep a man with such bouquet of illnesses in a job like mine.

So having resigned, I experienced a true euphoria for a time, maybe a month or two, I can't remember now. I was paid quite a good bonus for the work I'd done. I visited Japan, the Philippines, Australia and Ecuador, then I visited my father, mother and Judith. In short, I had the life of a typical holidaymaker, not thinking about the future.

But in reality I wasn't a holidaymaker and I had no idea what was waiting for me, but I didn't want to think about it, especially because everything around me was moving towards change: America was shaken by the presidential campaign of Barrack Hussein Obama."

<h1 style="text-align:center">03:29 A.M.</h1>

"Mr. Kold," the Lawyer looked quickly at the clock. "You are a very good narrator but I'd like to ask you a couple of questions. Do you mind?

"No, go ahead."

"You mentioned a few times that your father voted Republican. But what are your political preferences?"

Kold thought for a bit then decisively shook his head:

"I have to admit – I like the Democrats more than the Republicans, although you're right – I am from a family which traditionally votes for the Grand Old Party. Why? Probably because I support change and the democrats are trying to change the world for the best.

"President Obama is a democrat and reformer. He indeed is trying to change the world and I want to believe that he wants to change it for the best. Did you vote for him?"

Kold chuckled.

"I read Obama's program and familiarised myself with his biography, and I realised that this was what the United States should have had a long-long ago, back in the time of Martin Luther King. Without a black president our 'Miss Liberty' looked rather hypocritical, with a slightly powdered bruise and Ku Klux Klan hoods in the folds of her toga. I think you know what I'm talking about.

The Lawyer lowered his head in agreement.

"I have a good memory," Kold went on. "Thanks to Mr. Eisenberg, who forced us to memorise the Declaration of Independence, the Bill of Rights, the articles of the Constitution and the speeches of the great politicians of the past. He used to insist that brain is a muscle and needs constant exercise!

Basically, when Obama said: 'Now, understand, it is a choice. If people like me, if most of the people in this room, can't afford to pay a little bit more in taxes, then a lot of this stuff we can't afford. If we're insisting that those of us who are doing best in this society have no obligations to other folks, then, no, we can't afford it. I want to make sure that Malia and Sasha and your children and your grandchildren, that they're inheriting a land that has clean rivers and air you can breathe and that's worth something to me, that's something I want to invest in because when I'm all finished here and I'm looking back on my life, I want to be able to say, we were good stewards of the planet...' I remembered a speech by another black-skinned politician, which was pronounced more than fifty years ago. Thanks to Mr. Eisenberg – I still remember it every word. Are you ready to listen?"

"Do you mean Martin Luther King's 'I Have a Dream' speech?" the Lawyer asked.

"Exactly."

"Yes, I'll listen to it with pleasure.

Kold straightened, his face acquired a slightly tragic expression and he began to talk in a well-trained voice, reciting the whole of Martin Luther King's speech faultlessly.

"Five score years ago, a great American, in whose symbolic shadow we stand today, signed the Emancipation Proclamation. This momentous decree came as a great beacon light of hope to millions of Negro slaves who had been seared in the flames of withering injustice. It came as a joyous daybreak to end the long night of their captivity. But one hundred years later, the Negro still is not free..."

His voice soared as he was caught in the power of the rhetoric.

"... I have a dream that one day every valley shall be exalted, every hill and mountain shall be made low, the rough places will be made plain, and the crooked places will be made straight, and the glory of the Lord shall be revealed, and all flesh shall see it together..."

And as the speech went on, his whole body began to shake, and the sound of the American preacher's words reverberated through the deep bunker as if they would blast it open.

"'From every mountainside, let freedom ring!
And when this happens, when we allow freedom to ring, when we
let it ring from every village and every hamlet, from every state and
every city, we will be able to speed up that day when all of God's
children, black men and white men, Jews and Gentiles, Protestants
and Catholics, will be able to join hands and sing in the words of the
old Negro spiritual, "Free at last! free at last! thank God Almighty, we
are free at last!"'

"Bravo!" the Lawyer applauded. "Bravo to Reverend Martin Luther King and your fantastic memory."

"In Barrack Obama I saw a man who also has a dream," Kold said. "And I thought, you never know, maybe together we will be able to defeat the octopus and bring freedom back to America? Only one or maybe even two years later I realised that I didn't have any allies in that bureau and that Obama was a politician like all the others, no better than the Bushes, Clinton and the other recent presidents. But back then, before the elections, I was seized by a real sense of excitement, and I headed to Fort Meade to meet up with the Baseball player.

I'd never had any illusions about Mr. Jenkins. I always spoke to him very formally, understand me. Of course neither Obama, nor the octopus, nor my plans were mentioned in our conversation. I just told him that I wanted to continue my work in the system as a freelancer on individual contracts. So that if my health failed due to epilepsy I could always take a break.

"But are you actually well?" the Lawyer asked then added at once: "Of course, that's not a very tactful question but it's my professional duty to ask it."

"Everything's good," Kold nodded. "Although sometimes my legs hurt when its damp, but that's nothing really. So I will continue…"

FILE 014.WAV

IT workers – programmers, system administrators, and to a smaller extent 'metal workers'[7] and web designers – are special people. I am

---

7   Russian slang word meaning an IT worker specialising in repair, assembly and commissioning of computer hardware.

saying that without any hint of fascism or bolshevism, because I'm not making anything up. Everything is like it is. We are exceptional in the most unsightly meaning of the word. We are not like everyone else. We are a caste, but we're definitely not Brahmans. People hate us and worship us. In the past only usurers and executioners were treated like that.

If electricity suddenly disappeared from the Earth and the computer isn't needed anymore, we'll be the first ones killed. But while these ingenious machines exist, so do we, and we do it quite well.

There are a lot of us, but of course far fewer than there are plumbers or bankers. And they – along with housewives, accountants, owners of investment companies, policemen and even tax inspectors – all look the same, all have the same lamer's face, the face of a person who understands nothing about computers, and doesn't want to understand,. They all want just one thing: 'It needs to work!'. And they don't care why or how it happens. All of it is our headache, our job and our guarantee that we were, are and will be a treasure as precious as the lotus flower, because the modern world can't exist without us – and will slide into chaos without us.

I won't go overboard about our caste, since it's basically professional snobbery which even sewage workers have, and others don't have to know it.

But to make it clear how we differ from other people, here are a few IT jokes, which made me laugh like mad:

Every admin has to be a practicing gamer. Otherwise their conditioned save/load reflex will atrophy, which leads to interesting quests like 'how to restore the server's state this morning by having back-ups from last week'.

Or here's another one:

'Have you been to Acapulco? Then why did you come back so pale?'

'Because there was wi-fi in the hotel but not on the beach…'

Though that's more about internet addiction.

Then here's another one: If you find an error which is too time-consuming and tedious to fix – then just include it in the list of features".

Or here's another one, very childish:

A dog went missing. The dog's special features: Shift+2. Reward: Shift+4.

Did you get any of them?

And for dessert, an IT worker's prayer:

'God, give me a button to restart this world!'

So why am I saying all this? That's because a true IT specialist, even if he's just going to brush his teeth, never thinks about it like all other people: I'll just brush my teeth and then go to sleep.

No, a true IT specialist breaks down the whole process straight away into smaller pieces and creates and algorithm in his head: bathroom – door – basin – faucet – water – shelf – toothbrush – toothpaste… and so on and also inside this algorithm there'll be another one, the so-called sub-algorithm: shelf – toothpaste tube – lid (to toothpaste tube) – toothpaste – toothbrush – lid – toothpaste tube – shelf.

Humour is humour, but the harsh truth of life for me was the fact that IT specialists weren't just faithful servants of the octopus, no. They themselves were the octopus; they were living cells of its organism. And in order to defeat them I had to remember everything I knew and everything I could do.

That is why, in preparing for my fight with the octopus, I naturally began by creating an algorithm of actions for myself. Strategy, plan, projects – it is blah-blah-blah and lyrics.

Everything was precise and clear in my algorithm, and no disruptions were expected. Of course, I also input unexpected circumstances, the so-called *force majeure*, and also completely improbable situations best formulated in the tips for one of the earliest versions of Microsoft Office: that which suddenly disappears can appear by itself again.

In creating the algorithm, I used the general thesis that the octopus is a system: in other words it's 'a plurality of elements that are in relationships and connections with each other, and which form a certain integrity or unity'.

To defeat a system one needs another system, plainly. But one mustn't forget the law formulated by one of the first IT specialists, professor William Ashby. This law, which deservedly bears his name, says: 'When creating a problem-solving system, it is necessary for the system to have more variety than the variety of the problem being solved, or to be able to create such variety'. The larger the variety of actions available to a control system, the larger the variety of perturbations it can compensate.

In other words, it was possible to defeat the octopus only by countering each of its tentacles, each of its information channel, by an even a larger number of channels.

In my imagination it would be as if the octopus crawling in the dark, muddy underwater cavern was suddenly brilliantly illuminated by countless bright beams of light, shone by countless lanterns at the same time.

In situations like this an octopus will draw in all its tentacles, try to hide, and crawl into some crevice or a hole, or change its color to mimic stones or seaweed. If the illumination of an octopus' dwelling is prolonged, then the cephalopod can die from stress or hunger.

And that was exactly what I was hoping for. In the opposition of two systems, or more precisely, of the system and the antisystem I was going to create, the information rays would kill the octopus, like the light kills the darkness.

I won't say more about the algorithm I created. It has yet to run its course, and disclosing any more could harm me and the whole campaign for the octopus destruction. But I will tell you a few more things.

I initiated the first stage of my algorithm back in Fort Meade. For some reason the journalists who now write about me think I was copying secret information on something like disks or flash drives and then carrying them out of the NSA building in my anus.

Of course, it's complete nonsense. As an employee of the agency, I had high level access to classified information and access to databases and documents related to BRISM and many other projects. I was also able to use communication channels which completely encrypted content. So of course, I never risked using portable media devices.

So after resigning and becoming a consultant in a few companies working with the NSA and the CIA, I began to proceed with my algorithm. Hawaii came into the picture not because I liked it there, but more because it was a nice bonus.

Everything was essentially prosaic. The International Airport of Honolulu was the quickest stopover for Hong Kong, and that was an important part of the algorithm. Why? Very simple: China is also a system and I was going to use its potential in fighting the octopus.

But I met Middy by an accident. No, that's not quite right. I met her in line with the algorithm, but specifically by chance. I would've never made contact with a person who showed an interest in me. I have worked in the agency long enough and I wasn't that naïve to catch bait thrown at me.

I've already told you about the honey trap – so where was the guarantee that it wouldn't be used on me? This would've been a very easy way to hold their former employee on a short leash. The whistleblower doesn't just watch him but sleeps with him in the same bed.

At the same time, I needed a woman, a girlfriend – and not just for legitimizing my presence in Hawaii. After all, where else would a couple in love go. Not North Dakota!

As I've said, my relations with women have not so much problems as certain issues. Meeting on a street, in a café or a bar is not my thing. A few attempts to find myself a girlfriend through dating websites came to nothing. All contenders turned out in real life to be completely impossible – and one even turned out to be a man. Indeed, apart from prostitutes, only women with issues unable to arrange their personal life off-line seem to come to meet people on the internet.

When I went to Honolulu to find myself a little house with a view over the sea – not as fashionable as the bungalow at the foot of Mauna Kea, but still decent – that's when my legs began to ache awfully.

Maybe it was to do with some change in the air. I often react to the weather. I can stay awake all night before a thunderstorm. And if there's a tornado somewhere nearby, my head feels like it's about to crack like an overripe pumpkin.

I'd forgotten about the broken legs until then, although back in the hospital the doctor had told me that in time the healed bones may ache. That's normal and I should be prepared for it.

Anyway, I was looking for accommodation, meeting with realtors, estate agents and other intermediaries. Typhoon Ivica was circling in the Pacific Ocean, and although storms are rare on the Hawaiian islands, I got 'lucky' and the typhoon's damp breath had spoilt my life for a few days.

In search of salvation I went to a clinic, but they just prescribed me sedatives and painkillers. I'm not really a fan of pharmaceutical treatments because I think that nowadays there are enough chemicals in our food, water and air, and to stuff yourself with it in medication too is a step too far.

Still, struggling with the pain, I wandered through Downtown Honolulu. It was a warm, sunny day. Doors and windows were flung wide, and 'He Mele No Lilo', children's laughter and ringing bells were coming from somewhere.

I was already on my way back to the hotel to ask the receptionist to help me find some kind of a doctor-physiotherapist when I saw at the end of the street a sign saying: 'Massage Room 'Flexible Nene'. All types of massage. Pain relief. Yoga for beginners'.

The nene is the Hawaiian goose, a symbol of the state and the islands' business card. It's everywhere here: on shop displays, on cards, on advertisement booklets and posters. I couldn't quite imagine this goose being flexible so I headed to that massage room full of curiosity and hoping to get cured of my ailments.

A pleasant-looking but very plump Hawaiian woman with the indispensable floral lei necklace on her high breasts greeted me. She asked me for a long time what kind of massage I was interested in, but in the end just spread her arms helplessly.

'I'm sorry, mister, but we can't help you. We don't cure this kind of issue.'

'And how long did you have these pains for?' said a pleasant female voice behind me.

I turned round and saw a slim, you could even say thin, girl of about twenty-five, with huge eyes and prominent cheekbones. She didn't look like Hawaiian or hapa. In fact, she looked entirely European, with white skin, which was odd considering the local sun.

She was wearing a red dress with a deep neckline that showed off her figure well. I only looked at the girl for a few seconds – but judging from her posture and the way she held her head, I guessed she was a gymnast or a dancer.

Our conversation lasted barely half a minute. I said that in the past there was no pain, and she, with a very serious expression which looked quite comical, told me that things like this happen with a change of climate. It is linked to a cessation of circulation of earth energy in the legs, because I was torn from the energy system my body is used to. But a few yoga sessions under her direction and a relaxing massage with special 'Parachute' oil would solve my problems.

I knew quite a bit about yoga, but I'd never tried to do even the simplest exercises, suspecting that you should really have a competent instructor.

And it looked like fate had sent me such a person in this delicate girl with big eyes. I had no worries she was a spy sent from the agency or the CIA, because I ended up in Flexible Nene by accident, and not a single special service in the world, including Mossad and the FSB, would've been able to predict that. And of course I really wasn't going to tie my life to this masseuse! We just agreed on the first session, I paid an advance payment to the Hawaiian and then I asked the girl her name.

'Middy.' She offered me her hand. I introduced myself, gently squeezed her warm thin fingers – and got struck by a buzz of electricity.

She was emitting such energy that I at once began to sweat as if it was fifty outside not twenty-five. A wave of heat rolled through me, making me blush to the roots of my hair.

Middy noticed and smiling said:

"Your *Kundalini* is being restrained. Your *Sushumna* is blocked, and the seventh chakra in the top of your head is not receiving internal fire. But you have a good karma and great potential, Mr. Kold.'

'Joshua,' I said looking in her eyes. 'OK?'

It happens. You meet a completely strange person, talk to them for a few minutes and understand that this meeting has been arranged by the higher powers. This person becomes close to you.

That is exactly what's happened with Middy. Just a week later we went together to Kauai Island to see my new house and a month later she left her job at Flexible Nene and moved to my place.

…It was an odd bond. During the day I worked, spending six or seven hours at my computer. In the evening I learned the basics of yoga. During the night, I burned in the flame of Middy's love. Oh that girl, who had been studying yoga for ten years, can love like no other! And during my rare hours alone I was improving my algorithm, trying to exclude all unwanted or even fatal surprises.

Mostly, I was selecting my 'agents of influence' through which I was planning to publish the materials to expose the octopus.

Of course, my first and main candidate might have been Cassandzhi and his Mikiliks platform, but the sad fate of Banning persuaded me to reject this option. I couldn't take the risk, so I didn't even consider whether it all happened accidentally or whether Banning had become the victim of a very well thought-out provocation.

After studying a lot of materials and newspaper articles, I chose Greywold, attracted by his reputation as a socialist and his anti-system sensibilities.

'Indeed,' I thought, 'A man is living in the jungle in Brazil, in a huge bungalow over a waterfall. He swims every morning in a mountain lake, walks out with his nine dogs and two red cats, while a parrot and a few lovers are waiting for him at home. There's not a single security guard. And yet he publishes incriminating material which hurt the careers of more than one politician... Surely, he will gladly take a role of the octopus' denouncer, and the journalist's reward will be enough.'

I wrote a careful letter to Greywold and sent it using a closed channel with encrypted text.

There was no answer. I waited in vain for almost a month until I realised that this kind of method will not work with someone like Greywold. He thought too much of himself and his place in the world of information battles to pay attention to anonymous messages. I had to look for other ways. That is when I thought about Boytras.

Of course, Boytras was a heroic woman.

She had filmed five completely anti-system documentaries, including *'The Oath'* – about the horrible fate of the Guantanamo prisoner Salim Hadam. For that she was chased and harassed across the world and searched in airports, as they attempted to compromise her and even kill her a couple of times. But Boytras went on fighting. She was like a small but toothy seahorse, which bravely attacks the octopus's tentacles.

And she replied to me!

Then the algorithm went into action, and soon Middy and I were on our way to Hong Kong – as if for a trip. I still feel very guilty that I used Middy as a cover. From outside the situation looked very simple: a couple in love are flying to see Asia's economic wonder and have fun.

Middy, of course, had no idea I had planned a meeting in Hong Kong with Boytras and Greywold.

The Hotel Mira, where I'd booked a double room in advance, looked from outside like a super-modern tomb of Chinese emperors – firm lines, tinted glass, dark polished stone and sterile cleanliness.

Our room was wonderful and, having given the bed what it deserved, Middy and I separated for a while. She needed to top up her stock of eastern incenses, and there was a whole shopping district in Hong Kong where the materials of various esoteric practices were sold.

I stayed in the room with the excuse that I had some urgent work to do. To be frank, I was a little scared to tease the geese. Outside the hotel, I could've easily fallen in a trap. Anyway, I can't say I find modern Chinese cities like Hong Kong or Shanghai that pleasant for a stroll.

Maybe that is because I see China – the modern China, the PRC – without any piety or illusions. This is a totalitarian state with a quite specific socio-economic system and a strange ideology. They have their own special Big Brother and even when in other countries, Chinese people are still terribly frightened by it.

There were a few boys and girls from the PRC studying in my college – and they never went out anywhere, never took part in anything, not in pp fax wars, not in parties, because they were afraid that when they go back to their homeland, it will be known that they were spending time not studying but having fun.

Yet whatever the modern realities are, China has strength, power and incredible prospects. It seems like there are no heights which a modest Chinese genius, multiplied by Asian hard work and Eastern dedication, cannot reach, or won't reach in the near future.

'Showcase capitalism', built in China, has become effective and successful because of the local mentality. When studying Taoism, Confucianism, and various Buddhist practices still used by the Chinese, I was always amazed how they managed to refract these moral and sometimes highly moral teachings into their social consciousness and even married Marx's doctrine with the philosophy of Confucius.

At the same time, the main mass of the population – one and a third billion people! – live on a modest income. Even now many

Chinese homes do not have a TV and in many distant agricultural areas owning a car is, if not exotic, then a rarity.

But Chinese do not seek personal enrichment. They are not that interested in the material side of life in the same way that Europeans are, let alone we, Americans. A different system of values allows the Chinese to be much freer in this sense. To put it simply, they do not depend on objects and objects don't have power over them. Sadly, it's the other way for us Americans.

I was thinking this way. With its own independent politics, China in its hypostasis is an aggressive but wise dragon and will tear the American eagle's tail with its talons with pleasure if suddenly people from the NSA or the CIA tried to prevent my meeting with Boytras and Greywold.

It was also easier for them to defend their right to freedom of meetings here rather than, say, in Latin America, where the level of corruption among officials is sky high and you can easily be sold like a pedigree bull.

In China, officials are shot for corruption in stadiums in the presence of a huge number of people. I abhor cruelty and violence, but in this case the ferocious manners of the Chinese Themis were good for me.

I had arranged a meeting in the restaurant on the third floor of the hotel. Rolling *baoding* balls in my hand, these ones, would be a straightforward sign Greywold and Laura could easily identify.

The original plan for the meeting was more 'spy-thriller.' At an agreed hour in the entrance hall not far from the elevators, Greywold was supposed to ask loudly:

'Where can I get something to eat?'

I was supposed to be waiting around the corner and then hearing his voice come out and walk past him, holding a Rubik's cube. Greywold and Boytras would've followed me to my room, where our conversation would've taken place.

But at the last moment I cancelled this plan – partly because of Middy, who could've returned at any point, and partly for reasons of secrecy. Nobody has stopped bugging Chinese hotels rooms, but restaurants where people are constantly changing are normally only bugged when it is known that a certain person will be there – Steve taught me this back in Zurich.

Greywold was exactly as I imagined from the images of him on the internet – an arrogant intellectual, hiding a lot of insecurities, phobias and vices behind his snobbery. But Mrs. Boytras made a very good impression on me. She was a lively, direct and funny woman, absolutely convinced of her own correctness and righteousness of what she was doing.

We spoke for no more than forty minutes and during that time drank two pots of tea. Greywold had a cake, and Boytras smoked a few cigarettes.

I told them:

'You can't wait for someone else to act. I was looking for leaders, but I realized that leadership means being the first one to act. I don't consider myself a hero – because I am acting in my own interests. I don't want to live in the world where there's no privacy and there's no place for intellectual researchers and creativity. That's it.'

We discussed communication methods and actions for the next period and they left. Nobody tried to cut across them, nobody tried to stop, grab, handcuff them. Everything worked in line with the algorithm.

And a few days later, Middy and I returned to Hawaii."

"You constantly call the system you confront an octopus – why? In my opinion it's more of a spider's web," the Lawyer waved his hand in the air. "Nets, nets, which envelope the whole world."

"The Japanese," Kold said, slowly rolling a glass with a few drops of whiskey in the bottom, "have a big appetite for marine creatures. For them, seafood is the main source of protein, and it had an effect on their folklore and traditions, just like for us, people of European civilization, stories connected to the ancient agricultural rituals had their influence.

One of the main figures in Japanese mythology is Ryūjin, god of the seas, lord of the water element, defender and protector of Japan. It was Ryūjin who raised the famous divine wind Kamikaze which sank the invading armada of Kublai Khan. All rivers and lakes, all winds and sea currents, are subject to him. He has countless treasures, and owns all treasures from wrecks and all the pearls of the world.

Ryūjin has two hypostases, two images: light and dark. The light one is a powerful and just sea dragon, the protector of the weak and the saviour of those in distress. The dark one is a gigantic octopus – no weaker but mysterious and incomprehensible in his thoughts. Indeed, it's an octopus and not a squid! It's important, because for the Japanese, the squid represents something completely different.

Ryūjin-dragon is fair, honest and brave; Ryūjin-octopus can be crafty, cruel and libidinous. There is an ancient legend from the seventh century about the founders of the powerful Fujiwara samurai clan – about Fujiwara Kamatari and his son Fujiwara Fuhito, in which the octopus appears in all its beauty.

According to the legend, Kamatari's daughter was married to an emperor of the Tan dynasty. When old Fujiwara Kamatari died, the emperor sent three unbelievably beautiful pearls to Fujiwara Fuhito as a sign of mourning and grief. When Ryūjin has found out about this, he became enraged, because he considered all the pearls in the world to belong to him.

Turning into an octopus, he attacked the ship carrying the treasure, and stole the casket with pearls. Fujiwara Fuhito had to lead the search for the pearls, or it would've been disrespectful to the emperor.

In one of the villages, he met a young a beautiful pearl diver called Ama Tamatori and married her. Soon they had a son. The happy lovers remained living in the village since Fuhito couldn't return home without the emperor's gift.

Ama Tamatori was the most skillful pearl diver in all Japan. For her beloved husband and son, who deserved a better life, she swore to return the stolen pearls.

She reached the bottom of the ocean, and found Ryūjin's palace among the underwater rocks, guarded by the sea dragons. Ama began to play the shamisen and her music sent the guards to sleep. Then the brave girl entered the palace and stole the pearls from the casket. Ryūjin soon discovered the loss.

He turned into the octopus and chased after Ama. The girl cut her breast and hid the pearls in the wound… And after that versions of the legend differ. Are you interested?"

The Lawyer nodded.

"Very interested, Mr. Kold, especially since I suspect you're telling me this story for a reason."

"You're right – I do have a reason. So, according to one version, the more ancient one as I understand, the beautiful Ama escaped, because the blood spilling from her wound created a veil in the water and the octopus lost her trace. But after getting to the shore and giving the pearls to her husband and son, she died from blood loss. Since then all pearl divers in Japan are called 'Ama' and they always dive with naked breasts… well, topless, in memory of brave Ama Tamatori, and the Kamatari clan became one of the most powerful in the country.

According to the second version, the octopus caught the poor girl, wrapped her in his tentacles and was just opening his poisonous beak to tear her, when he was so dazzled by her beauty that he at once entered into sexual intercourse with Ame."

"The octopus?" the Lawyer was astonished.

"Indeed. You shouldn't be that surprised. This type of zoophile plot is typical for many nations, including the European ones. Remember Leda and the swan, the abduction of Europa by the Jupiter-bull… You're not thinking the bull took poor Europa across the sea just to walk with her in the meadows?"

"No," the Lawyer laughed. "I don't!"

"In Japanese art, the subject of the intercourse of a woman and an octopus is very popular. Starting from 17th century, there were multiple *netsuke*, drawings and engravings, dedicated to the subject. One of the most famous is *'The Dream of the Fisherman's Wife'* created by the great artist Katsushika Hokusai two hundred years ago. In that engraving, a naked woman is depicted experiencing an orgasm from the caresses of two octopuses. The larger one is giving her cunnilingus, and the smaller one is kissing her on the lips and stroking her breasts with its tentacles. When I was in Japan, I specifically went to the museum of Hamato to see this masterpiece.

"How disgusting," the Lawyer cringed.

"From the European point of view, it is of course disgusting. From the Japanese point of view, it's a grace of gods. From my point of view, it's a warning, a fatal sign," Kold frowned. "According to Buddhist canons, nothing in our lives happens without reason, bychance. All events, things, actions and symbols carry a deep meaning, which only truly devoted people can figure out. I have spent a lot of time in meditations and contemplation of eternity. In Hawaii. Middy and I used to spend hours sitting in the lotus posture back to back, sinking into blissful relaxation. And I understood that poor Ama Tamatori, who dared to challenge the octopus Ryūjin is me! I stole pearls from the octopus and now he sees me as his prey. It was a warning for me but I didn't heed it…'

"What are you talking about?" the Lawyer didn't understand.

"Banning's fate. You know that after the investigation and the court he stated that he want to start hormonal therapy and change his sex in prison? It's all because he was raped by the octopus! Banning is also Ama. He also stole a pearl but made an error – the tentacles got to him. And it looks like they'll get me too…"

"Don't worry, Mr. Kold, you know – you're safe here."

"The hour of the octopus is coming," Kold murmured, not listening to the Lawyer. "On the Yesibu islands people believe that octopuses rise from the depths in the gloomy hour before dawn. They entwine the fishermen's boats with their tentacles and drag them to the bottom. The hour of the octopus is coming… The morning is coming," Kold took the flat watch with a metal bracelet off his wrist and put it on the table in front of him. "There's no progress."

"Are you assuming the worst?"

"Of course. They will fly to Russia. I am actually sure they are already here! And they will come here, enter this room, will state me my rights. After that I will demand my lawful right for a telephone call and will get in touch with my father. I will tell him… I've thought it all through already: I'll tell him that I've never been a traitor and everything I've done, I've done for America and for the sake of America. Then they'll put handcuffs on me, will throw a coat over my hands and walk me to the elevator. We will go up, leave the terminal through the staff only exit and head to the USA in a military plane. Interrogation will begin in the air. They will try to find out what I have passed to your special forces, what I have told them. And of course they will not believe that I had other purposes, that I am not a defector but a whistleblower who has opened to the world the truth about them … about their crimes."

"Calm down. Have some water," the Lawyer filled the glass and put it in front of Kold. Kold, without even looking, slid the glass to one side, stood up, walked across the room to the wall and back and rubbed his chin nervously.

"I don't know if I'll have enough courage to finish myself off," he said hollowly. "But I don't want… I can't... go to American prison!

"That's not a constructive attitude," the Lawyer noted. "One needs to fight until the end. Besides. I'd like to say that an American prison is usually more comfortable than, for example, a Russian one. That, of course, still doesn't make it a desirable choice. But if the circumstances develop in this way…"

"Torture…" Kold moaned. "You still don't understand… I read the secret reports about Banning's interrogations, do you understand?! Of course, Banning, his actions, the passing to Cassandzhi of almost a thousand documents stamped top secret, has become one of those drops that overfilled the crucial cup! But when all the Rubicons were crossed and nothing could be stopped, I came across those files, those reports… It's awful! Awful…"

The Lawyer nodded with understanding.

"Mr. Kold, I still would like to remind you that even in the event of failure and your – lets call things for what they are – extradition to the USA, you have guarantees, and your persona and everything related to it will be under the close focus of the lawyers and journalists of the whole world. Finally, I will make every effort…"

"What do you think?!" Kold exploded. He jumped up and pulled off his glasses. His face was red and drops of sweat appeared on his forehead. "Do you think they use a Spanish boot, a funnel and a machine for crushing joints? Oh, the art of suppressing a man's personality and acquiring information has moved unimaginably forward since the Middle Ages, although the word 'forward' is out of place here. I don't know, and I don't want to know, what this method is called, but its essence is to completely destroy the personality of the suspect, to change his mind so much so that the values and beliefs he held, would have no meaning to him. Do you understand what I am talking about?"

"More or less," the Lawyer shrugged. "It has happened in our own history. After a few months in jail defendants in the open hearings of the 30s would become completely different people – not only readily confessing to everything they'd been charged with, but thinking in a completely different, strange paradigm. There was a time I used to study the complete texts of the trial transcripts, which, by the way, were published here with large cuts. I was always interested how they achieved it and couldn't work it out. Of course there was an ordinary physical influence – in other words, people were violently beaten up – but it looks like it wasn't the only thing. Maybe hypnosis, some kind of psychotropic drugs. Inside the NKVD there was a secret society carrying out this kind of research. But it was already too far from us. Officially torture is prohibited in your motherland and a huge number of human rights organizations, not to mention the state control bodies, are keeping watch on it.'

"First, Banning is kept on the military base in Fort Meade and he is being tried there. It's impossible for human rights organizations to control what's happening in there. Secondly, I repeat again – strictly speaking it's difficult to define torture. Everything begins quite innocently. Using simple tricks, the detainee is led to minor violations of the prison regime, so then, absolutely lawfully, they impose a penalty on him and transfer him to an isolation ward. After that they apply psychological pressure on him – turning music on, using certain frequencies and rhythms, with a special vibration stand to create vibrations in the floor of the cell. They spray special aromatic components that provoke physiological reactions in the human body, and also introduce certain foods and chemical drinks containing drugs that affect the mind.

After a few days in these conditions, the detainee becomes irritable, and shows aggression – and is provoked to a serious offence – for example, an attack on a guard. Of course, nobody is talking about a serious attack: just a simple push, a touch or any physical contact.

The next stage – and again completely legally and lawfully! – is a more serious punishment with use of special measures. The detainee is transferred to a tiny – one metre by one metre – cage and completely undressed. They don't turn the light off for days to keep him constantly awake. And they show him so-called 'educational films' in which pictures of violence and aesthetically unbearable scenes are interwoven with sudden sounds and bright, colorful combinations of geometric figures. It's called 'dissonance therapy'.

Drained this way psychologically and physically, the man falls into a state similar to a trance and his brain loses the ability to comprehend reality. At the same time, the zones responsible for the long and short-term memory slacken. To put it simply, the detainee begins to rave. That is when specially trained psychologists enter the game, and pull the information they need out of the man using leading questions.

The notorious 'truth serum' gives the same effects. But after using the 'serum' there is a high chance a man will turn into a vegetable – and how can you show someone like that in court? Modern techniques don't leave such obvious traces and the fact that the detainee may forget that he was a man or lose the last twenty years of his memory – well, that is a small side effect, a triviality, which doesn't bother anyone. I will tell you more!" Kold lowered his voice to a whisper. "Nobody knows what they do to the man, when he falls into a trance. Maybe Bannings was raped in order to develop his feminine side? Maybe he was forced to have oral sex and drink urine while he, in a changed state of consciousness, took it all for granted. In Guantanamo even worse things are being done to the detainees…"

Kold went silent as if regretting saying too much, then sharply burst out:

"Damn it! I won't go to prison. It's better to have asylum in Ecuador, Venezuela, Nicaragua, Cuba, here or even in North Korea – or let the killer with a poison stiletto come for me."

"Trust me, Russia is far from being the worst option." the Lawyer said. "And you shouldn't treat us with such distrust. There is another option for the development of your odyssey. I have some insider information that during the negotiations, the Russian side received an offer in regards to your future from unnamed but quite influential international organizations. Under the pretext that you have no documents, it's suggested that you are returned to Hong Kong, where you came from, and where official representatives of the National Security Agency of the USA are waiting. They'll meet you on the runway and might even board the plane. Then you'll be transported to the United States and put on trial – but not in Fort Meade like Banning, but in Washington. Moreover, the trial won't be just open but it'll be extra open – journalists will be allowed to the hearings, and there'll be internet streaming, etc. During the hearing, the court will hear about unlawful actions by the NSA and CIA against governments and citizens of sovereign countries and also against the USA's NATO allies and even against Americans themselves, including prominent politicians, top officials, senators, congressmen and members of the president's administration and even the president himself. The result will be to turn the process against you into a kind of new Nuremberg Tribunal, during which it's not Joshua Kold who is being judged but the National Security Agency, the Central Intelligence Agency and those members of the United States government who contributed to the creation of this situation. The main blow will be inflicted on the President of the USA, his team and his politics. What if the system was created long before Obama? It's very simple – he, when taking up his role, couldn't know about all these actions, but he's done nothing to stop them. The result could be impeachment, a scandal worse than Watergate, the coming to power of the Republicans' most conservative wing, the Tea Party, and the halt of behind-the-scenes political powers.

"And what… what will happen to me?" Kold's voice cracked.

The Lawyer shrugged his shoulders.

"In my childhood, I watched a movie directed by Sydney Pollack several times. Jane Fonda and Michael Sarrazin played in it. In my opinion, the name of this movie expresses some kind of principle often used in politics for people who serve no purpose to the elite, quite well. Do you know what film I am talking about?

"*They Shoot Horses, Don't They*", Kold whispered.

"Neither me, nor the Russian leadership approves of these principles," the Lawyer spread his arms and quoted the Bible: "But am I my brother's keeper? I think, Mr. Kold you should change your attitude towards Russia. The empire of evil has long gone. To be more precise, it never existed."

"Yes, I guessed that everything is not so one sided," Kold nodded. "And after that book by Dostoevsky you gave me, I thought, how little we know about each other. But Orwell wrote this for a reason: '…men in the mass were frail, cowardly creatures who could not endure liberty or face the truth, and must be ruled over and systematically deceived by others who were stronger than themselves". You know, he visited me before I left.

"Who did?" the Lawyer didn't understand.

"Mr. Jenkins."

03:55 A.M.

FILE 015.WAV

"I was just preparing to pass the folder with documents to Greywold to be published and I was convinced that everything was progressing as it should be. Middy was away – she'd left to visit her mother in Honolulu for a couple of days.

I don't know how the Baseball player managed to get to the island at such a late hour, although I think I might've heard the motor of the Coast Guard cutter.

He showed up in his usual manner – just appeared at the door and that's it. I concealed my surprise in order not to give him any trumps, invited him to come in and turned the coffee maker on.

As first, our conversation meandered, although I guessed straight away that he had come to pressure me to return to the mainland and to Fort Meade.

I can't remember exactly what I told him and I had an awful headache – the weather was changing – but I said something along the lines that two and two always makes four and I am a free man.

He laughed and he stretched out his hand with his fingers spread:

'How many fingers am I showing, Josh?'

'Four.'

'But what if America says that there are not four but five, then how many?'

I stopped short and went silent. I felt like ice cold water had washed over me. I recognised this dialogue, I recognised this quote, and I understood where it came from.

Damn! They know everything!

Or is it yet another improvization by Mr. Jenkins, another genius psychological move by him? This man with a perpetually weather-beaten face and white-teeth smile – the most wily and cunning man I've ever met. Even the Serpent Tempter in paradise wasn't as deceptive and cunning when he lured Eve.

In the meantime, he took a peach from the dish, bit off a piece greedily, wiped the juice off his lips with the back of his land and quoted Orwell again:

"The war is waged by each ruling group against its own subjects, and the object of the war is not to make or prevent conquests of territory, but to keep the structure of society intact'. As I understand our conversation will go quicker in this form, eh, Josh?'

'I don't like your tone, Mr. Jenkins', I muttered, trying to appear offended.

I finished the peach, put the wet stone on the polished surface of the side table and spun it round. The wrinkled stone looked like a human brain, spinning on its axis according to someone else's will.

We stayed silent for about ten minutes. The wind, which had been blowing fiercely since morning, had died down. The Baseball player got up and smiled, but his smile looked sad.

'You know, my boy, what a heavy feeling disappointment is… God forbid you from experiencing it.'

He stopped by the door, and leaned against the post. Again he quoted Orwell, but slightly altered:

"'A single – free – man always looses. That is how it should be, because every man is destined to die and it's his biggest flaw. But if he can submit completely, without reserve, if he can abandon himself, if he can dissolve in his job in such way that he becomes the job himself, then he'll become powerful and immortal.'"

I stayed silent.

"You reject an incredibly beautiful future," The Baseball player added.

"If you want to imagine the future, then imagine a boot, stamping on your face. Constantly!" I muttered, not able to contain myself.

"It's our last conversation, Mr. Cold," the Ballplayer sighed and began to speak in an official tone. "If you pursue a course of action aimed against the state or capable of harming the defence capabilities of the United Sates, then all enforcement measure prescribed by the law will be applied to you. Remember this. I hope you'll have enough prudence not to make mistakes. Goodbye."

I was tempted to utter something along the lines of 'See you in hell', '*Hasta la vista*' or '*Au revoir, mon ami*'. I don't know why, probably out of powerlessness. Technically, Mr. Jenkins was completely right: freedom, slavery – these are just words, figures of speech. During the time of Socrates and Heraclites, maybe these words had an obvious natural meaning, but now, in the era when the conventional and cyberspace merged to create a new reality, it was all out of date. Orwell died more than sixty years ago. It's silly to live according to his philosophic calculations and political settings, and it's even more silly to break your life and the lives of those close to you because of it.

I was sitting in the middle of the hall with my head clutched between my hands. The peach stone still lay on the coffee table, with tiny *Drosophila* fruit flies circling around it. 'Everything is so simple for them,' I thought at that moment. 'They mate, lay eggs, have some juice, eat some rotting fruit and die, and the new generation are already coming to replace them. And it goes on without an end…'

It was a night of crystal stillness. A huge moon rose from behind the mountain and spread its wide silvered path to the dark horizon over the limpid surface of the water. The lights blazed in my house, spilling their glow onto the bushes and the spreading Araucaria by the gate. Occasionally, cars raced along the road further down. I sat in front of the open door in the lotus position with my eyes shut. If somebody with a rifle happened to be on the hillside now and that somebody wanted to make a few shots, it would be hard for him to find an easier target.

I imagined the bullet from a .338 Lapua Magnum crashing into my skull, how the cartridge opens like a brass flower, and the steel core, after breaking through the bone, enters my brain and turns it into jelly, and, after making a few swift rotations, crashes into the back wall of my skull, then pulls out a piece of the bone together with bloody clots of what just a few moments ago was a thinking substance, the most complex and obscure thing in the universe. This substance flies across the hall.

Then two days later, Middy will come here in the morning and find my cold body with glazed eyes, with the *Drosophila* fruit flies circling above.

And that's it.

I opened my eyes and stared into the darkness for a few seconds. Then I jumped up sharply, threw the peach stone out of the window, shut the door, turned the lights off everywhere, and rushed to the bathroom. For a long time, at least five minutes, I washed my hands in hot water.

A day later I flew to Hong Kong without saying anything to Middy. I didn't tell her anything because she had become very important to me. It was the tightest constraint that I couldn't avoid while constructing the algorithm. Sometimes even a programmer must rely not on logic but on divine Providence. By leaving Middy, I took her out of the game. I hope she'll be happy and I also hope that one day we'll meet again.

But when sitting down in to the seat of the Hawaiian Airlines Boeing, I was completely calm. Maybe explorers and conquerors in the Middle Ages experienced similar calmness when heading into the unknown.

When your fate is in God's hands, there's no point in worrying, because nothing that will happen can be changed or reversed."

The Lawyer's phone began to vibrate on the table and the screen lit up.

"Just a moment!" The Lawyer pressed the button. "Yes! Good… Maybe it's already a good morning, yes."

He listened to the voice on the phone for a while, then it looked as if his face had begun to glow brightly from inside.

"Great!' The Lawyer smiled. "Yes, I'll pass it on straight away. Thank you. All the best!"

Putting the phone aside, he looked at Kold slightly archly.

"In Russia on occasions like this people say: 'You should dance, lucky man'. We've won, Mr. Kold. Your request has been met. I just had a call from the office of the head of the Federal Migration Service. Permission for temporary asylum in Russia for one year has been granted to you. The official document will be given to you in the nearest future.

"Temporary asylum?" Kold said intently, looking straight at the Lawyer. "Please, explain…"

"'Happily," the Lawyer said, smiling, and taking a few pieces of paper from his briefcase: "Temporary asylum: the possibilities provided by the federal law 'On Refugees' to a foreign citizen or stateless person for a temporary stay ion the territory of the Russian Federation."

Temporary asylum can be granted to a foreign citizen or stateless person in two events:

1) providing he has grounds for recognition as a refugee, and completes an application in writing with a request for temporary stay on the territory of the Russian Federation;

2) if the person doesn't have grounds for recognition as a refugee under the circumstances provided by the law of the Russian Federation 'On Refugees', but for humanitarian reasons cannot be expelled from the territory of the Russian Federation.'

In your case, Mr. Kold, we are dealing with the second point.

"Humanitarian reasons," Kold rubbed his chin in confusion. "Really… I never thought the moment would come when Russia would show humanity towards me."

"'Temporary asylum is provided for up to one year. The term of temporary asylum can be prolonged for each consecutive year by the decision of the territorial body on migration issues with which the person is registered," the Lawyer went on. "A person, who receives temporary asylum, and members of his family arriving with him, have a right to use living accommodation on rental conditions, to receive assistance leaving the Russian Federation and can also claim other rights, provided by Russian Federation law, by international agreements of Russia and by the legislation for Russian Federation subjects.

A person who receives temporary asylum in the Russian Federation has access to the internal labour market and can work without any special permission.'"

"'Oh, I can work in Russia and rent a flat here!" Kold exclaimed. He stood up, then sat down again and continued in complete confusion. "Honestly, I didn't believe… The algorithm… You see – it's been disrupted, it's broken! I didn't rely on Russia at all, I didn't even consider it. I saw it only as a point of transit. I had everything itemised… I was going to travel, using only the airports of the states not on friendly terms with the United States. China, Russia, Cuba – and from there Ecuador, Bolivia or Venezuela. I considered all three possibilities. These were three of the most likely countries, although, in line with the algorithm, I applied to twenty-one countries… But when they began to play for time and then France and Portugal closed their airspace to Evo Morales's aeroplane… Damn, I had been preparing to fly with him! And his plane was forced to land in Vienna and was searched as if it was an ordinary charter plane. Indeed, all animals are equal, but some are more equal and don't care for international laws. I thought then that everything was lost… And to be honest, I thought that I'll be here, in this underground prison, for the rest of my life. I did not suspect that you have such humane migration laws."

"'Congratulations, Mr. Kold," the Lawyer put the papers aside and stretched out his hand. "This is our victory!"

Kold looked at the wide palm for a few seconds and then weakly shook it. The Lawyer felt the American shivering.

The phone rang again.

"There's already an official statement from the Russian President," the Lawyer said after a short conversation, passing the tablet over to Kold. The voice of the Russian leader sounded in the room.

"'Cassandzhi and Kold consider themselves human rights activists who fight for freedom of information. Ask yourself a question: should people like this be handed over to be put into jail? Either way, I would've preferred not to deal with questions like that because it's the same as cutting a piglet's hair – a lot of screeching but little fur.

The Lawyer translated this difficult text, omitting the phrase about the piglet just in case.

"Is that all?" asked Kold with a rasping voice.

"Earlier the President said that you can feel safe in Russia," the Lawyer smiled. "He also sympathises with you, Mr. Kold. He said that you are an odd lad and condemned yourself to a quite difficult life. This is true and you know it. But our President thinks that time will pass and America itself will understand that it's dealing not with a traitor or a spy but with a man who has certain principles that can be considered in different ways. And maybe in this case some compromises will be found. But it definitely won't happen now."

"And thank God for that," Kold folded his arms on the table like a schoolboy, then smiled shyly. "A path of a thousand li, as is well known, starts with the first step. I have come part of the way but I have to carry on until the end. Do you know what I want now?" he suddenly changed the subject and without waiting for an answer literally blurted out: "An ice-cream cake with pineapples and vanilla syrup! My father used to buy cake like this when I was little and we lived in Elizabeth City."

"You look as if your cherished dream has come true," the Lawyer noted. "But in the meantime…

"'In the meantime, it's not the end; it's the beginning of a new cycle," Kold agreed. "Of course I understand it. I won't be surprised if a reaction from the White House will follow immediately."

"You're absolutely right. I was told that a briefing from the White House Press Secretary Mr. Sarney will start in a few minutes. I think it might be useful for both of us to listen to him."

"Yes, yes, of course..." Kold sighed deeply. It did not escape the Lawyer that he was lost in confusion again.

As the call signs of the official channel of the US President's press service boomed from the screen, Kold fell silent. But the moment Jay Sarney appeared in front of the cameras, gleaming in his Harvard glasses, Kold said hurriedly:

"They are not going to say now that Obama has managed to make an agreement with Mr. Putin and I will be extradited? Right?"

"This night has exhausted you, my friend," the Lawyer reassuringly patted Kold on the arm. "Don't worry. As far as I know Mr. Putin is not one of those people who change their decisions easily. Everything will be fine."

The Lawyer repeated last phrase in Russian and Kold repeated it like a mantra:

"*Vsio budet khoroshio...*"

In the meantime, Sarney's firm, confident voice resounded in the room:

"The Russian Federal Migration Service has officially confirmed that they have granted temporary asylum for a period of one year to Mr. Kold and have allowed him to leave the airport. We are deeply disappointed that the Russian leadership has taken this step, contrary to our completely clear and lawful demands, expressed at both official and non-official levels, to extradite Mr. Kold to the USA where he is indicted.

Mr. Kold is not a whistleblower. He was accused of the disclosure of classified information in accordance with three counts of criminal law and must be returned to the USA as soon as possible, where he will face all lawful procedures and where he will be provided with necessary protection.

This action by the Russian leadership undermines the long-term history of our cooperation in the area of the rule of law – cooperation which very recently was at a high after the explosion during the Chicago marathon."

"You see?" The Lawyer leaned back on the chair. "He hasn't said a single word about…"

"Wait!" Kold interrupted him rather crossly.

One of the journalists was asking a question:

"The Russian side has stated that they are not going to extradite him to the USA. So what are the next steps of the American administration in trying to bringing him back home?"

Sarney replied, without changing his facial expression:

"We will continue contact with the Russian authorities, expressing our extreme disappointment with their decision and making it clear that there is an absolutely lawful rationale for returning Mr. Kold to the USA, where he is charged with three criminal accusations in relation to disclosure of classified information. He is not a dissident. He is not a whistleblower. He was convicted of a crime. Upon his return to the United States he will be granted all the rights and privileges provided to those accused within the framework of our legal system.

We have expressed this point of view at an official level and in private conversations with representatives of the Russian leadership. Therefore I am confident that discussions will carry on."

"They are not talking about guarantees anymore," Kold said quietly, keeping his gaze on the screen.

The Lawyer decided he should not say anything. After all, his client is not a child and doesn't require consolation.

The briefing went on. The conversation came to the visit of the President of the USA to Russia.

"I am not prepared to talk today about the timetable of the President's business trips." Sarney said. "Obviously, events are taking an unwanted turn. But because we have a wide circle of questions, in accordance with which we interact with Russia, we are now looking into the expediency of this visit."

"'Tell me,' Kold asked suddenly, "Could a war start because of me?"

"Of course not," the Lawyer indulged in a smile. "In the history of our countries' relations there have been many more dramatic episodes, but on both our side and America's, there have always been sober-minded politicians. I will go further – even such hawks as for example, Senator McCain really don't want war. Politics is the art of possibility. Many people in it have a certain role but nobody wants to leave it and turn from tribune and demagogue into executioner and murderer. Especially because the same McCain had enough grief during the war in Vietnam."

"Speak of the devil," Kold nodded towards the screen. And there was a question in relation to McCain:

"Do you consider the actions of the Russian side as a conscious attempt to infringe upon the interests of the United States, as Senator McCain claims?"

"'We consider these actions as an unwanted development and we're deeply disappointed by it," Sarney rapped. "We've made it very clear that we have legitimate legal basis for returning Mr. Kold to the USA and that he will be granted all rights provided to those accused in our country within the framework of our legal system. As for the motivation for the actions of the Russian side, I'll leave it to the Russian authorities to clarify."

A few more questions followed straight away:

"What are the diplomatic consequences of this step? And what are the possibilities in this regard beyond the diplomatic?"

Sarney hesitated for a moment but quickly regained control:

"Your colleague just asked me a question about President Obama's visit to Moscow. I have already stated that I cannot tell you what our decision will be at the moment. We are judging the expediency of this visit in the light of this and other events. But for now I can't say what the decision will be."

"I would like to put a wider question," a large man in a blue suit asked. "In the light of this event have you considered rethinking the rebooting of the relationship between Russia and USA started by Hilary Clinton?"

"Our relations with Russia, just as with other influential countries in the world, are based on realism," Sarney looked at the audience victoriously and continued: "And it's absolutely clear that the so-called reboot in our relationship with Russia has brought positive results in relation to our national security and the interests of the American people. Thanks to that reboot we have Russian cooperation in the transit of cargo and materials to our military in Afghanistan. It has also provided us with cooperation in relation to Iran. It has provided Russian cooperation on a new agreement about the reduction of nuclear arms under START. And it has provided other forms of cooperation which benefit the United States, our people and our national security.

During the evolution of our relations with Russia over the last four and a half years, we have had conflicts. We have had disagreements with Russia, and we have always stated our position in respect of these conflicts and disagreements very clearly. The last time was over the situation in Syria. That is how things were in the past and that is how it'll be in the future.

Of course, those who assumed it wasn't worth rebooting our relationship with Russia after president Obama came to power, may today reiterate that the results achieved weren't worth the effort spent on them. But I don't think this is the case. And I don't think that anyone can convincingly prove otherwise."

"They would justify their actions even if the whole world found out that they were killing and eating babies in the White House," Kold said. "The octopus will never acknowledge that he is wrong. And at one point I really believed that everything would change with the arrival of Obama..."

"The most interesting bit is starting," the Lawyer nodded at the screen. There was a dialogue emerging.

"Jay, what do you think the Russians are trying to achieve?" a pleasant-looking blonde woman asked. "Obviously, when taking a decision to grant Kold asylum, they were not expecting their decision would be met with understanding in the White House..."

Sarney answered at once":

"Yes, I don't think they were expecting that."

"And yet they did it. Why, do you think?" the blonde was pushing the Press Secretary, but hadn't managed to confuse him.

"I was asked this question before," Sarney reassured her. "I am not going to invent motives for them. I guess the official representatives of Russia can explain them themselves. We are obviously disappointed in this development. We have a wide and important agenda for interaction with Russia. It includes the areas where we've achieved agreement and we cooperate, and it also includes areas where we have disagreements and conflicts.

We stated long ago, just as president Putin did, that we don't want the Kold affair to become a problem in our bilateral relations, because of their scale and importance. We are aware of this and will therefore continue moving forward in our relations with the Russian leadership."

The secretary announced a break in the briefing.

"This already looks like pouring water into mortar," the Lawyer spread his arms. "But in politics it's important to present a good face in a bad game. Mr. Sarney does it quite well."

"In the book you gave me, I liked one phrase," Kold said, looking at Sarney as he departed. "'To judge people impartially, we need to reject our preconceived opinions and our habitual attitudes towards the people and objects that usually surround us.' There in the White House, they think I'm just like everyone else, that they have calculated everything… Idiots! We are all different. Martin, Mitchell, Banning, Cassandzhi and I. Although there is one man I would associate myself with. He also wanted to make his country – and in the end the whole world – a better place."

"And who is that?" the Lawyer asked with interest.

"Guy Fawkes!" Kold stated solemnly, and his eyes began to glitter. "Since I was a child I admired this man who wasn't afraid to stand up against the cruel and unfair system existing at that time in England."

"People say that in English schools children still learn a rhyme about Guy Fawkes," the Lawyer noted: "'Remember, remember the fifth of November, gunpowder treason and plot.'"

"There are two of them," Kold said in his usual uninformative manner.

"Two of what?"

"Rhymes. They start in the same way but then… Compare them yourself, here's the variation where Guy Fawkes is a sneaky traitor:

Remember, remember the fifth of November,
Gunpowder treason and plot.
We see no reason
Why gunpowder treason
Should ever be forgot!

Guy Fawkes, yes, t'was his intent
To blow up king and parliament.

Three score barrels were laid below
To prove old England's overthrow.
By god's mercy he was catch'd
With a darkened lantern and burning match.
So, holler boys, holler boys, Let the bells ring.
Holler boys, holler boys, God save the king.

"Well, it doesn't lack historic truthfulness," the Lawyer smiled. "Guy Fawkes was a criminal."

"'He was a hero," Kold objected. "A second rhyme says more:

Remember, remember: the fifth of November.
Remember the gunpowder plot.
Centuries have passed but sadness and woe
Will forever be my lot.

The King and Parliament for death or pain
Were marked on this fateful day.
Just a sea of fire, and another land
Could send fate a different way.

The cellars are dark, and amid the stores
Sits powder, solid and black
But footsteps sound, "Guards to arms!"
Please, Lord, watch my back.

Run, run! But where? There's thick blank walls
And cries to the front and rear.
The heavens and fate protect the King;
So I'll pay with my head here.

Through the centuries, sadness runs
And will never be forgot.

So just remember the fifth of November
And the infamous gunpowder plot.

"Hmm," the Lawyer shook his head. "I haven't heard this version before. But it doesn't remove the essential truth: Guy Fawkes was plotting against the legitimate authority."

"I've heard that's happened a few times in Russia too," Kold's voice became sarcastic. "How many of your emperors didn't live long enough to become old in the last two hundred and fifty years? Four?"

"Three," the Lawyer smiled. "'Paul I, Alexander II and Nicholas II. Though, if you count Peter III, then indeed there were four. As for English history, apart from the execution of Charles I after at least a parody of a court, there've been many similar things. How about Edward II killed with a red-hot poker up his back passage? So I would argue with English people on how law-abiding they are. But you Americans don't take part in this argument."

"That is because in our political system the power gets passed on painlessly by the establishment and the new administration doesn't chop the heads off to the old one."

"Dear Mr. Kold," the Lawyer allowed himself some sarcasm too, "Today in this room we heard the words: 'This country, with its institutions, belongs to the people who inhabit it. Whenever they shall grow weary of the existing Government, they can exercise their 'constitutional' right of amending it or their 'revolutionary' right to dismember or overthrow it'[8] You understand that these lines potentially contain more scaffolds and axes than the whole of English and Russian history put together?

"Whose fault is it that we've became rams… I will quote Dostoevsky again," Kold closed his eyes to try to remember the words. But he quickly snapped his fingers and almost shouted: "'Power is given only to those who dare to bend and pick it up. But there's only one thing, just one: dare!"

The Lawyer didn't think it appropriate to pursue this slippery subject, especially because the end of the break was just being announced at the White House.

---

8   Lincoln's inaugural address, 1861.

The second part of the briefing began with a detailed question from a grey-haired man in glasses:

"Jay, you said Mr. Kold is not a whistleblower. But how about the fact that the House of Representatives voted for these programs and came close, it seems, to reducing them. During the hearings this week, the Chairman of the Judiciary Committee Patrick Lee cast doubt on them. And today, the president is meeting a group of legislators in White House, some of who also doubt these programs. So is it possible that Mr. Kold has in some sense done a service to the American people and to the nations of the world by declassifying these programs, if you take into consideration the public indignation they have provoked?

"'The first proper question!" Kold moved forward, staring at the screen.

"When a man gives an oath to keep the secrets of the United States, he has to keep them – and if he doesn't then appropriate consequences come," Sarney was looking over the heads of the journalists. "There are also established procedures for potential whistleblowers, for those who wish to give information about a violation. An unauthorized disclosure of classified information can bring great harm to the interests of our national security."

"Is that all he can say?" Cold was sincerely surprised. "Where did this guy come from anyway? I wouldn't trust him to advertise popcorn in a cinema."

The grey gentleman persisted:

"'But if he hadn't publicised these programs, then people would never have known about them. And we would not be discussing them today. And he would still be in the United States. But he dared to do it. He revealed these programs."

Sraney looked annoyed but his voice came out evenly and without emotion:

"Yes, we've found out much from this unauthorized disclosure of classified information. But even so, these programs were already being discussed and controlled by Congress and the courts, and they already contain protective elements to balance security and privacy. And the President has made it very clear that he wishes to achieve this balance. He supports this balance, considers that this balance has been found and he also thinks that there should be a discussion about these problems. And that is what he's engaged in now.

Today, as you probably know, he is meeting with members of Congress – the Senate and the House of Representatives, both Republicans and Democrats, to discuss these problems. Among the participants invited there are congressmen critical of the programs we discussed in sections 215 and 702 of the Surveillance Act."

"'Demagogy!" Kold shouted. "Ah, how I would liked to tell them in person. Vile hypocrites!"

"You will have this opportunity," the Lawyer said quietly.

"Without doubt, our intelligence services require adequate instruments to protect our national interests, to protect us from possible attacks," Sarney continued, "And, I assume, the majority of Americans will agree with them.

We also develop these programs in such a way that we lay in various safety elements and a multi-layer control system to guarantee that they do not violate the right of American citizens to privacy. This is the balance about which the President speaks. And this is the balance which underpins the implementation of these programs. With the agreement of the acting administration, the Department of National Intelligence has made efforts to declassify a significant amount of information after Kold's leaks. And I am certain that this process will continue. But I don't think that we can responsibly state that these programs, intended to protect us from terrorist acts, are not needed right now."

"So the President thinks that these programs should have been kept secret?" the correspondent asked.

"Again, you're mixing different problems. The fact that the Patriot Act and FISA are confirmed is well known. Congress is aware of these documents. The general public also knew about them. Certainly, there are details in these programs which the public has discovered as a result of the leaks. But the President is convinced that it's unacceptable to make extremely sensitive classified information public, because it can harm interests in our national security, and already has. It can endanger our citizens."

"He is wriggling like an eel in a fishing basket!" Kold noted with satisfaction, then turned to the Lawyer: "Although I have to admit that your analogy of the snake and the frying pan is better."

"I don't envy him," the Lawyer grinned. "You have made him sweat, Mr. Kold."

"Though who would envy me," Kold answered in annoyance, drumming his fingers on the table. "God knows, I didn't want this sort of fame and would've preferred the whole story not to have any publicity. I cannot imagine how they figured out it was me so quickly?"

"By using the same programs you informed Greywald about," the Lawyer suggested.

"Then in my case, they've worked extra efficiently…"

At that moment, another question came:

"Republican Senator Graham has called the release of Joshua Kold a change in the rules of the game in Russian-American relations. Has it really gone that far?"

Sarney sighed:

"I've already said quite clearly that we are deeply disappointed by the fact that the Russian authorities made this step, contrary to our clear and legitimate demand made at official levels and during private conversations to expel Kold from Russia and return him to the USA. Again, as I said before, I'm not going to make any guesses about the result of our discussions with Russian official representative on this and other questions currently on the negotiating table, except to say that we are deeply disappointed with the turn of the events. Thank you, ladies and gentlemen! Goodbye."

And without looking at the audience, Sarney quickly left the stage.

The Lawyer switched the TV off.

IN PLACE OF AN EPILOGUE

"Well, my friend, it's time to pack up," the Lawyer grabbed his briefcase, and snapped the lock. "I'll wait for you…"

"I had everything packed long ago," Kold said quietly. He disappeared through the door and came back a moment later with a small brown travelling bag. Kold put in on the floor by the table and froze, then nodded at the bottle: "There's still a lot left. Would you like a drink?"

"Thanks – I'll abstain."

"I'll have a drink, though. People say Russians consume a lot of alcohol because it's so cold here. It looks like I am going to be Russian, at least for the next year – so I should start getting used to it."

"It's a delusion, Mr. Kold, a stereotype," the Lawyer smiled. "According to statistics from the World Health Organization, Russia, despite its notorious awfully cold climate and no less notorious habit of drinking vodka instead of coffee in the mornings, is not ahead in terms of alcohol consumption. The countries of Southern Europe with their wine are far in the lead in this sense. So you can leave the whisky and begin your emotional preparation with Russian *kvas.*"

"*Kvas?*" Kold repeated. He sat down, poured himself two fingers of whiskey and drank it easily in small sips.

"It's the Russian Coca-Cola, but it was created seven thousand years ago and is made at home out of bread and water."

"God," Kold whispered, "*Kvas…*"

He turned towards the Lawyer and said in a voice deepened by whiskey and worry:

"You know, Theodore Roosevelt, the first American awarded the Nobel Peace Prize and the twenty-sixth president of the USA, once said: 'I foresee a great future for Russia. Of course it'll have to go through certain shake-ups and maybe severe shocks, but it'll all pass and after that Russia will rise and will become a stronghold of the whole of Europe, and maybe the most powerful in the world!' I think by opposing the octopus Russia and its President has made the big step towards the future which Roosevelt outlined for it."

"Arise, Count! Great deeds await you!" the Lawyer quoted the classic and smiled broadly.

Kold stood up slowly, picked up his bag and walked to the door like a sleepwalker. He looked back longingly and muttered to himself:

"The hour of the octopus... The time of the octopus... I hope it won't turn out that all my great deeds in life were only in this room..."

Moscow, August-October 2013

• • •

CONTENTS

Dear Reader,

Thank you for purchasing this book.

We at Glagoslav Publications are glad to welcome you, and hope that you find our books to be a source of knowledge and inspiration.We want to show the beauty and depth of the Slavic region to everyone looking to expand their horizon and learn something new about different cultures and different people, and we believe that with this book we have managed to do just that.

Now that you've gotten to know us, we want to get to know you. We value communication with our readers and want to hear from you! We offer several options:
– Join our Book Club on Goodreads, Library Thing and Shelfari, and receive special offers and information about our giveaways;
– Share your opinion about our books on Amazon, Barnes & Noble, Waterstones and other bookstores;
– Join us on Facebook and Twitter for updates on our publications and news about our authors;
– Visit our site www.glagoslav.com to check out our Catalogue and subscribe to our Newsletter.

Glagoslav Publications is getting ready to release a new collection and planning some interesting surprises — stay with us to find out more!

Glagoslav Publications
Office 36, 88-90 Hatton Garden
EC1N 8PN London, UK
Tel: + 44 (0) 20 32 86 99 82
Email: contact@glagoslav.com

Glagoslav Publications Catalogue

- The Time of Women by Elena Chizhova
- Sin by Zakhar Prilepin
- Hardly Ever Otherwise by Maria Matios
- Khatyn by Ales Adamovich
- Christened with Crosses by Eduard Kochergin
- The Vital Needs of the Dead by Igor Sakhnovsky
- A Poet and Bin Laden by Hamid Ismailov
- Kobzar by Taras Shevchenko
- White Shanghai by Elvira Baryakina
- The Stone Bridge by Alexander Terekhov
- King Stakh's Wild Hunt by Uladzimir Karatkevich
- Depeche Mode by Serhii Zhadan
- Herstories, An Anthology of New Ukrainian Women Prose Writers
- The Battle of the Sexes Russian Style by Nadezhda Ptushkina
- A Book Without Photographs by Sergey Shargunov
- Sankya by Zakhar Prilepin
- Wolf Messing by Tatiana Lungin
- Good Stalin by Victor Erofeyev
- Solar Plexus by Rustam Ibragimbekov
- Don't Call me a Victim! by Dina Yafasova
- A History of Belarus by Lubov Bazan
- Children's Fashion of the Russian Empire by Alexander Vasiliev
- Boris Yeltsin - The Decade that Shook the World by Boris Minaev
- A Man Of Change - A study of the political life of Boris Yeltsin
- Gnedich by Maria Rybakova
- Marina Tsvetaeva - The Essential Poetry
- Multiple Personalities by Tatyana Shcherbina
- The Investigator by Margarita Khemlin
- Leo Tolstoy – Flight from paradise by Pavel Basinsky
- Moscow in the 1930 by Natalia Gromova
- Prisoner by Anna Nemzer
- Alpine Ballad by Vasil Bykau
- The Complete Correspondence of Hryhory
- The Tale of Aypi by Ak Welsapar
- Selected Poems by Lydia Grigorieva
- The Fantastic Worlds of Yuri Vynnychuk
- The Garden of Divine Songs and Collected Poetry of Hryhory Skovoroda
- Adventures in the Slavic Kitchen: A Book of Essays with Recipes
- Forefathers' Eve by Adam Mickiewicz

More coming soon...